DEMON REVEALED

HIGH DEMON SERIES, BOOK TWO

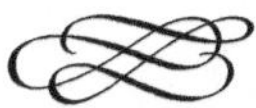

CONNIE SUTTLE

Print Second Edition (2018)
Print ISBN: 1-63478-063-9
Print ISBN-13: 978-1-63478-063-6
eBook ISBN: 1-93975-905-6
eBook ISBN-13: 978-1-93975-905-4

Published by:
SubtleDemon Publishing, LLC
PO Box 95696
Oklahoma City, OK 73143

Cover art by Renee Barratt @ The Cover Counts

To Walter, Joe, Larry, Lee, Dianne, Sarah and Mark.
Thank you.

ACKNOWLEDGMENTS

As always, this book is the result of collaboration. If it weren't for the support of my editor, my cover artist and my beta readers, it would be less than it is. All mistakes, as usual, are mine and no other's.

About the Author:
Connie Suttle lives in Oklahoma with her husband and a conglomerate of cats. They have finally banded together to make their demands, which has proven disconcerting to all humans involved.

You may find Connie in the following ways:
Facebook: Connie Suttle Author
Twitter: @subtledemon
Website and Blog: subtledemon.com

ALSO BY CONNIE SUTTLE

Blood Destiny Series:

Blood Wager

Blood Passage

Blood Sense

Blood Domination

Blood Royal

Blood Queen

Blood Rebellion

Blood War

Blood Redemption

Blood Reunion

Blood Destiny Series Boxed Set (Books 1-10)

Blood Recall

Blood Alliance*

Legend of the Ir'Indicti Series:

Bumble

Shadowed

Target

Vendetta

Destroyer

Legend of the Ir'Inditi Boxed Set

High Demon Series:

Demon Lost

Demon Revealed

Demon's King

Demon's Quest

Demon's Revenge

Demon's Dream

God Wars Series:

Blood Double

Blood Trouble

Blood Revolution

Blood Love

Blood Finale

Saa Thalarr Series:

Hope and Vengeance

Wyvern and Company

Observe and Protect*

First Ordinance Series:

Finder

Keeper

BlackWing

SpellBreaker

WhiteWing

~

R-D Series:

Cloud Dust

Cloud Invasion

Cloud Rebel

~

Latter Day Demons Series:

Hot Demon in the City

A Demon's Work is Never Done

A Demon's Due

~

Seattle Elementals Series:

Your Money's Worth

Worth Your While*

~

BlackWing Pirates Series

MindSighted

MindMage

MindRogue

MindMaster*

~

Black Rose Sorceress Series

The Rose Mark

Rose and Thorn

Black Rose Queen

Queen of Thorns and Roses

Future Wars Series

Buffer Zone

Black Zone*

Other Titles from SubtleDemon Publishing:

Malefactor

Transgressor

Underhanded*

by Joe Scholes

*Forthcoming

"*R*eah and I talked about it—that's how I know." Gavril wanted to shout at the adults. Reah had tried to tell Lendill Schaff about Nods Whitlin, but he'd ignored her, sure that Nods was only an illegal immigrant on Tulgalan. "She said there was no water shortage on Mandil. They were growing citrus in the desert so there was plenty of water to grow drakus seed. We pieced it together—she said somebody called the High Commander could have been in on this." Gavril sat in front of his mother, his father, ASD Director Norian Keef and Vice-Director Lendill Schaff. "She didn't contact you a second time because she was embarrassed after the first time." Gavril knew that feeling all too well.

"Whitlin won't be able to talk for a few days—Tory nearly crushed his throat," Norian grumbled. "Those wizards are refusing to talk—we can't force them. They're older than that stupid boy—I'm hoping he'll get upset and frustrated enough to tell us all he knows. As soon as he can talk."

"The wizards won't say anything?" Queen Lissa asked.

"The most powerful of them keeps asking about Reah. He stopped talking when I told him she wasn't any of his business." Norian was angry about the entire incident. Lendill had ignored Reah's warning;

she hadn't had enough courage to come to him again. Ry hadn't thought the information he'd gleaned was serious enough to call in agents and seven people died. Another eight were wounded.

"But how are they getting to Tulgalan?" Lendill knew he'd miscalculated—he should have gotten at least one agent to tail Nods. He might have learned a great deal from that. Instead, they were left to clean up bodies and attempt to explain to the Governor of the Realm of Tulgalan just why a wizard's battle had destroyed half of Taritha Village.

"I would have made the same mistake," Norian sighed. "She's only nineteen. We didn't give her enough credit."

∼

"Reah, my darling, wake up. Please."

I ached. All over, I ached. The pain wasn't unbearable now, but it had been. I remembered waking up occasionally; the pain had been so bad. I only recalled cool fingers against my feverish forehead before blessed blackness came again. A voice, now, asking me to wake. Calling me darling. Not Aurelius—he never called me that. I was attempting to puzzle it out in my foggy brain. That hurt too, I think.

"Aurelius is out on assignment again. I am here, pretty one." I was afraid to open my eyes. Afraid of the reality that I might have to face when I did. Perhaps someone would come to send me back to unconsciousness.

"No, darling. They'll relieve the pain, but you must wake. You must move and eat and answer questions."

I moaned. I didn't want to answer questions. I didn't want to think. Didn't want to *remember*.

"Hush, now. We'll get you through this."

"Wylend, go away." *That* voice I'd heard before. I was trying to connect it to a face and a name.

"Karzac, if that order came from anyone else, I would turn them into a goat." I opened my eyes a crack to see Karzac the healer glaring at Wylend Arden, King of Karathia. Why was Wylend here? Surely he didn't want me to cook for him that badly.

"I will explain it to you very soon," Wylend rose from his seat beside my bed, returned Karzac's glare and disappeared.

"Reah," Karzac sighed heavily, "I know you are in pain. I will try to relieve as much of it as I can, but the one who calls himself the Director of the ASD is clamoring to speak with you. I did my best to hold him off, but he keeps insisting that the ASD owns you. That I find repugnant in every sense of the word, and have considered asking a Larentii to put him through the pain you have suffered, just so he will have some idea of what he is asking of you." Karzac's green-gold eyes were kind as he reached out to touch my shoulder. The pain lessened. He put his hands on my neck, then, causing the pain there to drop dramatically.

~

"What am I going to do?" Tory wanted to slam his body into a brick wall. Then back up and slam it into a brick wall again.

"Bro, I have no idea." Ry watched his taller sibling carefully. Lissa had asked Ry to watch Tory—he wouldn't be able to reconcile his feelings with what his Thifilathi had done. He should have realized the full moon was close on Tulgalan, and when he'd forced the Thifilathi to deal with the shooter, it had taken over completely.

"I've ruined everything," Tory moaned.

~

"Drink this." I saw the same cook was still working for the Queen of Le-Ath Veronis, and he didn't look happy as he handed a drink to me. It looked like mush.

"Reah, it's protein and berries. Drink it—it will help with the headache." Karzac was still fussing over me—he'd folded me to Lissa's private study, where I was scheduled to meet with Director Norian Keef and Vice-Director Lendill Schaff. I felt awful and my nervousness made me feel as if I'd heave up anything I might attempt to swallow. The cook disappeared through the door and my hand shook as I lifted the straw to my lips under Karzac's watchful gaze.

"Healer, we'd like to interview our agent in private," Vice-Director Schaff told Karzac the moment he and Director Keef swept into the room.

"You are telling me this because I am Lissa's mate, just like the Director here," Karzac snapped. Lendill Schaff received a daunting glare, in addition to formidable sarcasm from Karzac. "Be assured I can make your life just as much hell as the Director's here," the healer muttered and folded away.

"I don't know what to do about that," Norian Keef cut his eyes toward the space where Karzac disappeared, raked a hand through thick, brown hair and sat on Lissa's office chair with a sigh. Lendill Schaff sat on the edge of Lissa's rather large, hand-carved desk and crossed arms over his chest, staring at me. I quailed before his gaze and set my drink aside—I no longer had enough strength to hold up the glass.

"Reah, you should have brought me the additional information— Gavril told us what you came up with," the Vice-Director snapped. "That was information the ASD needed to revise our records and update the information you'd given me before. Clearly, I would have taken a closer look at young master Whitlin had you done so. Yet you withheld that information. I don't care how embarrassed you were at calling me the first time, or how reluctant you might have been to contact me a second time. Had you shared your information with Rylend, he could have brought it to my attention. You did not." Lendill was angry. I felt dizzy and ill.

"Now," Lendill went on, "we have one of our prisoners asking for information on you. Considering that you failed us in this, we are going to escort you to the dungeon, with the hope that seeing you will jog wizard Bel's memory a little." I looked up at Lendill in alarm. What were they going to do? I was in no shape to walk to the dungeons. I couldn't even walk across the room. I also had no desire to be a part of a coerced confession from Bel—I still cared about him. He hadn't shot me—in fact Bel had been trying to stop Nods when Ry and Wyatt attacked him.

"We will hold you up if you have difficulty walking," Lendill must have seen the look on my face. He wasn't going to put his hands on me. I didn't want his hands on me. Right then, Karzac or one of the Larentii might have been the only male hands I would allow. I struggled down the hallway, jerking my elbow away from Norian Keef and teetering dangerously as we reached the stairs leading to the dungeon. There wasn't anything left in my stomach to heave up, otherwise I might have stopped to do so halfway down the steps. My breaths were short and labored by the time we reached the bottom, where the wide, flagstone floor of the hall that ran the length of the cells stretched before us.

My vision grayed and I struggled to clear it as we walked down that hall. Bel had been placed inside a cell about halfway down. "Reah?" His voice was barely a whisper as I lurched to a stop before the bars that held him back. He was leaning against a wall of his cell near the bars. I saw he didn't touch the bars—likely they were spelled, preventing Bel from using his power.

"Bel?" I wanted to weep, but there weren't any tears. My voice was dry as sandpaper.

"Thank the gods, Reah, I thought you were dead." Bel bumped his forehead against the wall and closed his eyes.

"We might be persuaded to keep her alive—if you consent to tell us what you know," Lendill now had my neck gripped in his hand. That brought a pain-filled whimper—the puncture wounds where Tory's teeth had penetrated my neck were still blazingly painful.

"Don't hurt her!" Bel shouted, standing straight and glaring at Lendill.

"You have no right to demand anything!" Lendill shouted back. "She is our conscript—we can do what we please with her. Tell us what you know!" He removed his hand from my neck and gripped my right shoulder, just where the ranos-shot had entered. And then he shook me—hard. I shrieked, dropping to the floor in excruciating pain. Then I began to convulse.

Consciousness can be a fleeting thing—I was aware for brief moments, and during those moments, I realized I had no power over my body. None. It was jerking uncontrollably. At times, I saw the lights in the ceiling overhead in blurry brightness, at other times I saw the shoes Director Keef wore. All while my body jerked in spasms that I couldn't stop. My teeth clacked together and I bit my tongue several times. I heard shouting. Men's voices. Men. They had brought me to this. All my life, men had controlled me in one way or another. My mother had died, leaving me alone and unguarded. Perhaps her lot hadn't been that much different from mine. I don't know how long the seizure lasted; I only know that unconsciousness came after what seemed an interminable amount of time.

"Do not attempt to give me excuses. I am a breath away from killing you both." Kifirin stood in front of Norian Keef and Lendill Schaff. "I care not that you were attempting to get information the only way you could. Do you wish to go and explain that to our little one in there?" Kifirin flung an arm toward Reah's bedroom. It had taken two Larentii, with Karzac helping, to get the seizures to stop. Karzac had yelled first, before Kifirin arrived. They hadn't waited for her to drink the protein smoothie—it was liberally laced with sugar. Reah had been dangerously hypoglycemic and that, combined with the stress, the forced walk to the dungeons and Lendill's pain-inducing grips had triggered the seizures. "If the Larentii hadn't come, she would be dead now. Is that what you wanted?" Kifirin blew angry clouds of smoke as he glared at Norian and Lendill. While it was dangerous if any High Demon blew smoke, when the god of the Dark Realm produced his smoldering breath, lives hung in the balance.

"We didn't realize how bad off she was." Norian hung his head.

"And yet you failed to ask. You were only interested in what you consider your own gain, here. I warn you, this is a larger game than even you realize. And on many levels. I am leaving. If I stay, my anger with you will grow and you will die. I leave you with your lives. For now." Kifirin's dark eyes were filled with stars. Norian knew that the god was passing judgment. Kifirin folded away as Norian and Lendill stared.

"Norian, if you had grown six heads, I might have been less surprised." Lissa glared at her mate. "And Lendill? Where the hell did that come from?" Lissa paced inside her bedroom while Norian watched.

"That wizard cares about Reah. We can't beat a confession out of him and our treaty with Mandil prevents compulsion to force them to confess, so we went in another direction to get information." Norian realized he stood on unsteady ground with Lissa.

"So, instead of punishing the criminal, you punish the innocent to get what you want?" Lissa stopped pacing for a moment.

"We thought the healer had taken care of everything," Norian grumbled, sitting on the end of Lissa's bed.

"Norian, she was shot with a ranos pistol. Those things can kill Ra'Ak spawn, remember? And then she was claimed by a High Demon. I'm vampire, Norian, and I didn't get over those puncture wounds in my neck for days, even with a Larentii's help."

"Your son did that," Norian defended himself with what he knew.

"Yes. He's High Demon. I admit it. That's how they claim their mates. That's how I have two sets of teeth marks in my neck, thank you very much. If Lendill had investigated that stupid kid to begin with instead of ignoring Reah, then people would still be alive and you'd likely have more information than you do now. As it is, you have nothing. You don't know where they were staying, where their supply is kept and who got them onto Tulgalan to begin with. Don't point the finger anywhere except where it belongs, Norian Keef."

"Lissa, if you were still working with me," Norian was back to grumbling.

"I put in my time, Norian. Part of that was when I was pregnant with Gavril. Gavin still has a fit over that. At least Ildevar allowed me to serve twenty-five years instead of the original thirty. I'm done with that, now. I have a planet to run, Norian. That's my job. Why don't you go and ask your current Liaison, the King of Lavareal, if he'll go out and catch criminals with you?"

"He wouldn't bother, and he'd be less than useless anyway," Norian sighed, thinking of his current overseer. Norian had gotten Ildevar Wyyld to agree to make Le-Ath Veronis the permanent base for the ASD—it had better security than any other Alliance world and he preferred being closer to Lissa.

The lot of Liaison for the ASD—although it was merely an empty title in most cases—was assigned to rulers of Alliance worlds for periods of thirty years. Lissa had been the only hands-on Liaison in Norian's lengthy experience as Director, and since her life and the rule of Le-Ath Veronis had been placed on hold for so long, Ildevar had shortened her tenure by five years.

"Back to your treatment of Reah," Lissa came to poke a finger in Norian's chest.

"We've done this before with quite a bit of success," Norian defended himself. "We just didn't realize how bad off Reah was. We were going to explain and apologize afterward—it has to look real in every sense before we try to get a response from the criminal."

"Oh, that was real, all right. And maybe you can apologize to Reah, but if I were in her shoes, I don't think any explanation would be sufficient and I sure as hell wouldn't forgive it." Lissa stalked out of her bedroom, leaving Norian to stare after her.

"Fuck," Norian muttered and got up to go find Lendill.

"Torevik, do not force me to call Jayd to help restrain you." Tory was blowing smoke, as was his father, Gardevik Rath.

"They nearly killed her!" Tory shouted at his father—something he'd never done.

"Son, I realize the Thifilathi is speaking right now," Garde worked to calm himself and his son. "Think on this for a moment. You are to blame as well—she wouldn't have been so weakened if the Thifilathi hadn't chosen to claim her when it did."

"That's still no excuse for dragging her out of bed and then doing —*that*." Tory wanted to pound Norian Keef and Lendill Schaff into pulp. "And they won't let me see her." The last statement was nearly a wail.

"Son, they're worried she'll have another seizure. Seeing you when she opens her eyes could be too much of a shock."

"But you said it was important to apologize right away. And to keep on apologizing until she believes me."

"Son, she's really sick right now. We have to wait until things are better where Reah is concerned. She isn't just suffering from the claiming—ranos injuries usually kill. If Aurelius hadn't given her his blood, we'd have a body instead of a live quarter-demon."

"Are they going to tell me when things are better, Dad? Are they?" At least Tory had stopped breathing smoke.

"Son, I hope they realize how important that is to both you and Reah."

～

"Reah?" That voice I knew right away. Perhaps the only real friend I had. Gavril was there beside my bed. I had to work to open my eyes— I still felt dizzy and confused.

"Chash?" I wanted to reach out to him, but my hand wouldn't obey my will. Gavril reached out and took it for me. My voice too, was dry as a desert.

"Reah, you need to wake up and have lunch with me. Karzac says he's going to put in a feeding tube if you don't wake up."

"What?" Now I was even more confused.

"Reah, just wake up, okay?" Gavril's dark eyes—his father's eyes— were begging me.

"Chash, I can't move." Even speaking made me feel tired.

"I'll help you—just let me know if I hurt anything." Gavril had an arm beneath me, pulling me to a sitting position. I was shaking and holding onto Gavril as he piled pillows behind me. He was stronger than he looked.

"Mom says I'm the only person you might be glad to see right now," Gavril brought me a small bowl of food. "Mom made this—she calls it chicken and dumplings. She says its comfort food."

"Sounds good, Chash." I'm not sure how we ended up that way, but Gavril was behind me after a while and I was leaning on him while I brought the spoon to my mouth. He even helped a couple of times when my hand shook too much. Was he only twelve? Twelve going on forty, I think.

"You'd do the same for me," he said, after he got me back down on the bed.

"I would," I murmured, my eyes closing. The food had been good— the dumplings were light and the broth seasoned just right. Lissa was a good cook. Exceptional, even, for a vampire.

"Reah, baby, wake up." I knew that voice and it frightened me. "No, avilepha, don't be scared." Tory was at my bedside, lifting me up. "Dad says I have to earn back your trust. Since I was the one who destroyed it." I discovered I had enough moisture in my body to produce tears. "Baby, you need a bath. I promise I won't hurt you. Ever again," Tory was murmuring into my hair. I couldn't fight him—I didn't have the strength. Aurelius had bathed me before, now Tory was doing the same, lowering me into a tub of warm water after undressing me carefully. A puckered and sunken spot on my right shoulder now marked the ranos pistol wound. The hole was closed, leaving a mixture of red and purple bruises behind.

"Karzac says it'll go away," Tory soothed as I stared at it in shock. "It'll just take a few weeks, I think, for your body to regenerate." Tory was on his knees on the floor beside the tub and I wept while he washed me, although he was careful with what he touched. "Baby, you don't have to forgive me. I know I let it take over—I couldn't control it after a while. I'm sorry, Reah. More sorry than I can ever say." He was wiping tears off my face with the washcloth.

"Your hair is growing out," he rinsed it carefully, allowing his fingers to wander down the back of my neck. "Is it tender? Does it still hurt?"

"How about I stick my teeth in the back of your neck the next time I turn," I snapped at him. His fingers stilled.

"You could do that. I give my permission," he kissed my forehead gently then leaned me forward, kissing the back of my neck.

"None of that." Karzac was there immediately, his hands on his hips. "I have never struck anyone in my life, but that may change quickly."

"Karzac, I wasn't going to do anything," Tory muttered.

"And you will not, until I give permission," Karzac growled. Karzac waited until Tory got me out of the bath and wrapped in a huge towel. "Now, we will check on things," he said softly as he ran his hands over me.

"Little girl, things are coming along—it is the High Demon in you most likely," Karzac said after checking my neck and shoulder. His hands brushed over my abdomen and more private areas, making me blush. Tory was watching, and that made it worse.

"No, avilepha, Karzac won't hurt you," Tory held my head against his wide chest.

"The wounds will be healed in another two weeks, I think," Karzac washed his hands after the examination. "Reah, if Shannon and Cleo were not pregnant right now, I would have them come and deal with this immediately. As it is, we will be forced to wait for the healing to come." I didn't know who he was talking about and didn't want to show my ignorance by asking.

"I'll put my girl to bed," Tory said after Karzac left. "Karzac has a mental check on you, baby. If I get out of hand, he'll be here with a baseball bat, I think."

"What's a baseball bat?" I asked wearily. The bath and examination had worn me out.

"I'll take you to a game sometime—the vamps from old Earth play it all the time. They have leagues and the competition is pretty stiff."

"What does *avilepha* mean?" I had one more question as he covered me up in my bed. They'd put me back in the bedroom I'd had at the palace—Gavril had said that Tory almost had a meltdown when someone suggested moving me to my house. Gavril had eventually convinced me that Tory was nearly suicidal over what had happened.

"It is the High Demon's language—it means *my love*. M'hala means *my heart. Hala avilepha, m'seidra camethei refieoru* is the declaration of love from the male High Demon to his female High Demon mate. *It means my heart's love, you are mine forever.*" Tory lifted my left hand to kiss it.

"What do you call," I shivered, almost unable to voice the remainder of the question. I didn't have to.

"*Nelimalu*—the claiming," Tory kissed my hand again. "It is violent, m'hala. I had already asked my father to do what my uncle had done for his twin daughters—arrange for anesthesia and aftercare. The Thifilathi took matters into his own hands. Reah, I never meant to hurt you—not like that. I wanted to hurl myself into a wall or off a cliff afterward. It almost made me crazy. Connegar arrived and put me under for a while, then Mom had Ry watch me like a hawk afterward. I am so sorry, love. The Thifilathi will never do that again. This is the way Kifirin made us—to claim our mates in Thifilathi form. Dad says it ensures that all the babies a High Demon female bears will belong to her mate and no other. Something in the Thifilathi saliva makes changes in the female's body and it will only recognize his seed after that."

"Tory, what are you saying? What about Aurelius?" I was upset again.

"Aurelius knows, m'hala. In fact, he was demanding that we find a way to keep you from suffering during this whole thing. We all know how that turned out." Sarcasm coated Tory's words.

"Where is he? Are you sure that's true—that I can't have anyone else's babies?"

"I shouldn't have said anything," Tory muttered. "I should have known this would upset you. I can't say that for sure, love, since you're not a hundred percent High Demon. I do know that the High Demon females—all of them in the past—have only borne their mate's children. And Aurelius is on assignment—I can't say where because even I don't know. He belongs to the Saa Thalarr and they keep that information to themselves. It's to protect them in the long run. He might have told you if you'd been here, but you weren't. Even if you knew, you wouldn't be able to say it to another person—knowledge of that race protects itself."

"Tory, I don't know how I feel about this. Before—well, before things happened, I think I cared about you and worried over what Aurelius might think. Multiple marriages are allowed on Tulgalan, but mostly it is the men marrying more than one wife. Rarely is it the other way around, although it is allowed, just as the other is. I thought I was betraying Aurelius when I felt something for you. But now," I sighed helplessly.

"Reah, it will take time. It does with every High Demon female who is claimed. The pain and hurt have to go away, and the male has to make amends and try to regain his female's trust. It is a long road, m'hala. Say you'll take that road with me. Give me a chance, Reah. What you see in front of you now is the only thing that will touch you from now on. I know how to be gentle, avilepha. I will give you only pleasure from now on. The pain is over. My claiming marks are beautiful, love, and a reminder that you suffered in the claiming. The Thifilathi is satisfied. He will not harm you again."

"Tory, how do I know that? I only recently learned I am part High Demon. I don't know your race." I tried to roll over and turn away from him. What was I supposed to do? Just believe everything they said? Why hadn't they warned me about this ahead of time? Why?

"I wanted to talk to you. Dad and Uncle Jayd wanted to wait until closer to time so you wouldn't have a long period to worry over it. Once the Thifilathi has chosen his mate, he will hunt ceaselessly for her until he finds her. It is always better if he can claim her under controlled circumstances."

"So, your father," I began.

"Well, Kifirin placed my mother in a healing sleep, so she wasn't awake for the claiming," Tory sounded embarrassed. "She woke in pain, though, and she wouldn't let anyone touch her at first. Uncle Reemagar finally found her and convinced her to let him heal as much as he could. That's how that happened. Mom doesn't know that Dad told me," he added. "Mom has Kifirin's claiming marks too. He put his teeth in her neck first."

"But she has other children," I pointed out. Erland Morphis was Ry's father, and Gavril was Gavin's son.

"Ry and I were born to surrogate mothers, using Mom's DNA in donor eggs. The Larentii manipulated them—they were Mom's eggs when they were finished. Sissy came the same way Ry and I did. Gavril came the traditional way. But Mom isn't High Demon. She's vampire, but before that, she was a quarter Bright Elemaiya and a quarter Karathian Witch. We think that had something to do with all this."

"But I'm only a quarter High Demon." I pointed out.

"But you have every one of the High Demon gifts, according to Kifirin. Now that Aurelius has given you blood, you're immortal. That was the only thing we were all worried about."

Tory had just let something slip that I didn't know. "When did Aurelius give me blood? I don't remember that." Tory saw that this upset me.

"Hush, baby—I didn't realize he hadn't told you. I think he gave it the night you spent with him. Did he give you something to drink?"

"Yes, but it was fruit juice."

"That's how they give it to those who aren't vampire or werewolf—in juice of some sort. It helps mask the taste. Think about it, Reah—have you had to void, since then?"

I had to think for a moment to realize what he'd been asking me. It dawned eventually. "No," I replied, "but that was sporadic before then. I've gone for days before without having to—you know."

"It's the High Demon in you—your body was almost completely efficient, just as mine is. Now, that is complete and you won't age past a certain point. You may look like you're in your early to mid-twenties eventually, but no older than that. You're not susceptible to diseases anymore, either." He turned me gently until I was looking up at his face again. "Reah, I love you. I think I was hooked the minute I first saw you. My Thifilathi certainly made his feelings known during the full moon only a few days later. If you hadn't still been recovering, things might have happened sooner. I don't know whether that would have been a good thing or a bad thing. That's why the female High Demons are kept away from the males for the most part—so they won't be taken unaware or by the wrong one. You weren't locked up, Reah. It was only a matter of time." Tory's blue eyes looked right into mine as he bumped his forehead against mine. "We belong together, Reah. I hope you can get over the claiming someday and come to love me." He flouted Karzac's orders and kissed me before folding away abruptly. I lay there and stared at the ceiling for a very long time afterward.

"She didn't scream or call me names, and she only cried a little," Tory sat heavily on one of his mother's guest chairs inside her study. Lissa watched her son's face—he wasn't as upset as he had been before going to visit Reah. Karzac had already been by, saying that Tory had bathed Reah without taking too many liberties.

"Honey, take it slow, all right? I know you want to be with her right this minute, but she has to digest all this first." Tory's eyes were a darker version of Lissa's sky-blue. With his dark hair, he looked quite handsome. "Torevik Rolfe Rath, are you listening to me?" Lissa was attempting to get Tory's attention.

"I'm listening, Mom."

"The problem we'll have, I think, is working things out between Reah and your Uncle Norian. Not to mention Lendill." Lissa was testing the waters; Tory knew what Lendill had done. Sure enough, a curl of smoke came from Tory's nostrils at the mention of Lendill's name.

~

"Lord Morphis, what did you learn?" Erland Morphis knew things had become serious if Wylend was calling him *Lord* Morphis.

"Lissa says that Karzac has estimated around two weeks for recovery, my King," Erland bowed respectfully, flashing a thousand-watt smile. His son had inherited the same smile.

"I almost don't know how to go about this—I've never found anyone that I wanted in this position before," Wylend sighed.

"I heard she didn't react badly when your great-grandson went to make amends with her. That may be a good sign."

"Will it not be awkward, though?"

"No more awkward than the Falchani twins."

"Well, there is that," Wylend agreed. "I do not intend to interfere or encroach upon her relationship with Torevik."

"You will not. You are quite busy, my King. I think things can be worked out." Erland was still smiling.

"I am most displeased about the length of time she has remaining with the ASD."

"Norian does seem to have a tight grip on her. Do you think that might be worked out in some way?"

"Look into the rules for me, Lord Morphis."

"Of course, my King."

CHAPTER 2

Gavril was snuggled against my left shoulder as we sat in bed, doing research for his latest report. I was feeling better and wondering with much trepidation when the Director or Vice-Director might summon me. I'm sure Karzac had made them aware that I'd be healed enough for duty in another week. They had weeks on Le-Ath Veronis—a seven-day period instead of the eight-day that Tulgalan employed. It depended upon the planet, its government and how they wanted their months divided. Le-Ath Veronis had twenty-eight day months, exactly. Tulgalan took thirty-two days in their moon turns and fourteen moon turns to travel around its sun.

"Here—it says that Wasternell nearly destroyed itself with chemical warfare around three thousand years ago," I pointed out the specific passage. We were reading through archaic records translated directly from an old language that was extremely difficult to wade through. My thoughts turned to Aurelius too, and whether he would return before I was sent out again by the ASD. Tory came to see me often, and we went to the pool area or the arboretum. He mostly wanted to sit with me pulled against him. We talked. He told me more about the High Demons and their history. I was still having difficulty reconciling it as part of my history, too.

"We need to find the reason for their war," Gavril was bringing me back to the present.

"Wars are usually over land or money or something of that nature," I leaned my cheek on Gavril's shoulder.

"I should have known I'd find you two together." Lissa walked into Gavril's bedroom. That was our favorite place to study. My stomach felt queasy suddenly—this is how I'd learned the last time that the Vice-Director wanted to see me. "Reah, Vice-Director Schaff wants to talk to you in my office. Do you need assistance getting there?" This time was no different from the last, except too many things had happened since then.

I didn't need assistance, as much as I might want Gavril or Tory to go with me. I shivered at the mention of Lendill Schaff's title. At least my strength was returning and my shoulder wound looked much better. Karzac kept reassuring me that the scar would disappear completely in a few weeks.

"Re, don't worry," Gavril whispered as I slid off his bed. While most boys his age might have coverlets depicting sports teams or musicians or some such, Gavril's was a studious deep green with matching pillows. He'd picked it out himself—I'd asked about it.

"Thanks, Chash." I gave him a quick hug before walking past Lissa and out Gavril's door.

"Reah, we'll be sending you to Pheslik—drakus seed is showing up there, now," Vice-Director Schaff got right to business. He had such a handsome face and it covered the demeanor and cruelty of a viper. I did my best not to shiver in his presence, or give myself away when all I wanted to do was weep. I also wanted to ask him about Bel, Hish and Max, but that might bring about more abuse.

Gavril might know if the wizards from Mandil were still being held in the palace dungeons. I hoped so—I wanted to see them. Alone.

I had my doubts, somehow, that Bel was in this as deeply as Director Keef seemed to think. I worried over Bel and the others—were they being mistreated? Vice-Director Schaff had certainly done his best to mistreat me. I'd never had a seizure in my life, even when Edan was doing his worst.

"You'll be going out again with Rylend and Torevik, but under an assumed name this time. I'll have your new ID and credit chip waiting when the healer releases you." That was my dismissal, so I rose, gave the best respectful dip of my head I could and walked out, my legs feeling like rubber.

"How did it go?" Norian Keef walked in only moments after Reah had gone.

"She'll never trust us again," Lendill sighed.

Aurelius was leaping from one tree to the next, using vampire speed. Spawn were littered throughout the jungle and he couldn't take all of them at once. They were easily confused—these were young, having been taken from the local population not long before. Aurelius figured they were less than a month old—barely having sloughed away their human appearance. A concentrated effort had been made to take over this portion of the population—Birimeran technology was in its infancy, but it was there, in the highly populated areas in the north. Here in the southern jungles, the native population was less educated and more superstitious. Those still retaining their humanity spoke of the spawn as gods or godlike, with the speed and agility that any Ra'Ak spawn gained when turned. Aurelius had already asked for help and it was scheduled to come soon. He hoped it came—*now*.

Something didn't feel right on the way back to Gavril's room. It wasn't just the discomfort I felt after listening to Vice-Director Schaff. This was wrong, somehow. Really wrong. As in, someone was in trouble or something. It only got worse as I walked along until it had my stomach cramping. I'd never felt anything like this before, unless it had been—well—on Mandil. I had to think back; it seemed a lifetime ago, although it hadn't been very long at all. People I cared for had been in danger, and then, "Aurelius!" I was shouting his name as something happened that I never expected to happen. Not without help or instruction.

Aurelius was backed up against the bare cliff face—he realized that the spawn had only been herding him through the trees when he reached that spot. More had been waiting there and he was cut off. Piles of spawn dust littered the rock and shale around the cliff, but there were too many of the creatures remaining for Aurelius to turn his back on them and attempt to climb. More could be waiting at the top, he realized; he was too afraid to use the ability he had to *Look* and find out.

Six spawn attacked at once, forcing Aurelius to use his speed and vampire claws to behead them. His eyes were red and he was hissing, he knew. While that might frighten any normal humanoid, it had no effect on spawn. If they were instructed to attack, then they would attack, with no fear for their lives. Aurelius knew something was directing these—they never acted in concert like this without something more intelligent behind them. More came walking out of the jungle, stalking him. Aurelius might have been able to take down fifty or so alone, but there were more than that. Many more. Aurelius prepared himself for what was to come.

"Aurelius!" I was shouting his name and my Thifilatha was running through a rainforest, even as I swept spawn aside with my arms. I was burning them, too, whenever I touched them—they were screeching and dusting if they came in contact with any part of me. There had to be hundreds of them, at the very least. With my height as Thifilatha, I could see Aurelius backed up against a rocky cliff, fighting them off the best he could. If Gavril hadn't described what vampires looked like when they fought, I might have been frightened. Aurelius' fangs were showing, as were his lengthy claws. His eyes were red, too—Gavril had explained that it happened whenever a vampire fought or was in danger. Aurelius was dealing with both those things.

"I'm coming, my love!" I was using Aurelius' endearment for me. Stooping low, I flung out my arms and killed another swath of spawn. Some thought to attack me. It was their last thought. Aurelius was still fighting—I think he was regaining hope that he might live over this. I was nearly there, too, when the spawn that had been waiting at the top of the cliff leapt over the edge, dropping down upon Aurelius.

Aurelius stared in shock as Reah, in full Thifilatha, leapt toward him, her beautiful, translucent gold wings spread out, catching the spawn that now fell from the sky. The ones that hit her wings burned and winked out of existence, like fireworks on a clear, summer night. It might have been lovely to watch, except for the shrieks the spawn made before they dusted. Aurelius stood at the foot of the cliff while Reah stood over him at fifteen feet in height, spawn striking her wings by the dozens, bouncing against her head and body before screaming, burning and dusting.

Spawn dust hit the cliff face like a sandstorm, causing Aurelius to hunch down and cover his head to keep blasting particles from his eyes. He hoped the mass dusting wasn't blinding Reah—she'd come to protect him. There wasn't any way he might have lived over this, otherwise.

"Reah my love, are you going to change back now?" Aurelius patted one of my huge, gold-scaled arms. I'd sat down wearily against the cliff face after the last of the spawn had been killed. The piles of spawn dust surrounding us were several hands high. I'd learned, too, after changing this time, that I truly could burn what I chose and hold back the burning if someone I trusted wished to touch me while I was Thifilatha. Aurelius was touching me now.

"Four feet," Aurelius read my thoughts and nodded at my estimation of how deep the spawn dust was that lay about us. "And I am grateful you can hold back that talent you seem to have," he added with a tired smile.

"Auri, please teach me your measurements sometime," I sighed. I wanted to hold my head in my hands—it hurt. Karzac was going to have a fit when we got back—he hadn't released me yet, but there wasn't any way I would leave Aurelius here to die. I loved him. I knew that for certain, now—my heart had squeezed horribly when I'd seen him fighting off hundreds of spawn, trapped against the cliff face as he was. "Are there anymore spawn?" I asked after a moment, when Aurelius hadn't answered me.

"No, love. You killed them all."

"You got your share."

"I got what I could. Now, change back, please. I can't hold you when you're like this." He looked up at me.

"She doesn't know how." Someone else was there with us, suddenly. Someone I didn't recognize. "I have seen you, young one, but each time you were asleep or unconscious."

I blinked at him; he was beautiful to look upon. I could also see the aura and power surrounding him. Struggling into a kneeling position, I placed my forehead on the ground at his feet. Somehow, I knew what he was, even if I couldn't put a name or words to it.

"Few know to bow to me nowadays," he said, smiling a wondrous smile. "My fault, I'm sure. Young one, rise up. I will teach you to come back to yourself."

"I am Kifirin, Lord of the Dark Realm," the god told me later, after he'd shown me how to regain my normal shape. Aurelius had watched both of us carefully as Kifirin had worked with me. It only took concentration on my part—visualizing what I wanted—and it happened. Kifirin was more than handsome as a man—he was the most beautiful creature I'd ever seen.

"Little one, you were foretold long ago," Kifirin said as I searched for something to cover myself. Turning Thifilatha destroys whatever I am wearing at the moment.

"That sounds like a child's tale," I muttered at Kifirin's statement.

"But this foretelling only came to me." Kifirin's smile might stop many a heart, I think. "It is not time, yet, to explain that tale. I will go." Kifirin disappeared as quickly as he'd arrived.

"What did that mean?" Aurelius took his shirt off and wrapped me in it. It bore rips and tears but it covered most of me—likely because I could wrap it around myself twice.

"Auri, I don't know and my head hurts," I rubbed my forehead.

"I'll fold us back, then," Aurelius' breath was warm against my temple as he kissed me gently and lifted me in his arms.

"Aurelius, I'm sorry—we didn't know how bad it was and there wasn't anybody we could have sent that quickly." Someone named Kiarra paced in front of Aurelius and me. Her hair wasn't as white as mine, but it was close.

"It doesn't matter now—my Reah came to get me," Aurelius was smiling down at me. I sat beside him inside Lissa's office—it was the second time I'd been inside it within a day.

"Young woman, if this had been for any other reason, I would be chewing you out, right now." Karzac flung the door open so hard it bounced against the doorstop and almost hit him in the shoulder. He glared at it and it stopped just short of his body. That look could quell anyone or anything into submission, I think.

"Karzac, I'm sorry and I have a headache. Can we still be friends?" I asked in a small voice.

"You saved one of ours. Even so, I would have been your friend anyway," Karzac placed a warm hand against my forehead. The pounding headache subsided, then disappeared. "Little one, if I yell at you at any time, it is only because I care about you and you have frightened me. There will be no other reason. Do you understand?" He had my face in both his hands, his green-gold eyes staring into mine.

"Yes," I nodded. He still held my face in his hands, after all.

"Aurelius, did she injure her Thifilatha in any way? Are her wings intact?" Karzac turned to Aurelius.

"She was whole," Aurelius assured my healer. "As am I. I would not have been, however." Aurelius gripped one of my hands in his.

Kiarra left us after a while, leaving Karzac with us. Tory walked in and together he and Karzac explained the events on Tulgalan to Aurelius. They also informed him of what had occurred since then. Aurelius growled when he heard that Nods had shot me, and then growled again over Tory's claiming. Tory flushed, embarrassed to give Aurelius the truth. I know I was embarrassed, too, although Karzac insisted that none of it was my doing. Then we went over what had happened with Norian Keef and Lendill Schaff.

"The ASD has some answers to give me," Aurelius' voice was nearly unintelligible and his eyes were red.

"Master Vampire, you need to hold that back—they still have a tight grip on our young one, here." Karzac jerked his head in my direction. "I do not wish to cause her more grief than she has experienced already."

"If they allow their argument with me to interfere with their fair treatment of Reah, then they aren't much in the way of men." Aurelius rose from his seat, dropping my hand. He was angry—dangerously so. Karzac had insinuated that the Director and the Vice-Director might treat me worse if Aurelius voiced his concerns. Was that what would happen? It made me want to cry.

"Baby, hush." Tory gathered me tightly against his side. "They haven't treated me or Ry badly."

"You are sons of a queen, and the sons of Director Keef's mate," Karzac grumbled. "Of course you will not be treated as any conscript might be treated. Reah is a rare treasure and they intend to use her any way they can."

"Is that what you think?" Norian Keef slammed the door so hard against the wall it crushed the doorstop and split the fine wood of the door.

"Yes, that's exactly what I think, Director," Karzac spat. "Tell me what you did when you forced that child to walk through the entire palace and then down two flights of steps to the dungeon, when she shouldn't have been on her feet at all. Tell me what that second of yours was thinking when he dug his fingers into a ranos pistol wound. Tell me what you were both thinking when you stood there for minutes, watching our little one go into convulsions and nearly die. Were you hoping that your prisoner would confess something right then? As I hear it, he was shouting at you to help her!"

Norian's face held guilt. There wasn't any other way to describe it. I was wiping tears away—only now was I hearing the incident described. I hadn't been lucid enough at the time to say exactly what had happened. And Karzac had been warning Aurelius about voicing his opinions to Norian Keef. Well, Karzac's temper had just gotten the better of him.

"We will not be treating agent Nilvas worse, now." Norian ran fingers through his brown hair. He was slightly shorter than Karzac, and there was still something dangerous about Director Keef. I wouldn't want to be on the opposite side of Karzac's anger, however. Who knew what the physician might be capable of doing?

"You've already done that. How can the worst become more so?" Aurelius' eyes were so dark a red they were nearly black.

"Vampire, it was not my intention to cause that much harm. Neither Lendill nor I knew how bad off she was. We thought the healer, here, and the Larentii had taken care of things. We were wrong."

"And you did not ask." Karzac was still furious. Nothing Norian Keef had to say would make up for what Karzac might consider gross negligence and outright endangerment. I'm not sure how I knew that, but the information filtered into my mind somehow. And Director Keef—he was angry as well. Angry with Karzac, angry with Aurelius, angry with Lendill and angry with himself. Surprisingly, I didn't detect anger with me and that caused me to wonder. I was still pressed tightly against Tory's side. I shivered in his embrace.

"Norian, are you destroying my study?" Queen Lissa walked through the door.

"I am surrounded by people who wish to destroy me," Norian grumbled.

"And I might be convinced to help them if you are frightening Reah," Lissa pointed a finger at her mate. It made me wonder how they'd become mated to begin with. Director Keef's actions so far hadn't spelled out an ideal mate for the Queen of Le-Ath Veronis. Not in my eyes, anyway.

"He's a lion snake shapeshifter, and he wasn't always this awful." Lissa turned her gaze to me.

"Lissa, the fact that you gave away that secret would have you imprisoned, if you were one of my conscripts," Norian snapped. "And thank you for calling me awful in front of my employees."

"She already thought that, don't you think? Norian, this isn't your normal conscript. You know that." Lissa flung a hand in my direction. "She's nineteen, for fuck's sake. She didn't tell anyone while she was growing up that her brother, who is actually her father, was doing his best to beat the life out of her. I think she can keep your secret, Norian Keef, as well as keeping her own." Lissa's eyes were now just as deep a red as Aurelius' were. And what had she said about Edan?

"Oh, no," my vision went dark.

"Reah, don't pass out, baby," Tory was patting my cheek while Karzac rushed over, placing fingers against my forehead.

Vice-Director Schaff was standing next to the sofa when I woke. I blinked up at him, wanting to cry. Was he going to hurt me again? That's what Edan had done. If I passed out after he hit me, he'd hit me again when I woke, just for fainting in the first place.

"She thinks you will harm her. State your business and leave." Karzac was still there and handing out orders. Tory was there, too, as was Aurelius. My head was in Auri's lap and Tory was blowing clouds of smoke from his nostrils.

"Reah, we wanted to tell you soon. About Edan Desh. Addah had the DNA tests run shortly after your birth. He suspected even then. We figure it was the reason he sent you to Edan. His mistake was never telling either of you what he'd found—that Edan was your father. We suspect foul play, not only in that but also in your mother's death. We are currently investigating Edan, Marzi Desh and the physician who attended your mother. We are very close to bringing charges against them—for rape, murder and child abuse. You no longer have to level abuse charges—if other, more serious crimes are committed, the abuse victim doesn't have to be involved. The state will prosecute." Lendill nodded curtly to Karzac and strode swiftly from the room.

"I was born of rape." That fact settled into my brain—it was so much like Edan to do something like that and so much like his mother Marzi to convince him it was a good idea in order to get rid of another, whom she saw as a rival.

"Reah, you can't let that upset you," Aurelius now held me on his lap. "None of this was your doing, love."

I saw the wisdom and reason in his words—it did nothing to keep my heart beating at a more steady rhythm or my mind from going in circles. They'd killed my mother. She hadn't wanted to leave me, perhaps. Her death was something that had plagued me over the years, and Marzi's whispered "You should never have been born," when I was six now made more sense.

"Marzi probably wanted to tell Addah that my mother had gone to bed with Edan," I mumbled, even while Aurelius kissed my temple and held me tightly against him. "But when my mother became pregnant, I guess other things prevented it."

"Reah, stop thinking about it, baby." Tory went to his knees in front of Aurelius and me. "We're trying to get you back from the other things. This shouldn't have been dumped in your lap just now."

"No time would have been a good time, my love." Aurelius stroked hair away from my face. I suppose it was growing out a little.

"Reah, I don't want to place you in a healing sleep but I will if this overwhelms you," Karzac was still there.

"I just feel cold," I muttered. I did feel cold.

"It would help if you'd drink some hot tea with Tory and me." Aurelius rose easily, even with me still in his arms. He was vampire—he was strong.

"I want to come." Gavril poked his head in the door. "Master Morwin wouldn't let me leave my lessons early. I got here as fast as I could." His dark eyes held a silent apology for me.

"Chash, don't worry about it." Aurelius set me down and Gavril and I were hugging each other tightly.

"I heard all that stuff; my hearing's really good," Gavril said. "Reah, it doesn't matter how you got here. Where would Aurelius and I be if you hadn't been born? I'd have taken that shot instead of you—you shoved me out of the way. Believe me, anybody brave enough to go pound on a High Demon in his smaller Thifilathi to keep him from killing a witness gets the highest marks in my book."

"She was pounding on me? I don't remember that," Tory grumped.

"And yelling at you. I think if she hadn't been your mate, you might have killed her, too." Ry walked in. I hadn't seen him for a while—he'd stayed out of the picture while Tory had been courting me.

That is how I ended up being escorted to the kitchens by a High Demon, a vampire, the child of vampires, a Karathian warlock and a healer. The cook was the same, I saw—he still hadn't gotten his job on the light half of the planet.

"You're the one who made the fish," he said when I walked in, supported by Gavril on one side and Aurelius on the other. Tory allowed his younger brother to help me down the long warren of hallways into the kitchen. "I am Chef Harding," he held out his hand. "I can never get the fish to come out right," he said.

"You're only cooking it a little too long," I said. "Make the sauce first, then do the fish. It always turns out better that way."

"I don't suppose I could get your sauce recipe?"

"Not that one," I said. Gavril and Aurelius let me go. "I can show you one that won't get you involved in a lawsuit with Desh's, though."

That's how Chef Harding and I collaborated to make fish with a new sauce and serve it to our audience. Karzac had held Aurelius back. "We will allow this—it is a distraction," he whispered. I heard but pretended I hadn't.

"This is amazing," Chef Harding moaned with pleasure as he tasted his portion.

"I am happy with this," I agreed—the recipe had been bubbling in my head for a while—I just hadn't found the time to try it. We had a menu planned around the fish before all was said and done. Norian, Lissa and Lendill came into the kitchen right then and I was proud of myself—I didn't slam plates down or grumble as I served the Director and his second-in-command.

"I'm immune to poisons, so you'll have to kill me a different way," Norian's half-grin was a little on the wry side. Lendill said nothing at all.

"Permission to speak freely, Director?" I asked.

"Permission granted."

"I wouldn't stoop to killing you," I snapped. "You're not worth spending the rest of my life in prison over, or dying on one of the worlds that still hands out the death penalty. Vice-Director, I hope your life is never in danger. I might have second thoughts about saving that tight ass of yours." Skipping to get to Aurelius had been easy—I don't know why I hadn't thought of doing it before. I skipped away now; it was a simple feat to accomplish.

"Bel?" The light was dim inside his cell but bright in the hallway just outside it, making it difficult to identify the wizard. Bel was sitting on a cot shoved against the back wall, his gaze locked on the white wall opposite his cage. His expression was a hopeless one—he didn't expect to get away from his Alliance prison.

"Reah? Thank the gods—they wouldn't give me any information on you. We thought you were dead." Bel stood and walked toward the bars, staring at me as if I were a ghost.

"No, just almost there for a while," I said.

"Reah, this isn't what it looks like," Bel said, holding out his hand to me. He was careful not to brush against the bars of his cage.

"I was hoping it wasn't," I said, grasping his fingers in mine. "But I have to tell you, it doesn't look so good from the Alliance standpoint."

"I know. Reah, you have no idea how bad things are. The High Commander is in charge of things on Mandil, now. The Prince Royal is little more than a figurehead. Has been for a while, now." Bel shook his head in dismay at his own statement. "We didn't realize until later that three of the Prince's wizards aren't Mandili—they came from somewhere else. They were hired by the High Commander, and everything the Prince said or did was funneled straight to that stinking pile of—well. The High Commander paid the desert villages to raise drakus seed alongside their citrus crops. It was easy enough to accomplish." Bel squeezed my fingers.

"The Prince came to the Rangers shortly before you came to us, Reah. He asked us to place ourselves under the High Commander's authority. If it hadn't been for the drakus seed, the High Commander would have ordered the outlying villages to empty and come to Crown City long ago. He wasn't willing to let all that go—he just hadn't calculated on the strength or the tenacity of the enemy we faced. He didn't know what they were. He sent us and those other two cohorts to the desert outposts to protect the locals and their drug crop. Those fool wizards the Prince has don't have much in the way of protection against spawn. The High Commander almost destroyed Mandil."

"Bel, are you telling me you were undercover? The whole time?"

"Reah, please believe me. We'll die over this—they're sending us back to Tulgalan for judgment, didn't you know? One of those kids who died was the son of a High Council member. They'll sentence us to Evensun for that reason alone. Leave it to the High Commander to recruit shit for brains Nods Whitlin."

"You're telling the truth, I'd know if you weren't," I said. He *was* telling the truth. I'd been able to tell truth from a lie since I was six. I'd known Marzi was telling me the truth when she'd whispered her poison in my ear. "But what were you going to do? I mean, there had to be some sort of plan, didn't there? After you reported back to the Prince?" At that moment, I was desperately hoping there was a plan.

"Reah, we—the Rangers—were hoping to take the High Commander's wizards down, as soon as we figured out what they were doing and who they were selling to. We don't have any contacts with the Alliance—all we have is a shaky treaty to leave each other alone and a few wizards who are still loyal to the crown. I don't know if our ability will be enough—we've missed Lin and Jorvis. More than you can ever know. We miss you, too, Reah. I don't know what it was that we saw that night; I only know that without it, we would all be dead."

Both of us gasped and turned as we heard the footsteps coming down the hall. "Go, Reah," Bel hissed. "You don't need to be caught here!" I took Bel's advice and skipped away.

"Can we believe this?" Lendill Schaff held up the small chip from the hidden camera, wiggling it suggestively at Norian.

"I think we can," Norian grinned. "Reah gets us what we want and we didn't even have to do anything for it."

"Except act like assholes," Lendill muttered, handing the chip over.

"Yeah—we have a lot of begging and scraping to do after we get this cleared up."

"If we get it cleared up. The more drakus seed that gets out, the more deaths it leaves in its wake. If this becomes widespread, the entire Alliance could fall. The Alliance worlds are looking to the ASD and the Alliance armies to deal with this. It has become too large a problem much too quickly, and we have too little intelligence to kill it swiftly. They'll break away and try to handle the problem themselves if it looks like we can't." Norian rubbed his forehead—he felt a headache coming on. "Ever since those fools on Campiaa decided to form their own Alliance by accepting every black-hearted planet in the known universes, we've been under attack. If we can't get this cleaned up soon, the Reth Alliance could die a painful death. They're trying to break us up, Lendill. Any way they can."

"Then I have a suggestion," Lendill smiled.

"What's that?" Norian was willing to listen to anything at this point.

"We're sending the prisoners to Tulgalan in three days. Let's stage a breakout along the way and attribute it to those rogues we have in custody. Let's arrange for a quick death for our shooter, too. He killed all those kids—not the Rangers." Lendill had come to think of the captive wizards in those terms—Bel and Reah both had referred to them that way.

"And we'll send ours back to Mandil with them—Ry and Tory both, in addition to Reah. They already know Reah, that won't be a stretch, and we'll say that those three were captured in the bust—rival dealers and such. Maybe those three, combined with the Rangers who work for the Prince, can successfully bring down those rogue wizards and then the drakus seed farms can be destroyed." Norian liked the idea. Very much. "What do you think, Lendill?"

"I'm all for giving it a try. How much danger do you think they'll be in?"

"Some, but remember Tory and Ry can transport themselves away at any time. Reah, too, unless I miss my guess. How did she get into the dungeon otherwise?" Norian was grinning.

"I'll call them in for a meeting," Lendill agreed.

"We have a change of plans—you'll be going farther undercover than you've ever been before," Lendill paced as he made the announcement. "You'll have a new destination, too."

"Where is that?" Ry asked. He wasn't huddled against Tory; I was. He wasn't terrified of Vice-Director Lendill Schaff; I was. Ry, Tory and I took up the sofa in Queen Lissa's study as we listened to Lendill Schaff and Norian Keef.

"We'll tell you in a moment," Lendill assured us. Norian was seated behind Lissa's desk, his fingers steepled. He was watching all three of us—very carefully. Some sort of plot was going on here; I just didn't know what it might be. "First, I want to show you some images recorded yesterday." He held up a tiny chip.

I stared openmouthed as the entire conversation between Bel and me was played on the screen that popped out of a credenza behind Lissa's desk. Norian had moved aside so we could get the full picture. Why had I been so stupid? Why? I wanted to bang my head against the low, wood table in front of Tory, Ry and me. Tory moved his arm until his fingers were covering my forehead—he'd read my thoughts and was taking preventive measures. I'm sure I presented a lovely picture for both Lendill and Norian—my gaping mouth coupled with Tory's hand.

"Reah, you should learn that we have cameras everywhere—even if Lissa is unaware," Norian chuckled. Well, it was fine sport I'm sure, making fun of my stupidity and inexperience.

"We're not making fun of you," Lendill pointed out. "If you had realized there were cameras, we wouldn't be in possession of vital information, now would we?" He was smiling. That smile twisted my heart and made me feel ill. He tapped a button on Lissa's desk, making the vidscreen go blank and slide back inside the credenza.

"Now," Lendill went on, "all three of you are officially under arrest."

CHAPTER 3

Vidscreens had been brought and hung on the walls opposite our cells. We got a very clear image of Tory, Ry and me, all being led away in cuffs toward the dungeon. A reporter was telling everyone in the Alliance how we'd been a part of the drakus seed fiasco on Tulgalan, which had nearly destroyed Taritha Village. They'd even recorded an interview with a tearful Silva. "I knew something was wrong with them," she wept. "They killed my Danthus."

A lie was in her words, and I figured it was an attempt to draw attention to herself, somehow. It made me feel ill.

"Don't let it get to you," Bel's cell was on my right. He, Hish and Max had all been brought into Lissa's office after cuffs were placed on Ry, Tory and me. All of us had been made aware of the plan before being hauled down to the dungeon, in full view of Nods, whose cell was located just off the stairs. He had plenty of guards around him, too. I wondered if he knew that most of them were vampires.

"Did you tell?" Nods was standing at the bars and shouting at Bel as he walked past, his head down, his wrists cuffed.

"We can't get anything out of these," Lendill snarled at Nods, who backed away in fear. "Maybe we'll have more luck with you—looks like you have your voice back, now." Nods looked guilty and frightened, giving me the idea that he hadn't said anything until now. He glared at me, too. "So, trying to take our business away, huh?" He accused. Somebody had already been talking within his hearing. Norian had plotted this with a master's hand; I had to give him that. Nods was to be sent back to Tulgalan to face justice. At first they'd thought to kill him, but then thought it better if he made the journey to Tulgalan. He was the shooter, after all. The rest of us were merely accomplices.

Now I sat and watched what everyone else in the Alliance was watching—the newsfeeds about how Ry, Tory and I had been engaged in a drug turf war, trying to take down a rival for the drakus seed trade. Seven people had died as a result, including Danthus. I was sorry about him—he'd seemed level-headed, whereas his brother Inis hadn't. Inis had survived, somehow. Is that the way it went, more often than not? I shook my head.

"Baby, don't let them hurt you." Tory was on my other side. Karzac had been down once already, complaining in a language I didn't understand the entire time. Norian and Lendill had watched while Karzac looked me over, putting his hands on me to ease aches and pains.

"She'll be ready to travel tomorrow, but that's all," Karzac looked as if he wanted to punch Norian as he walked through the door to my cell.

"Your concern is noted, healer," Norian sounded snippy. Karzac then proceeded to hold a lengthy conversation with Norian, still in a language I didn't understand. Norian looked well and truly chastised when Karzac was finished and stalking away.

"I've offended the healer," Norian muttered, before he and Lendill followed Karzac.

"Reah, come here, baby." My cell lay between Bel's and Tory's. Tory was holding his hand through the bars between our cages. I walked over and sat down next to him. He was barely able to kiss my forehead between the bars. "It'll be all right," he soothed.

"I send you after information, and I see this on the vids instead?" Wylend Arden looked as if he were about to tear his luxurious private suite apart. Erland watched the King of Karathia pace.

"My son is part of this too, I'll have you know," Erland pointed out. "As is Gardevik's. I can assure you, I couldn't see for the smoke billowing from Garde's nostrils when he learned of this. All I can say is that Norian Keef and his Vice-Director will be very dead men if this does not turn out in a satisfactory manner."

"I will be there before you, and they will suffer before they die," Wylend agreed.

"Reah, promise you will come back to me. Promise." Aurelius was stroking my face. He'd folded aboard the Alliance ship, run by ASD operatives—all of whom were trusted by Norian and Lendill. I didn't know how far to extend that trust if I were honest with myself.

"Auri, I will do everything I can to come back to you. I promise that," I said. I had no idea if any of us were going to live through this.

"I love you," Aurelius whispered and then disappeared before either of us could weep over the parting. I was shaking afterward.

"Very nice. Now get in your cell," the ASD agent snapped. He'd been watching us the whole time. Norian had given official permission, as he'd called it, for a visit before I was hauled off to Tulgalan. Meekly I entered my tiny cell and the door was shut and locked behind me. If I hadn't known that I could skip away from my cell, my claustrophobic Thifilatha would likely have been beating the door down.

I had no way to gauge time as we traveled—I was sealed off from the others inside the cell—there was barely enough room for the narrow bed and the food dispenser in the wall. No room to walk, pace or worry. No windows, either, so no way to communicate with my fellow prisoners. Except Ry and Tory had mindspeech.

Don't fret, avilepha. Tory's voice came; he was talking in my head after reading my thoughts.

Reah, it will be fine—you'll see. Ry was now weighing in.

Oh sure, you've done this a hundred times, probably, I said right back to them. Not that it would do any good.

Reah? Did you just say something? Tory sounded shocked.

Did you hear me? I was shocked, too.

I heard you. Ry's mindspeech was thick with disbelief.

Holy crap. I used one of Gavril's favorite phrases. I hadn't been allowed to see Gavril—I'd been handed a comp-vid and we'd said good-bye that way. Gavril had been about to have a meltdown, as was I. He said much the same thing Aurelius had, asking me to promise to come back. It was so hard, saying that good-bye. Now I tried something else. *Bel, can you hear me?*

Reah? Shock was a mild word—astonished might have been closer to the mark. *You have mindspeech, Reah?* He thought to ask the second question.

It seems so, I answered. *What about Hish and Max?*

Not all the wizards have it—Delvin has it too. Hish and Max don't.

Where is Delvin?

Keeping the High Commander happy with his shielding tricks, Bel muttered mentally.

Poor Delvin. I thought Hish was the only one who could shield.

Hish is much better at it—Delvin's shields are weaker and he can only protect himself and one or two others. The High Commander is only worried about his own skin.

So Delvin is good enough for that and Hish can risk his life elsewhere?

Yes.

You know the High Commander is a coward.

Reah, don't say that to anyone other than to me or Delvin. And then only mentally. Understand?

That sounded worrisome. Did Bel suspect some of his own Rangers? I was going to have to talk to Tory and Ry about that. I did. Immediately and at length. I told them about all the Ranger wizards who still lived, and what their talents were.

"Where are you going?" Wald asked. Edan was shrugging into his heavy coat; it was snowing outside. Edan's half-brother Wald didn't want to open the restaurant alone that evening.

"To the nearest constabulary station," Edan grumbled. He'd seen the vids, just as everyone else had. The name didn't fit, but he'd know that face anywhere. Reah had managed to get herself into too much trouble. It sounded as if she'd found a bad crowd after she'd been sent to who knew where by the idiot who worked for the Governor of the Realm. Edan had no desire to claim a daughter as his mother demanded. This was his excuse—he was ready to hand fabricated information to the constabulary and the ASD—that would absolve him of any responsibility where Reah was concerned. She was nothing to him, and he'd see to it that Addah Desh could never lay claim to her talents, either.

"Edan, someone here to see you," his assistant cook, Mardin, showed a man into Edan's office.

"I don't have time," Edan snapped, smoothing out the collar of his coat. He backed up quickly when the ASD badge was shoved in his face.

"Well, Edan, you managed to drag me into your little mistake, didn't you?" Marzi Desh hissed at her son.

"As if you didn't force me into it," Edan snapped back. The two had been left in an interviewing room together. Lendill was smiling as he watched the vid-recorder. They were about to give him everything he wanted and he wouldn't be forced to ask a single question. The rest of the family could be kept quiet if Lendill promised to keep this out of the news. He had an interview set up with Addah Desh the following afternoon.

It's time, Reah. I'd fallen asleep but Tory's voice in my head woke me.

All right, I said. The whole thing had been carefully planned. Ry would provide the initial explosion—Bel said he didn't know if he could control his blasts well enough. We didn't want to breach the hull of the ship—that would come later, just for show. The whole ship shook anyway with the force of Ry's blast. Cell doors popped open. Only a few remained locked. Nods' door was one of those. I was out of my cube quickly and running down the hall. Tory, using the strength any High Demon possessed, ripped off spelled cuffs—they held no power against him. Or me. I ripped my cuffs off. Ry didn't need Tory's help—he'd been the one to spell the cuffs to begin with. I hadn't known that until Norian Keef let it slip.

Bel, Hish and Max were all glad to get rid of the cuffs—I could see that. The ASD agents were shouting and running toward us—we had to make this look good. They were firing laser pistols at us, too, causing pieces of the ceiling and the walls to explode outward. I ducked as some of it came my way.

"Get us out of here!" Tory shouted at Ry. Ry didn't even blink as he folded every one of us away.

"The wizard was stronger than we anticipated," the Captain of the prison vessel declared. He was a mid-ranking ASD operative. The news vids were showing images of the blasted-out hull where all but one of the prisoners had escaped. That prisoner was shown as he was loaded into an armored vehicle before being driven to the local cell that awaited him.

"It is most fortunate that this particular prisoner did not escape— he is the reported gunman," the reporter noted. "As you can see, three ASD agents were killed during the escape." Norian watched the newsfeed—it had been a stroke of genius, finding three bodies to transport. None of his agents had been injured during the escape. The breach in the outer hull had been made by his own agents aboard ship, shortly before they reached port on Tulgalan. All on board were well away from the blast that created the hole in the side of the ship.

∼

"Are you sure the compulsion will hold up?" Norian turned to Rigo, one of Lissa's vampire mates.

"Oh, yes. And no word will ever reach Mandil that we violated the treaty in that way. Nods will not reveal any secrets other than what he's told us already, after I placed compulsion to be truthful."

"Yes. I couldn't believe what came out of his mouth before you stepped in," Norian offered Rigo a grim smile. "The wizards who planted those lies in his mind were quite powerful, according to Lord Morphis." Norian turned back to the news on the vid-screen. Erland Morphis had also stated that no wizard or warlock could outdo an old vampire on compulsion. It was information Norian squirreled away. It might prove useful, someday.

∼

"My Prince, we managed to escape with a little assistance." Bel indicated Ry, Tory and me with a quick gesture. "These were arrested with us and have agreed to help."

I was frightened that the Prince might recognize me, but I was dressed scruffily enough and Bel had nearly shaved my head again. Tory hugged me after my hair had been whacked off for the second time.

"What can these do for me?" The Prince sounded less than hopeful as he looked the three of us over.

"This one holds power greater than mine," Bel nodded toward Ry. "These two can provide shields than no wizard can crack." He pointed toward Tory and me. "If you stand with them, your protection will be assured."

"They can protect me in this way?" The Prince was intrigued and rose from his seat. The High Commander had borrowed the wizards who normally guarded the Prince to investigate an attack. All of them were loyal to the High Commander, of course, and left when the High Commander asked.

We'd created the diversion the High Commander was investigating, blowing out a section of the western wall surrounding Crown City. Ry had used just enough power to make the wizards believe their current opposition was behind the attack—a few of the lesser-talented wizards still opposed the High Commander and his cronies. The High Commander had fooled the citizens, but other wizards were not so easily taken in.

"The boy will not be so easily noticed by the others," the Prince was eyeing me carefully. I prayed he wouldn't see me as female.

"No, my Prince. He can run errands for you—he has experience in this area, along with toting sums. I understand he also has good cooking skills." Bel flashed a smile in my direction. I wanted to kick his shins.

"So, a late-night meal might be had, should one be required?" The Prince sat down, still keeping his eyes on me.

"The taller one can serve as a bodyguard to me and the others," Bel bowed slightly. "The wizard we will keep among us—he will stand in for Pell, who needs to go home to his wife. She is about to birth her first any day."

"Will the disguises hold?"

"Certainly, my Prince."

"Then it will be so. Boy, come. You will carry messages for me this afternoon." The Prince snapped his fingers at me. I went.

"Where did *that* come from?" There was no mistaking the contempt in his voice as the wizard looked me over. The Prince's wizards had returned after checking the hole blown into the wall. At least one wizard was instructed to stay with the Prince, unless the High Commander pulled him away. It was a ruse, to make the Prince believe he was being guarded. Neither the Prince nor I were fooled.

"I needed a boy to run messages and cook for me late at night when I am hungry," the Prince snapped. "It is such a chore to have my cook awakened when it is late."

"That is certainly true," the wizard agreed.

"I can only imagine that he will cook for my wizards as well." The Prince examined his fingernails. "Boy, send for my valet." He made a bored, shooing motion with his hands. If he were acting, he deserved an award, I think.

"Yes, my Prince." I bowed low, as required of one with little or no status.

"Scurry," the Prince waved a finger. I scurried.

"As required, my Prince." I'd brought the valet, who seemed less than enthusiastic.

"My nails need work, Malvis," the Prince held out a hand.

"I will see to it," Malvis settled next to the Prince, lifted a kit from a deep pocket inside his black robes and set to work. Malvis was used to this sort of thing, it appeared.

"If you do not need me," the wizard bowed slightly to the Prince Royal.

"No," the Prince sighed. "Feel free to amuse yourself." The wizard, dressed just as richly as the Prince, left the room quickly.

"Malvis, this one can shield us," the Prince grabbed my arm with his free hand and dragged me over. "How large is your shield, boy?" The Prince hissed.

"Fourteen hands or so, in every direction," I said, nearly breathless with shock.

"Enough for all of us, if needed," Malvis kept his head down, trimming the Prince's nails carefully.

"We just need warning before they make their attempt," the Prince muttered angrily. "Bel will do his best, as will the others, but we are treading dangerous ground, my friend."

"Your father would have died quickly, had he faced this," Malvis agreed softly. "He would have attacked and they would have killed him immediately. We must lower our heads to them, making them think we are feeble sheep."

"They are taking credit for destroying our enemy in the desert, when it was Bel and his Rangers who performed that magic for us," the Prince huffed. "Does the High Commander think I do not see through his lies?"

"His wizards are lazy," Malvis nodded. "They have talent, yes. They do not have the stamina for the long road."

"Boy, what is your name?" The Prince turned to me.

"They call me Re," I replied.

"Re, this is Malvis who once advised my father, the Prince Royal before me. Now he advises me, disguised as my valet. We have been setting ourselves against the High Commander and his drug-trafficking thieves for a long while, now. It is my hope that we win this battle, else we may all be dead and the High Commander will dance upon our graves."

"My Prince, I will work to see that does not happen." I bowed to him.

"Boy, I hope your shield works, we may have need of it," Malvis said, not lifting his eyes from his task.

"Some of the old wizards are attacking the fields in the desert—I want you to go out and take care of that problem." The High Commander handed Bel his new assignment.

"Shouldn't be difficult," Bel replied casually. "Get your things together," he ordered the Rangers. Tory, too, lifted a pack to his shoulder.

"Where did that one come from?" The High Commander gestured toward Tory.

"Bodyguard—good with shields," Bel said. "Not much good with other spells, though."

"Good enough." The High Commander just wanted Bel and his Rangers to take care of the problem he was encountering in the desert —they were losing crops and it was nearing time for the harvest. If the few remaining wild wizards kept attacking, the workers he'd sent out to tend the crops wouldn't go out to pick. They'd be too frightened. The High Commander needed as much drakus seed as he could raise. Their recent encounter with an unexpected enemy had devastated some of his fields. The High Commander swept aside his black robes and stalked out of the meeting room, leaving Bel and the others to tend to business.

"Reah has mindspeech. Do either of you have that talent?" Bel swung his pack over his shoulder. Ry looked at Tory and then back at Bel, a huge grin on his face.

∾

"I wish I had your talent, my friend. Someday, perhaps, you'll tell me how you came by it." Bel stood inside the walls of the outpost where he'd served with Commander Aris. He still had no idea what had happened to the man. He addressed Ry after Ry had folded all of them to the outpost.

"Perhaps someday, I'll consider telling you. Is this where we're staying?"

"For the night, at least." Bel, Hish and Max dropped their packs inside the barracks they'd used before. "Pick a bunk. We'll have to feed ourselves tonight. Some food—not much—is still inside the keepers."

∾

"Tell me again why we didn't bring Reah with us?" Hish was doing his best to chew the meat they'd cooked.

"I think I should ask her to teach me a little of what she knows," Ry was cutting his meat into tiny pieces, hoping that would make it easier to consume.

"How do you know her, anyway?" Bel was curious.

"Reah is my mate," Tory was trying his best to consume his dinner.

"You're joking." Bel almost dropped his fork.

"No. But she has two. I'm the second one."

"She's only nineteen."

44

"We know," Ry admitted. "Tory and the other one are recently mated to Reah."

"So, she wasn't just any conscript when she landed here," Hish said, cutting into his meat with difficulty.

"Well, she was at the time. Worked in a kitchen for the Alliance. It wasn't until she got back that the ASD latched onto her." Ry was about to give up on his dinner.

"So, she has us to thank for all that battle experience?" Max grinned.

"I believe that's true," Tory agreed.

"We have a cook where we're going—we'll stay in the largest village. You'll get a look at the drakus seed fields while you're there. The villagers the High Commander relocated spend most of their days pumping water for the plants." Bel gave Tory and Ry the information they needed. Ry had tiny cameras affixed to his clothing —nobody from Mandil would even think to look for them—the technology was beyond them. The Director and Vice-Director would be getting live feeds from Ry if he wore either of the two vests he'd brought with him.

"Who guards the fields at night?" Tory asked, sipping the wine he'd poured; they'd found a few bottles left behind after the evacuation.

"Pell is there—he sleeps during the day and guards at night. You'll take his place," Bel nodded at Tory. "Mind you, I don't want any of the attacking wizards killed—we want to bring them in with us. We may need their help when the time comes. I figure the High Commander will wait until the harvest is done before making his move."

"What about the army?" Ry asked.

"Right now, the Station Commander is still loyal to the High Commander. Evlif Gorth is a reasonable man, though. I'm hoping that when the final push comes, he'll send his troops in the right direction. The High Commander hasn't done much to make Station Commander Gorth respect him." Bel shoved his plate away with a sigh and sipped his wine.

❧

"She's no family of mine—I got the papers making that a fact not too long ago." Addah Desh was rude to Vice-Director Schaff.

"Then ponder this—let her identity slip, even in the slightest way possible, and you and I will have a discussion with the local magistrate over child labor law violations within your restaurants."

"What?" Addah Desh almost came out of his chair. His face was turning slightly purple, too. Lendill wondered if he might be forced to call Emergency Medical for assistance.

"I have all the records, Master Cook Desh. Your son did not pay her properly and worked her long hours from the age of eight. No child is to be employed in a service industry establishment that exists to bring in income—not under the age of fourteen. At age fourteen, that child is only allowed to work a maximum of three clicks per day. Your granddaughter was forced to work for six to eight clicks per night, depending upon which night. The money you sent to your son to pay her was funneled directly into his accounts and not paid out. Not in the proper manner, anyway. He may have slipped her a few credits now and then, but it would not have been sufficient. All his expenses are accounted for. No salary was paid to Reah Desh. She may as well have been a slave—he treated her as one. And beat her, as you know, whenever he was angry. A trait gained from his mother, don't you think?" Lendill toyed with the comp-vid under his hand—all the pertinent records were there if Addah Desh wished to see them. "Your granddaughter—your flesh and blood—and you allowed this to happen. What do you think you will do if this is leaked to the media?"

"You're saying that Edan raped her mother—at Marzi's urging?"

"Yes, I have that confession on a vid chip. They were quite eager to blame the other, in an effort to reduce their own charges. And then Marzi paid the physician to slip a blood thinner into your youngest wife's medication—it appears she learned that the baby might have been Edan's and threatened to go to the constabulary after the birth of the child. Marzi didn't want to be implicated and at the time she was protecting your eighteen-year-old son. That no longer is the case. She feels Edan has failed her, since you have cut them out of your will. You suspected this all along, didn't you, Master Desh?"

Addah Desh deflated. All his bluster and pompousness—gone. He hadn't realized he might be included in the charges, alongside Marzi and Edan. Fes was poised to take over Desh's number two, after Edan's arrest. Addah had no desire to lose business because Edan and Marzi had gotten caught. Now, he might be accused of knowledge of a crime, without reporting it. It could ruin the entire family.

"I should never have married Raedah. I knew Marzi was more jealous of her than any of the others." Addah sighed. "And then she died, leaving me with a motherless child to raise. I had the tests run, so I knew she wasn't mine. Yes, I had suspicions, but I chose to ignore them. I wasn't aware that Edan was harming the girl and not paying her. I swear I didn't know about that."

"Your granddaughter isn't a criminal. Someday, perhaps, you'll learn what she truly is." Lendill Schaff stood and lifted his coat.

"Word will not come from me or any of mine," Addah Desh voice sounded defeated.

"See that it doesn't—much depends on this," Lendill Schaff walked out the door.

"We haven't gotten drunk together in a long time." Norian looked at Lendill. They'd returned to Le-Ath Veronis and now sat in a bar in Casino City.

"True. What did Reah say about not saving me?" Lendill was half-drunk already.

"She said she'd think twice about saving your tight ass."

"She said my ass was tight?"

"Those were her words." Norian was beginning to slur his s's.

"You think she looked at my ass?"

"Well, that was the impression I had. I don't think she knows you well enough to speculate on your spending habits."

"I saw the vid—they cut her hair again."

"I know."

"She doesn't like that."

"It's the only way she'll pass as a boy."

"You didn't treat Lissa like this."

"I know." Norian tapped his glass so the bartender would give him a refill. "I just crawled right into her bed as the lion snake one night." Norian hiccupped.

"I wish I could do that."

"Lissa would have your head."

"I wasn't talking about Lissa."

"You'll sleep here." I was given a closet next to the royal suite. The Prince's bedroom was surrounded by those of his three wives. Guards stood outside his doors and I was going to sleep in a closet. A small cot had been brought in, but it didn't look comfortable. I'd had better at the military station. Clothing, too, had been brought—a young boy's clothing by the looks of it. Blue and gray, like the uniforms worn by the other servants. I hugged myself tightly as I sat on the edge of my cot, surrounded by my meager new wardrobe.

Auri? I sent. He was far away and unlikely to hear. It surprised me greatly when an answer came.

Reah? When did you gain mindspeech?

Yesterday, I returned.

Reah, you sound lost, love.

I am lost. Aurelius, they have me sleeping in a closet.

Lara'Kayan, it will not always be so.

I know. But it is small and closed in. I shivered, just thinking about it.

Love, I am only a thought away. If it becomes unbearable, call out to me. I will help you get through this. Try to sleep, love. You are still not fully recovered. A promise lay in Aurelius' words—a promise to get back at Norian Keef, somehow, for sending me out before the healer thought I was ready.

I'll try, I sent and crawled into my tiny bed. I was nearly asleep too; I was more tired than I thought when another message came. *I love you* was sent to me, and it was no voice I'd heard in my head before that moment.

"Wake!" The side of my small cot was kicked, nearly upsetting it. I stared in alarm at one of the Prince's wizards. "The Prince wants something to eat. Get up and cook!"

There would be no sympathy and even less patience from this one —he had a cruel mouth and disdain in his eyes. I rose, slipped into the clothing I'd worn earlier and followed the wizard to the kitchens. I cooked. The kitchen was well stocked and I was used to what Mandil had to offer already. Cutting thin slices of fowl, I dredged them in flour, fried them quickly and made a sauce to go with them, in addition to fresh fruit and sweetened cream. The wizard and the Prince were both staring at me as they tasted their food.

"Where did you learn to cook, boy?" The wizard demanded.

"My family taught me." I hung my head. I was telling the truth.

"And why did they turn you out?"

"My father had many sons. I wasn't necessary," I said. Well, it had actually been my grandfather—I knew that now.

"Then we will be glad of the surplus," the Prince declared, eating the rest of his fowl with delight. The dessert was a plus—he liked that very much. As did the wizard. I was allowed to return to my bed as soon as the plates and utensils had been cleaned and put away.

"Re, wake up." The voice was whispering right next to my ear, causing me to gasp and sit up in alarm. I was crushed against a uniform I recognized. "Re, hush," Delvin held me tightly against him so I wouldn't scream.

" $\mathcal{L}$ ittle girl, be still," Delvin gripped me tightly against him, whispering the words. "Come now, get dressed, the Prince wants his errand boy."

I wanted a bath, but that wasn't to be. I was set to running errands immediately, before I got breakfast, even. I was hungry, too—I hadn't gotten any of the food I'd cooked the night before, and I hadn't gotten dinner, either. That was why my stomach was growling as I handed a message to Malvis.

"You haven't eaten, and my guess is you haven't gotten a bath, either." Malvis had given me a good sniff when I arrived at his quarters. He had a small room down the hall from the Prince's suite.

"Yes on both, Master Malvis," I ducked my head respectfully. He was older, with silver in his dark hair. His brown eyes, too, looked wise to me, as if he'd seen many things during his life.

"Then come, we will go to the private bath together." That frightened me into immobility. Malvis took one look at me, grabbed my hand and led me along. We went into the Prince's private bath, which was decorated with beautiful tiling and gold fixtures. The bath was large—at least twenty people might have fit around the edges comfortably. A bit of steam wisped up from the surface of the water.

"Little girl," Malvis hissed, "Never let those wizards know you're female." He shot the bolt behind us, locking us in. If I'd been inside the bath alone, that might have frightened me. Malvis was there, so that helped.

"How did you know?" I muttered, not looking at him.

"I know a great deal. The others are fools and do not look past the surface of things. That will be their downfall. Come, we will bathe and then I will take you for breakfast. The Prince only thinks of his own belly, most of the time."

The bath felt good to my still-aching muscles. If I were anywhere except where I was, I might have fallen asleep. I stayed awake, cleaned myself and dressed right alongside Master Malvis. We walked out of the baths together and down to the kitchens, where servants were busily preparing for the noon meal. Malvis and I were served a decent breakfast, cooked fresh just for us. I carried a message from Malvis to the Prince when we were done.

"Ah, Malvis, you are my conscience," the Prince muttered after reading the note. "Re, you will remind me from now on if you have not eaten." I nodded at the Prince Royal.

"These are the fields." Bel swept his arm out as Tory and Ry stared. The drakus seed plants seemed to go on forever.

"And this is only one of many villages doing the same thing?" Ry attempted to keep the shock from his voice. He couldn't see the end of the drakus seed fields. Citrus trees were off to the side, but those were the only other fields he could see.

"This is the largest, but there are others nearly as big," Bel answered.

"How many?" Tory didn't like what he was seeing.

"Hundreds. Some of the villages were emptied by the demons that we fought, but the High Commander sent out others to take their place as soon as the danger was eliminated. They have worked to revive the crops. There will be a yield from those fields as well."

"Not demons—spawn," Tory corrected absently.

"How do you know they were not demons?" Bel was curious.

"He knows," Ry provided the answer.

"With the weather here, the fields can be replanted in a moon-turn, with another yield in two. That means four harvests per full turn," Bel whispered. "The plants need sun and a lot of water. We have both."

"Were the plants native to this world?" Tory asked.

"No. They were brought in. The High Commander and his wizards, I think." Bel didn't sound happy about that.

"What do you know about the wizards? The ones who were imported?" Ry wanted to learn as much as he could about them—he might be forced to fight them and needed to know what their strengths and talents were.

"We don't know much except they can do blasts of power when they want—they'll execute someone that way if they're angry."

"And they can move about like I can—perhaps farther, even," Max offered. "I don't know if they must have specific targets as I do—I can't take people far and I have to have a fixed target in my mind. Moving objects is much easier than moving people. If I'm too tired, it's useless."

"So far, these wizards seem unimpressive," Ry grumbled. "How did they get here to begin with? Were they transported in a ship or did they arrive by other means? Have you seen them? Do you know their planet of origin?"

"We're not supposed to know they're from somewhere else, so the answer is no," Bel snorted angrily. "And if you haven't guessed, we don't get a lot of space travel on Mandil."

"So, how did you get to Tulgalan?" Tory crossed arms over his chest.

Bel coughed. "We, uh, dug up Reah's escape pod. We have a few people loyal to the Prince who are good with technology. They recharged the pod and equipped it for us. We're not sure how Nods made it to Tulgalan—but when we caught up with him, we told him the High Commander sent us. One of Pell's talents, besides creating big holes in the ground for people to fall into, is convincing people that something was their idea. The High Commander is pretty sure he told us to do exactly what we did."

Tory almost choked, he was laughing so hard. Ry, too, was grinning hugely. "Man, that is epic," Tory slapped Bel on the back.

～

A hand was clapped over my mouth and I was hauled into the kitchen after I'd slept two clicks. The Prince wasn't hungry but the wizards were. The High Commander, too, had come with them. I was terrified the High Commander would recognize me, but he barely noticed. Someone else was there whom I hadn't seen before, and everyone was bowing to his every whim and calling him Arvil. He seemed puffed up to me—like Addah used to act around someone he felt was less important.

The wizards—three of them, plus the High Commander and the one they called Arvil, all received flat bread with sauce, cheese and vegetables. I had to cook it in a shallow iron skillet in the oven, and the trick was getting the crust to the right amount of crispness. I ended up making two at a time—they were eating the food faster than I could make it.

"This is excellent, I had no idea your food here was this good," Arvil licked his fingers. The flat-breads were designed to be eaten with your fingers, after all. I'd served a light wine with the late meal, too, and it went over well.

"Most of the food isn't this good," the night wizard grumbled. I called him the night wizard, since he hadn't given me his name—I didn't know the names of the others, either. Nobody had introduced us. The night wizard was the one with the cruel mouth. Another had reddish-brown hair—he was the day wizard, while the third had gray hair. He was the evening wizard. Delvin had taken the day wizard's place that first morning when I woke. Day wizard had something else to do then, I suppose.

"We expect you to invite us over if you are having a late snack from now on," gray-haired evening wizard grumbled.

"Everything hinges on whether the Prince is hungry or not, and if this one keeps his mouth closed." Dark-haired, cruel-mouthed night wizard had a kitchen knife pointed at my throat.

"You don't threaten your cook—you get awful food," Arvil took the last piece of flat bread.

"I'd better not get awful food," night wizard was still threatening me. I wanted to snatch the knife away from him and do some threatening myself. I'm sure the Director and Vice-Director would be extremely angry if I killed anyone before they could spill information, so I held back and nodded meekly instead. When I was allowed to go back to bed after cleaning up, I sent tired mindspeech to Tory.

Reah, why are you up so late? Tory's sending was weary. He'd had a long day, too.

Tory, someone new came in tonight, and the others were calling him Arvil. No last name or anything, and I still don't have names for the three wizards.

Tory didn't reply for a while and I wondered if he'd fallen asleep. He hadn't. *Reah, don't give yourself away to that one—Arvil. Try not to come to his attention, all right, avilepha? Promise me.* Somehow, that made me worry. Tory had heard that name before, but he wasn't explaining it to me. Maybe it was better if I didn't know.

All right, I returned, sounding more grumpy than I'd intended.

Go to sleep, baby, Tory's mental voice faded.

You think she heard right? She didn't mistake that name for another? Norian Keef and Lendill Schaff both had mindspeech, and Tory had sent the information as soon as he'd told Reah to go to sleep.

I can't imagine why she'd mistake that name for another, Tory was tired and didn't want to get into a debate with Norian and Lendill over it.

Did she know how long he's staying, or where? Lendill was getting in on the conversation.

Ask her yourself—I think she gave me what she had. Tory sent a mental yawn.

She won't talk to either of us, Lendill insisted.

I wouldn't either, if I were in her place, Tory returned.

"As you can see—the harvest is nearly ready." The High Commander had brought his visitor to the drakus seed fields. Ry's cameras were sending vid feeds directly to Norian and Lendill the following morning, and Norian could see for himself that Reah hadn't misheard —Arvil San Gerxon was on Mandil.

It was still too early to take him—Norian had already sent mindspeech to Ry and Tory. Too many others were involved in this— some Norian and Lendill could only guess at. They were getting a good look at the High Commander and his three wizards, however, and Lendill was running their images through his comp-vid even while he and Norian watched.

"It's a good thing Ry is disguised—Arvil would recognize Erland's son in a heartbeat," Norian muttered.

"What could Arvil do to Ry, even if he did recognize him?"

"No idea. Probably nothing on a personal level. What would he do to Mandil?"

"Something to think on," Lendill agreed.

"On another note, where do you think all his usual thugs and bodyguards are?" Norian asked as they watched the High Commander take his guest through rows of drakus seed.

"Most likely back at Crown City—perhaps the High Commander doesn't feel comfortable around them and ordered them to stay behind."

"Or those wizards are on Arvil's payroll, and the High Commander only thinks he pulls their strings."

"More than likely that's the case," Lendill agreed. "Have you ever seen so much drakus seed in your life?"

"My friend, we've only seen small plots before, because the punishment for growing this drug is so severe. I am astounded at the breadth of this endeavor." Norian shook his head over what he saw through Ry's vid feed.

∿

"The seed is close to harvest," Malvis was kneeling, massaging the Prince's feet and ankles. The massage looked wonderful—I'd never had anything like that before. The Prince was dressed in gold silk and he and Malvis were talking—albeit quietly, since the High Commander and his three wizards were away, tending to a problem at one of the outer villages. At least that had been their excuse.

The Prince was unaware of Arvil's presence until I informed him quietly before running my morning errands. One of those errands had taken me to the military station, to Station Commander Gorth's office. He didn't seem to recognize me either, and I wondered about that. I was glad, but it still made me curious. I'd seen Dane and Dory in the distance while on my way back, and was extremely happy they were helping others patch the hole in the station wall and ignoring message bearers. It might have been nice to talk to them, but I had no idea if I'd frightened them the last time I'd seen them. Making contact certainly wasn't a good idea.

"Re, I would very much like to take my midday meal on the patio," the Prince waved an arm. "Invite my wives." I nodded and he and Malvis were deep in quiet discussion when I went out the door of his suite to inform the kitchen staff.

∿

"You are wishing to go to the summer house in the mountains, are you not?" The Prince looked at each of his three wives later over a meal of spiced meat wrapped in flat bread with fresh fruit on the side. At first, they looked at one another in confusion, before turning back to their husband. "Yes, husband, that is indeed what we desire," the oldest dipped her head obediently to the Prince.

"Well, it is early, but I suppose I must humor my wives," the Prince smiled indulgently. Two of the kitchen staff stood nearby, and I think the entire charade was for their benefit. I had no way to tell who might report to the High Commander regarding the Prince's actions. "And since it is such a fine day, why not gather your things and leave this afternoon? You keep telling me you wish to stop at Hedil to buy silks."

"That is indeed what we wish," the youngest was giving the Prince a heart-melting smile.

"Then that is what you shall have. Malvis will see that you have plenty of money to spend. Go now—the light will still be good in Hedil if you leave soon."

I helped load their things into the Prince's coach later—the vehicle was solar powered and all three wives had guards, several attendants and two drivers to take them on their way. The Prince waved fondly at them as they drove off, then retired to his suite, pulling Malvis and me inside with him.

"Re, the Station Commander will arrive shortly, asking to speak with me regarding a thief he is holding in his cells. See that he is brought to me promptly." The Prince breathed a troubled sigh and flopped onto a chair laden with silk cushions inside his suite. The fabrics and rugs that furnished it would have fetched a fortune on any Alliance world—all of it had been handmade from the finest materials Mandil could supply, and in beautiful colors. Mandil created some of the best natural dyes I'd ever seen.

"As you will it, my Prince." I bowed and walked out of the suite. The Station Commander came half a click later, and I escorted him to the Prince Royal's suite.

"We move now," the Prince was standing and dressed as if he were going to do battle. A lot had happened in half a click, it seems.

"Re, stay steady." Delvin had come and dropped two ranos rifles into my hands. The Prince's palace was now prepared for a siege. Several of his servants had been arrested and escorted to the holding cells at the military station. Two hundred soldiers and recruits now knelt behind windows, doors and any other opening, waiting for the High Commander and his wizards to return. I sent mindspeech to Tory and Ry, sounding hysterical, I think. I had no idea things would happen this quickly.

We already have the message from Bel—Delvin informed him the moment the Prince called for him and the Station Commander, Tory replied. *Reah, don't do anything foolish, avilepha. We will be there shortly.*

~

"I didn't expect it to happen this quickly," Norian grabbed the jacket to his uniform and bolted through his office door, Lendill right behind him. Ry had sent the message to Norian as soon as he'd gotten notice through Bel's mindspeech.

"They'll attack the palace first thing, to get to the Prince." Lendill was racing down the hallway behind Norian.

"Are you ready?" Norian shouted to his six handpicked operatives. They were all armed and ready as Norian burst into the meeting room. They'd been watching the live feed from Mandil, just as Norian and Lendill were.

"Ready, Director," his senior officer replied, shifting a laser rifle onto his shoulder.

"Let's go." Few knew that Norian could fold if he were forced to do so. This situation called for that talent. That particular gift had come from Lissa—it was something she could give should she desire it. She had given it to protect Norian after she was released as Liaison for the ASD. Norian used the gift sparingly.

~

Even now I may never know exactly who alerted the High Commander, and the Prince wasn't aware that Arvil had brought additional troops with him when he'd come to Mandil. Some of those troops were wizards, I discovered, and any one of those seven power wielders were capable of alerting Arvil to the Prince's troops, all of whom were armed and waiting for his return to the palace.

Arvil and his allies folded in, the wizards with him sending out blasts as they landed, while the seven additional wizards Arvil brought joined in. Delvin stood beside the Prince and Malvis, pretending to hold up a shield. I was the one protecting the four of us as blasts and poison gas spells were hurled in our direction.

The troops the Station Commander placed around the palace were being killed by the dozens; they had no protection other than their rifles. Those still alive were making inroads against the non-wizard attackers, until they drew the attention of Arvil's wizards. The wizards would carelessly toss a spell in their direction, and they had no hope to survive those blasts.

Bodies, none of them whole, littered the palace and surrounding courtyard. The High Commander and Arvil were now surrounded by all seven wizards, and were being shielded by one of them—Delvin shouted that information over the din and chaos that continuously erupted around us.

We now fought in the courtyard before the Prince's palace; there were fountains and elaborate stonework there, all of it being blown to bits as each blast landed. Bel, Hish, Ry, Max and Tory finally came, and to my surprise, Director Keef, Vice-Director Schaff and six others armed with laser rifles were with them.

Bel had brought some of the hedge wizards from the desert, but all of them immediately moved to protect the Prince's regular troops, who were being slaughtered. Ry was hurling blasts of his own at the seven wizards, attempting to get to the High Commander and the one called Arvil. That divided the attention of the High Commander's wizards; half of them turned to fight off the new threat. Tory was providing a shield to his group, just as I was shielding mine. Hish was forced to help whenever huge chunks of stone and other debris blew upward and then rained down around us—I wasn't any good against a physical threat—only the magical ones in my current form.

Don't turn! Tory's voice sounded in my head—somehow he'd known I was thinking about it. Fleetingly I wondered why—I couldn't see that either side was winning this fight, and my Thifilatha would certainly turn the tide in our favor. Tory, too, could turn and do the same. A large, decorative fountain was hit right after Tory's mindspeech came and the Prince, Malvis, Delvin and I ducked as water and chunks of stone blasted toward us. An arm came around my waist and I was physically pulled away from the Prince's side. Delvin's hand came over my mouth as he rushed me toward the knot of wizards surrounding the High Commander. If Delvin hadn't held me in the tightest of grips, I'd likely have been left behind. As it was, my Thifilatha still trusted him at that moment and I was jerked—not folded, *jerked*—so far away from Mandil I couldn't have said where we were when I landed.

"Reah," Delvin's voice whispered in my ear as I saw others land around us—all the wrong ones. "Reah," Delvin repeated, "Don't give yourself away." The High Commander, Arvil, the seven wizards—all of them surrounded me. "I swear I'll protect you. I *swear*," Delvin whispered again before letting me go. I jumped backward, knocking into Delvin again as Arvil pulled a ranos pistol from his belt and shot the High Commander in the head. Delvin's fingers closed on my shoulders once more.

"You won't fail me again," Arvil snapped at the headless torso. The ranos pistol had obliterated the High Commander's head, and blood and bits of bone were scattered everywhere. I could only stare in horror, my gaze darting from the High Commander's body to Arvil and then back again.

"At least one part of the plan went well," Arvil placed the pistol back in his belt and moved closer to run his eyes over me. "You belong to me now, *boy*. You'll be put in my kitchen—my last cook met with an unfortunate accident."

My mouth was open in surprise, I know, as I twisted in Delvin's grip and stared up at him. Bel suspected one of his, but he hadn't suspected this one. Delvin knew I felt betrayed—he could read it in my face.

"Where the fuck did they go?" Norian was shouting as his six, Bel and the remaining wizards corralled what was left of the High Commander's cronies.

"Campiaa, where else?" Tory was blowing smoke as Ry attempted to calm his brother. "They took Reah!" Tory shouted at the sky.

"Send her mindspeech—tell her to cooperate with them," Norian issued orders quickly. "This is our opportunity to see who is involved!" The Director was in charge and he was seeing the possibilities.

"What if they hurt her?" Tory was coming after Norian, his hands clenching and unclenching while smoke poured from his nostrils.

"Tell her if they are about to harm her, to get away. Otherwise, I want her to stay!" Norian wasn't backing down.

"Tell her your fucking self!" Tory shouted.

"I'll tell her, she already hates me," Lendill offered. The Prince Royal, with his trusted advisor Malvis, watched the exchange with interest.

"Bel, take your wizards and fire those fields," the Prince issued the command.

"As you will it, my Prince." Bel bowed quickly and gathered his remaining Rangers and wizards. Delvin had betrayed them, taking Reah with him and the others. Bel was hoping that Delvin still had a decent bone in his body and thought to protect Reah, since he'd been the one to grab her before they'd disappeared.

Don't change, Reah, don't fight them and stay where you are—we need intelligence from your current location, Vice-Director Schaff's mental voice was loud and frightening in my mind. I jerked when I received his mindspeech—I was terrified with Delvin and the others surrounding me. All but Delvin still thought I was a boy. *Reah, did you hear me? Answer me!*

I think I whimpered aloud before I answered Lendill Schaff's mindspeech. *I hear you,* I returned as best I could.

Reah, if they hurt you, you have permission to come away from there. If they do not, you are in a position to hand all of them to us. We need names, Reah, and anything else you can get for us. Do this, Reah. It's important. Remember the oath you took, when you came to the Alliance. You swore to protect it. Protect it now, Reah. You are duty-bound.

I shivered at his words. He expected me to stay and funnel information to him. *Are Tory and Ry all right?* My mental voice was sullen.

They are well. This is an order, Reah. Send information to me or to Director Keef—he can send and receive mindspeech, just as I can. If you desert your post, you will be committing treason.

He threw his trump card in my face. I was already considered a criminal by the Alliance. Now I might be guilty of treason if I didn't stay among these thugs and listen for what little I might glean while working inside Arvil's kitchen. I wanted to weep for being in so far over my head in all this. I couldn't. I could only stand in front of Delvin and shiver.

"I'll take the boy to the kitchen," Delvin gripped my arm so hard it hurt.

"He can have the sleeping quarters next to it," Arvil waved a hand. "Go ahead, but get back here quick—we have to make plans to pull the seed from our fields on Birimera instead."

"They'll expect breakfast when they rise, but that varies," Delvin said as he dragged me down a dark hallway. "This is Arvil's private home," he added. "And it's a fortress with guards around it at all times. Hop when he tells you, Reah, and cook as well for him as you cooked for us."

"You've been here before," I muttered, not looking up at Delvin's face.

"Yes. I have been here before."

"I regret cooking for you," I said.

"Reah, don't," Delvin hissed. "It was hard enough to do this to Bel and the others—they don't have a chance against what's coming. Keep your head down and don't aggravate Arvil. That will keep you alive just as well as anything I can do for you. I swear I'll protect you as much as I can."

I wanted to yell at him about empty words and false promises, but I didn't. I was stuck on Campiaa for the moment and had to fit in as best I could.

"This is the kitchen," Delvin hauled me inside. It was smaller than I thought it might be—the parts of Arvil's private home we'd gone through to get to the kitchen were much more spacious and better furnished.

"This is a cesspit," I moaned as I looked around me.

"He doesn't spend where he doesn't think he has to," Delvin snapped. "Reah, don't fight me or Arvil San Gerxon over this. Make do with what you have. Your sleeping quarters are next door," he pointed to the left of the kitchen. "At least your suite has its own bath. I'll try to find clothing for you. Be ready to make breakfast in the morning." Delvin left me standing inside Arvil San Gerxon's nearly archaic kitchen while tears slipped down my cheeks.

They said they were going to pull seed from Birimera, I sent. I was still wiping tears off my face as I made my report.

Thank you. Lendill's reply was curt as he cut off the communication.

~

"She's crying," Lendill sighed. "Don't tell Torevik. I think he'll take both our heads."

"I'd stay away from Aurelius too, if that sort of thing worries you," Norian observed. "Let's help the others burn drakus plants."

~

"Father, I am having enough trouble with my son over this. You need to stay here and help us convince him to wait." Gavin hadn't been on this side of things before. Aurelius had always been the reasonable one. Now his vampire sire wanted to go haring off to Campiaa to rescue Reah. Gavin would have done the same in Aurelius' place, but Gavril was panicking over Reah's abduction, too.

"Director Keef is leaving her there—she has already gotten vital information for them. In fact, one of the planets where they are growing drakus seed is the one on which you fought demons last." Aurelius jerked his head up at Gavin's words.

"At least we don't have to wake our cook." Arvil grinned as he led his contingent of wizards into his kitchen about a click later. "We'll have a decent meal tonight."

"Possibly not, Lord Arvil," I bowed to him as respectfully as I could. "Your thermostat is broken on your oven, Lord." I pointed to the digital readout on the outside of the oven, and then, using a mitt, pulled the thermometer from the oven. The reading was very different.

"Also, four of the six units on top of your stove do not work, I am sorry to say." I led him to the stove and showed him that only two were glowing red while the others were dark, although all were turned on. "These floor tiles are loose and crumbling," I toed one with my shoe, "because the dishwasher line is leaking. The dishwasher is also inoperable for other reasons. You have hard water here, Lord." I pointed out the calcium deposits around the base of the sink faucet. "I will serve you the best meals possible, Lord, but I must have decent equipment to work with in order to do so."

I was risking my life, I felt, telling him these things, but I would rather be killed over this than serve up poor food.

"Why do I not have a decent kitchen?" Arvil must have been in a good mood; he was smiling and tossing a hand in the air. "Come, boy, we will walk to my casino next door and you will use their kitchen tonight. I will see about getting these things replaced and repaired."

That's how I was allowed to see the guards surrounding Arvil San Gerxon's home, which was every bit as large as the Prince's palace on Mandil. A very high wall surrounded it, I discovered. We were led through a narrow gate, and a huge casino was revealed once we passed the high walls surrounding Arvil's mansion. Lights flashed and glittered around The San Gerxon I; it fronted a sandy beach and an ocean beyond that. I might have liked to go and watch the water, but I was commanded to cook instead.

"Master San Gerxon," the cook on duty bowed to his employer as we walked inside his kitchen. We were seeing the night cook, as it was quite late when we arrived. The day cook would likely be better and more highly paid.

"Don't worry yourself, we have a cook with us—seems my kitchen needs updating, so we'll borrow yours for now." The cook didn't like it, but acquiesced to Arvil's wishes, standing aside and bowing us through with as much dignity as he could muster. He watched carefully too, as I took stock of what he had and then quickly prepared the same fish I'd helped Harding make on Le-Ath Veronis.

When night cook Xiri got a taste of what I'd made—I let him have a bite when I poured sauce over the fish on nine plates—he closed his eyes and sighed with pleasure. "Master, we could sell this for many credits in your best restaurant," Xiri exclaimed. I made a small plate of food for him after serving the others.

"Re, teach him how to make it," Arvil waved a hand. He'd tasted the fish, just as the others had. Arvil also had a communicator in his hand after his fourth bite, telling someone that he wanted his kitchen completely updated, beginning the next morning. He offered to pay extra if it were finished quickly.

"There, Re—you will have a working kitchen soon. Meanwhile, I think we'll put you up here in the casino until the kitchen's finished and you will cook for me when I am hungry."

"I will, Lord. Some of my best dishes take time to prepare,

however. I will start one tomorrow morning, and finish it once you let me know when you wish to eat your evening meal."

"That sounds reasonable," Arvil grinned. "Is there more wine?" I poured more for him and topped off the glasses of the other wizards, Delvin included. I barely looked at him as he was served. How thankful was I that he hadn't learned I had mindspeech? If he'd known, he would never have brought me here—he might have tried to kill me instead. That talent was a double-edged blade, in every sense.

I'd never gotten to stay in a hotel before—even if it were attached to a casino. An electronic voice woke me in the morning, after asking me what time I wished to rise the night before. Delvin was pounding on my door before I was finished cleaning up. He handed several suits of clothing, shoes, toiletries and other items to me when I opened the door.

Delvin was trying to patch things up with me, but I wasn't having any of it. I was barely civil as I thanked him. I know, I shouldn't anger him—he was the only one who knew I was female and held my life in his hands, or at least my safety. Regardless, Lendill and Norian now knew who the traitor was.

"You think to teach me how to cook?" The day cook, Kiasz, had arms folded angrily across his chest.

"No, Master Kiasz," I bowed respectfully to him. "I am only here to prepare the evening meal for Lord Arvil, at his bidding. His kitchen is undergoing renovations, so he instructed me to come here. He is expecting only the best from you as usual," I did as much flattering as I could.

"Don't get in my way," Kiasz snarled and moved aside. I made preparations to make the slow-cooked rib roast. I watched it carefully too, throughout the day, beginning vegetable preparations when it came closer to the dinner hour. Master Kiasz glared triumphantly at me when Arvil ordered his midday meal from Kiasz directly. It mattered not to me. I just didn't want the pompous day cook to ruin what I was making. Silently I thanked Aurelius for taking away the need to visit the facilities.

I'd gauged Arvil's evening meal very closely, and the plates of food were served at a long table inside the kitchen, just as it had been the night before. Xiri had come on duty, but Kiasz had stayed to see how things went. The tender rib roast was served with sauce, buttered squash and longbeans with a leafy salad after. Dessert was oxberry puff tarts—I had no idea how they'd gotten oxberries but I wasn't going to argue. Xiri accepted his plate with a huge smile. I respectfully asked Kiasz if he were hungry, hoping that this wouldn't turn into another episode like the one I'd experienced with Master Cook Wyn.

"The sauce is incredible," Xiri didn't waste time voicing his opinion. Kiasz had a frown on his face as he ate—that is until he tasted the dessert.

"Boy, I know not who taught you to cook, but he must have been a master," Kiasz was eating more of the oxberry tart.

"He was," I hung my head.

"His father had too many sons, so this one was turned out," Arvil was enjoying his food and gloating over his new prize.

"How many sons did your father have?" Xiri was curious.

"Twenty-seven," I answered truthfully.

"Mercy," Kiasz muttered. "We will gladly accept the surplus. How old are you, boy?"

"Nineteen, but the physicians say I will always be small."

"That's why his father turned him out; he was the runt of the litter," cruel-mouthed wizard pointed toward me with his fork.

"As you say," I ducked my head. I learned then that Master Cook Kiasz had no love for that particular wizard—he began to treat me well from that moment on. Xiri, too, wanted to learn what he could from me, so he befriended me as well.

I kept wineglasses filled and handed out a second round of desserts to all of them. They were quite full and slightly drunk when they rose from the table to leave. "Re, be in the kitchen at my home tomorrow morning—my contractor wishes to speak to the cook about where everything should go. And another meal tomorrow evening will not go amiss. Inform Delvin, here, if it will be from this kitchen or the one in my home." Arvil walked out, followed by all the others except Delvin, who handed me a chip necklace.

"This will get you through the gates and allow you to purchase small things such as treats and haircuts," Delvin informed me. I hadn't looked at my hair lately—it was depressing to do so. I nodded—he was telling me to keep an eye on it and not let it get very long. "I'll be in the kitchen tomorrow morning, so you can let me know then what you want to do." Delvin walked out after the others.

"I will clean up," I sighed and went to stack plates on the long table.

Xiri shouted at some of his night help, who came quickly to do it for me. Kiasz patted my shoulder and left—he was just as weary as I was and looking for his bed. I left right after he did—I wanted a shower to clear away the smells of the kitchen. I also took the last bit of the roast with me—Xiri packed it up and gave me a bottle of wine to take with me.

"That smells delicious." A man spoke to me as I rode up the elevator to my room. He was elderly—his hair was white and thinning.

"There's enough for two—are you hungry?" I lifted the bottle of wine. I might have never done something like that, but I didn't feel anything bad from this one. We ended up sharing a meal inside his suite—he was wealthy, I could see that right away.

"You cooked this?" The man was astounded over that fact. "The wine is perfect with it, too."

"Yes, Master Griffin." That was the name he'd given.

"Well, Re, should you ever need employment," he handed me a card.

"I will keep this," I said, putting it into a jacket pocket. I left shortly after, picking up the boxes and disposing of them on my way out.

⁓

"She's fine, father, stop fretting." Griffin folded into Wylend Arden's study only a little while later. "I had dinner with her earlier. As long as they don't know she's female and as long as she keeps them happy with her cooking skills, she'll be fine."

"Son, I realize the logic in your words, but the heart doesn't hear those things very well."

CHAPTER 5

"Master Arvil's contractor will be here shortly." Three men were inside the kitchen when I arrived after walking from the casino the following morning. The one I spoke with was short with dark, curly hair. He wasn't much taller than I and I learned he was Oldam the plumber. The other two were cabinet workers—I was getting new cabinets, in addition to the appliances. Oldam showed me that he'd replaced the water line to the dishwasher, installed water filters and softeners and had replaced the faucets, fixtures and the sink. A new stove and dishwasher were already there, too, I saw.

"Does the stove work?" I asked.

"Yes—we had it done last night," Oldam replied.

"I have a chip to buy new dishes and pots and pans," another man walked in, dangling a credit chip in his fingers. I stared, I couldn't help myself. Dark eyes studied me as I gaped. He was more than handsome, with a straight nose, a strong chin and a sensuous mouth. He looked to be in his late twenties, but I was hopeless at gauging anyone's actual age. He was taller than Ry but not as tall as Tory, but then very few were as tall as Tory.

"Some of the old things will still work," I muttered. I couldn't take my eyes off him, for some reason.

"Too late," he grinned, making me catch my breath. His smile would turn any woman's head, I think. "I dumped that junk yesterday," he said, continuing to smile at me. "If we leave now, you might get enough to do dinner tonight," he added.

"Call me Teeg," he said later as we wandered down aisles in an exclusive shop that sold high-end pots, pans and dishes. I watched him walk—he was unconsciously graceful, moving fluidly, like a jungle cat might while stalking prey. "And money is no object." He was grinning at me again. I almost forgot that I was to behave like a nineteen-year-old boy. His smile was melting something that was better left frozen.

"This," I stopped at the stainless-steel cookware. One of the brands available was manufactured on Tulgalan and considered one of the best. I was used to working with it. We pulled everything I needed off high shelves with help from the sales staff. We also got two cast-iron skillets in different sizes, cooking utensils, two sets of dishes and glassware, fine crystal wineglasses, drinks glasses and a multitude of aprons, kitchen towels and supplies. The total was staggering when we were done.

"Only the best for Master Arvil," Teeg grinned at me again. I couldn't help it—I smiled back at him. "That's better," he said. The store was delivering our purchases, so we went to find something to cook at a nearby grocery. I think I will always remember that day with Teeg—the top of my head came midway on his upper arm and he smiled at me often, his white teeth flashing in a grin at times as he asked me about this thing or that.

He was dressed nicely, too, in a charcoal knit shirt and black slacks with matching boots. The fingers on his hands were long, well-shaped and used to working, I could tell. His dark hair curled slightly and was cut and styled very well. It made me worry about my own makeshift haircut that had left barely a finger's width of white hair on my head. Perhaps I'd find a barber, just as Delvin urged me to do.

"I'll come by to speak with Master Arvil about what else needs to be done," Teeg said after we dropped the food purchases inside the kitchen. "You want a work island, don't you?"

"Of course I want an island," I muttered, lowering my eyes. No need to show him my disappointment that he was leaving.

"I found some natural stone that would go well on top of your island," he was smiling when I looked up at him again. "There's enough of it to do the countertops too." I nodded mutely at his suggestion. I think I stared at his back the entire time he walked away, disappearing through the kitchen door after a few ticks. He walked with silent grace out of Arvil's kitchen. The same thought kept racing through my brain as I watched him disappear from view. How was he here on such an outpost of criminal activity? How?

"Re can have what he wants within reason, including an assistant," Arvil was happy with his veal dish. He and his wizards ate with good appetite as Arvil spoke with Teeg. "Xiri has already asked to spend some time over here."

"What do you want, Re, besides an island and new countertops?" Teeg was grinning at me as I poured more wine for Arvil.

"An assistant to prepare breakfast would be nice," I said. "That way I won't be spending all day every day cooking."

"Then ask for a day off," Teeg suggested. That stopped me cold.

"You may have eight-day off—I have dinner with my casino managers on that night," Arvil said. "And only worry about dinner unless I ask for something else the day before. This veal is excellent. Is there any more?" Arvil got more veal. Teeg left after a while, leaving Arvil and his wizards to finish their dessert.

If I'd thought Arvil San Gerxon was a benign autocrat that liked his meals, I was shown something different the following day.

"You let it slip, didn't you?" Arvil's assistant was there and cringing as Arvil shouted at him. The cruel-mouthed wizard and Delvin were also there inside my kitchen as I worked out a menu for the following week. The cabinetmakers faded from the kitchen quickly. I started to leave but Arvil barked for me to stay. "You need to learn, boy, just how things are around here," he snarled. Arvil nodded to cruel-mouth, who lifted his hands.

Even I didn't expect the assistant to scream as he burned alive. I think I dropped to the floor in the corner where I stood while the poor man screamed out his last and died on the kitchen floor. "Clean up the mess," Arvil shouted at Delvin afterward. I stared at Delvin in shock. He'd willingly given himself to this, and dragged me along with him. He didn't even look at me as he and cruel-mouth dragged Arvil's charred, former assistant away. I hadn't even learned what it was the man supposedly did to earn a death such as this.

No, the wizard blasted him with flames and he burned to death, I sent to Lendill later when I could breathe normally again. *I don't know what he did.*

We raided Birimera yesterday and burned a hundred drakus seed fields, Lendill returned. That made me swallow uncomfortably. If Arvil remembered that he'd said that within my hearing, I could be next. *Reah, that wizard can't harm you with his power,* Lendill reminded me.

I don't have protection against a physical attack—you told me not to turn, I reminded him.

Reah, we said you could leave if they are about to harm you. Make sure it is real harm—you've given us good information so far. I wanted to ask what he meant by real harm. Had his and Director Keef's little escapade that caused my convulsions been classified as something other than real harm? I was too afraid to ask.

I have to go to work, I said instead, cutting off the mental communication.

"We can't salvage this," Teeg said later as he examined the cracked and burned tiles. "You don't have to tell me what happened," he muttered softly. I'd knelt beside him so he could show me the damage. My new assistant had cleaned what was left of the floor after the body had been carried away.

"I didn't even know his name. Will his family be notified?" I asked.

"Re, people who work here generally don't have families," Teeg stood and lifted me by grasping my arm in his fingers. "Eight-day is tomorrow. Why don't you come by? I've been thinking about going up the mountain for some fresh air."

The mountain was an artificial ski slope north of Campiaa City. "Here's my address," Teeg flipped a card in his fingers before handing it to me. "Come early."

I was at Teeg's apartment shortly after breakfast. Thinking of him had kept me awake the night before, and that hadn't happened to me often. I considered sending mindspeech to Tory and Aurelius, but then Teeg thought I was a boy. He wasn't one to be attracted to young boys or men—I don't know how I knew that about him, but I did.

"Come on in—I'm almost ready." Teeg led me inside. A snowboard leaned against the wall just inside the door, and a bag that held clothing and equipment lay next to it. His apartment was nice too—it looked comfortable to me.

"You do this often?" I looked around me as he disappeared down a hall. The kitchen was small, but it would do for him. I got the idea he didn't do a lot of cooking for himself.

"Whenever I get the chance." He was back with three sets of dark glasses in his hands. "One of these should fit," he settled one pair over my nose. "No—too big." He tried the others. "Better." He grinned while I tucked the glasses inside my jacket pocket. I usually wore a jacket if I didn't have my cook's apron or coat on. My breasts were small, but my nipples did show occasionally. That might be a giveaway if anyone were looking.

A shuttle ran every few ticks, hauling visitors up and down the mountain. Teeg ran his chip over the scanner for both of us. The ride was nice, lasting half a click. The tourists and locals on the shuttle were chatting away while Teeg and I rode in companionable silence. I was busy looking out the window—we'd taken seats so I could see the ocean. It sparkled below us as I peered over the edge of the cliff running alongside the road.

"Didn't get to see the ocean much?"

"No." I chewed my lower lip as I turned in my seat to look at Teeg. He seemed so familiar at times, but I knew that was silly—I'd never met him until a few days before. I worried that Arvil might be asking him to spy on me and was determined not to let anything slip. Arvil didn't need to learn anything about me. Delvin already knew too much and he could easily get me hurt or killed. That thought made me frown. He'd promised to protect me, but then he'd betrayed Bel and the others. How could I trust that?

"You had such a frightened look on your face just then, Re." Teeg leaned down to stare into my eyes. I wished I could have told him my worries and fears. He seemed such a good man, but he was on Campiaa. Was anyone on Campiaa good? Who intended to be there?

"It's nothing." I turned to stare out the window again. The ocean had lost some of its sparkle.

"It didn't look like nothing," Teeg murmured, but he didn't push it.

I used my chip necklace to pay for ski rentals. This was something I'd never done or ever dreamt of doing. I watched Teeg slip his feet into the slots for his feet on the snowboard and go skimming down the artificial snow. He appeared so agile as he made sweeping arcs, snow spraying from the edge of his board.

The ones who'd rented the equipment to me had given me a brief lesson, but that information was deserting me now as I gazed down the side of the mountain. It looked steep from where I stood. Sighing, I hopped to the edge, turned my skis and let myself drop over the side.

My ankles were unprepared. That was the excuse I gave to Teeg, who was laughing when I reached the bottom of the slope. I'd fallen at least six times before reaching the bottom, too. "Come on, you'll get the hang of this." We took the lift back up the mountain and I watched with envy as Teeg went down again. He must have done this hundreds of times. I was about to give it my second try.

"Not too bad for a first timer," Teeg teased as I returned my rented equipment later. My legs felt as if they were made of rubber as we walked out of the rental hut. "Next time, we can go swimming." Those words almost had me stopped in my tracks.

"I don't swim," I made the excuse. I knew it was a lie. Teeg probably did too. "Well," I amended, "I don't like wearing the suit—I have knobby knees."

"Ninety-pound weakling?" Teeg grinned again. I didn't understand the phrase. "Never mind," he chuckled. "That joke is a lot older than you."

"Thanks for inviting me," I said when we climbed off the shuttle later.

"I'll walk you back to The San Gerxon," he offered. That was the name of Arvil's casino—The San Gerxon. I knew I should refuse—any young man would have done so. I didn't, and I hoped it wouldn't bring me harm later on.

"I'll see you tomorrow—we'll finish up those base cabinets. Then I'll get the stone cutters out to take measurements so we can fit the countertops," Teeg promised as I reached for the door to slip inside the casino. I thought I might stop by and see if Xiri was on duty before heading back to my room.

"I need to go grocery shopping again tomorrow," I said.

"That's fine; I'll be there before you leave." Teeg sounded so confident. I wished I had a fraction of his confidence. I felt as if I walked a knife's edge every moment I spent inside Arvil's palace. After I'd seen his assistant burn with nobody to even care that a man had died, well—I had truly seen why Campiaa had the reputation it did.

"Don't think about that," Teeg watched my face carefully. "That's why I invited you out today—to get it out of your mind. Don't fall into that pit, Re." Teeg turned away and jogged down the steps leading to the casino. I wished I could forget. The poor man's screams still echoed inside my head.

"Re!" Xiri was truly glad to see me, I think. Xiri was tall and thin, and with the tall hat he wore as night cook, he looked even taller and thinner. He had reddish-brown hair that curled around the edges of his hat, making him look somewhat comical. When he threw out his arms in greeting, he made me smile.

"We have an order for dessert for guest Wilffin," one of the assistants informed Xiri, interrupting his hug.

Xiri cursed softly and let me go.

"He is very difficult to please," the assistant explained as Xiri turned toward the pastry prep area.

"Then let's give him an assortment," I said. We ended up sending six smaller desserts on a single plate, including a generous portion of the oxberry puff tart with sweet cream.

"Now we sit back and wait for the complaints," Xiri fanned himself and sat down on a stool.

"Well, I need to go back—I went up the mountain today and my ankles are angry now," I smiled at Xiri. "Some people are impossible to please. Just remember that what makes them happiest is seeing the misery of others. Don't let them win." I patted Xiri's arm and left the kitchen. It was advice I should take for myself, but it was so hard at times. So very hard.

"There's my cook." Arvil was raiding the keeper when I trudged down the hall toward my small bedroom. It did have a decent bed, its own bath attached and a tiny closet. There wasn't much space for anything else.

"Can I get you anything, Lord Arvil?" I asked politely.

"Can you make a simple sandwich?"

"Of course." We walked back to the kitchen. Arvil was served an ox-roast sandwich with all the trimmings. Delvin and two other wizards who were with Arvil received the same. It made me wonder where the other five were. I knew better than to ask.

"You know, that seed is coming right along on Kliiver," Arvil said casually as I put clean dishes away. I didn't even look up at his comment—his words were a lie. He was attempting to trap me, somehow. I wasn't about to take that bait.

"Goodnight Lord Arvil," I said and walked toward my bedroom. Oh, they'd been careful, going through all my things, but I had a good memory and my only other pair of shoes weren't quite in the same spot inside my closet. They did suspect me. I wondered if I should send mindspeech to Lendill, and then decided against it. He'd just tell me to keep doing what I was doing unless they tried to kill me. I wanted to skip away from Campiaa so badly right then it made my head hurt.

~

"Would you like breakfast? Have you eaten yet?" I asked Teeg when he showed up the next morning.

"I wouldn't mind," he said. He had a plate of food sitting in front of him quickly. I'd poached eggs and served them over toast points with sauce and shaved ham. Fresh fruit went with the rest, and Teeg ate everything.

"That was perfect," he sighed, handing the empty plate back to me. The cabinetmakers had finished their job, so we were the only ones inside the kitchen right then. I wanted to tell him what had happened the night before so badly, and knew I couldn't. Teeg was loyal to Arvil, who was paying him for his services. I was nothing to Teeg.

The dishwasher worked perfectly, I thanked Teeg for that fact, wrote out my list and headed for the market, my new assistant right behind me. He was only a few months older than I was—nearly twenty he'd said, and his name was Neele. Neele told me all about how he lifted weights in his spare time as we rode the pub-trans to the market. Neele was two hands taller than I was, broad across the shoulders and narrow at the waist and hips. I believed him when he said he worked out. He had a scar over his right eye that I was determined not to ask about. He turned many a female head as we shopped for our needs and stopped to talk with two that seemed quite forward. Neele had a date before we ever left the store.

"That turned out well—maybe I'll ask her if she has a friend to bring for you, Re." Neele was grinning at me. "When's the last time you had sex?"

"Not that long ago," I muttered, hauling bags up the steps of the pub-trans. "And I prefer to make my own dates. Thank you for thinking of me, but I'll find my own. Woman." Neele snickered at my stumble. He thought I was embarrassed to admit I'd have a hard time finding a date. I let him continue thinking that.

~

"This soup is exceptional." Arvil was asking for more and we hadn't even gotten to the main course yet. The market had gotten fresh shrimp so I'd bought some, although they were small. These were perfect for soup or salads. The main course was redfish that I'd only seen imported from three Alliance worlds. It made me wonder if Campiaa was doing business on the black market with some of those worlds. I knew which ones supplied the redfish, so I resolved to send that information to Lendill. He might yell that it was unimportant. I knew where that opinion had gotten us before.

"We have a little errand to run after dinner," Arvil was dipping up the last of his second helping of soup. "Delvin here tells me you're a pretty good shot, Re."

"He doesn't miss," Delvin said, causing Neele to stare at me. "We're having a problem with the same enemy we had on Mandil," Delvin went on. "Our fields are under attack, so we're taking you with us to see if we can't rid ourselves of that little problem."

At that moment, I wanted to shout at Delvin. Scream at him and beat on his chest. What was he doing, telling Arvil San Gerxon things like that? He was determined to get me killed. I just knew it.

"Well, I normally don't go out with my wizards," Arvil smiled as I set a plate of fish in front of him first. "But after Delvin said you were such a good shot, I had to see this for myself."

"I don't have suitable clothing," I said, placing other plates around the makeshift table Teeg had brought in from somewhere.

"I got something for you this afternoon," Delvin grinned. "Boots, too."

"Then I'll go," I said.

Cruel-mouth folded us. I had no idea what world we stood upon when we landed, but it held the scent of plowed fields. I couldn't see trees anywhere near and sprinklers were sending jets of water far out into the fields in a circular pattern. In the moonlight, the mist off the water looked spectacular.

"They're heading this way, Master Arvil," one of three men who'd approached us when we landed bowed respectfully to Arvil.

"You have the ranos rifles ready?"

"Several for each of you."

"I will not be shooting, I will be watching," Arvil snapped.

"Of course, Master Arvil." The man bowed again. I knew why Arvil wouldn't be shooting—he couldn't see the enemy. The wizards and I could. Silently cursing Delvin for perhaps the hundredth time, I slung one rifle over my shoulder and accepted the second, checking the charge readout. It was ready.

"Heads up," the gray-haired wizard called. I'd already sighted the lights—they were blinking as they walked toward us.

"These have been charging once they're hit," Delvin said quietly beside me. "Be prepared." I wanted to tell him what he could do with his information.

"*Af te Jufaleh*," I said instead. Tory had given me the meaning for the High Demon words—they meant *go to perdition*.

"Re, you'll have to tell me what that means sometime," Delvin grinned and lifted his rifle.

"Be happy to," I muttered my reply and sighted my first target.

Arvil was laughing and clapping his hands with glee as I emptied my first ranos rifle in very little time, dropping it at my feet and allowing the second rifle to slide off my shoulder. I aimed and fired it just as quickly as the first. Spawn eye lights were winking out every time I fired. Arvil couldn't see the enemy but cruel-mouth was telling him, with corroboration from the others that I wasn't missing. Arvil was getting his money's worth, I think—the best of food for his table and a marksman right along with it. Somewhere in the Alliance records were my marksman's medals—I'd earned everything they could give out to a recruit. They would have been given to me had I gone to any job except the one I did—there wasn't any need to wear medals such as that on a cook's uniform.

"They're charging!" One of the wizards shouted. We'd already killed hundreds, but even I could see that some of Arvil's wizards were poor shots. They could see the enemy, they just couldn't hit them. That left holes in our defense. If we'd had Bel and the others there, we wouldn't be having this trouble. We didn't have Bel—Delvin had lied to his friends and now worked for the enemy.

My rifle emptied just as the spawn were about to hit us. Cruel-mouth raised his hands to send out blasts, but even I knew that was useless. Arvil was screaming for someone to get him out of there when I used the butt of my rifle to knock the spawn back that seemed determined to get to Arvil San Gerxon. I kicked the next one and punched another in the face before a fresh rifle was tossed to me. I started shooting just as fast as the weapon could fire, mowing down anything that came near us.

Arvil might have still been shrieking, but I shut it out after only a few ticks, concentrating on killing spawn. A fourth rifle was handed over when the third ran out, and I killed the last three that rushed us. "Fuckers," I muttered angrily, slinging my rifle over my shoulder and going to examine a deep pile of spawn dust in front of us.

Aurelius had said four feet to me once. This pile was nearly as tall. I remembered that I'd asked him to teach me his measurements. There'd been no time for that. We'd had no time, Aurelius and I. Tory and I barely knew one another. I missed both of them with an ache in my heart. I thought of Teeg, too. I wished I could truly call him friend —that we could be that, if nothing else. I had no friends. Not on Campiaa, anyway.

"Not bad, huh," Delvin clapped a hand to my shoulder as I examined the piles of dust surrounding us. "Not bad at all. Even for a girl."

I turned so swiftly toward Delvin he didn't have time to blink. "Bastard!" I shouted and punched him right in the face.

"Reah, he guessed." Delvin held the piece of cold steak to his eye inside my kitchen. Arvil San Gerxon was grinning hugely—he had a new toy to play with—*me.*

I wanted to hiss at Delvin and hit him again. I couldn't—Arvil had already informed me that he would forgive the hit I'd delivered to Delvin's left eye—I was allowed one punch after killing most of the spawn attacking his fields. I wanted to tell him they weren't attacking his fields, they were attacking us. Arvil had warned me not to hit any of his wizards again, unless he ordered it. That was just perfect.

"Reah, that's a pretty name—Reah," Arvil grinned at me. "From now on, you can dress any way you want. And grow your hair out. Nobody will touch you unless you want them to. Years ago, Erland Morphis had a female bodyguard. Nobody got past her. Now, I not only have a female cook, but she can protect me, too. That's priceless." Arvil sat down, still beaming at me. I didn't give myself away when he mentioned Ry's father, but I did wonder how Arvil knew of Erland Morphis.

"It would be better if I bought her more of those black leathers," Delvin said. He removed the steak from his eye for a moment, revealing the black and purple bruise beneath. "A more feminine version, anyway. You'll be ready for anything," Delvin chuckled at the look on my face.

"Sure, leathers are so comfortable to cook in," I said sarcastically.

"Now, now, children, mind your manners," Arvil still sounded gleeful.

"Well, you can wear normal clothes when you cook," Delvin conceded. I wanted to thank him for giving his permission in the most sarcastic way I possibly could, but Arvil might be running out of patience soon. I had no desire to see anyone else burned to a crisp while screaming in agony.

I went to bed shortly afterward, but before I futilely attempted to sleep, I drew out what I'd held in the pocket of my leather pants and examined it. Perhaps it was luck, perhaps it was my death. I'd tripped over something when I'd gone to examine spawn dust in the field surrounding us. It turned out to be part of a sprinkler pipe. I'd lifted a piece of it up after nearly tripping over it in the damp soil, and then slid the small chunk carefully into one of my pants pockets. It held a serial number—most things did that were manufactured by the Alliance. Contacting Lendill, who was grumpy at being wakened, I sent the serial number to him through mindspeech. I hoped he was awake enough to record it for research later—he was certainly interested in the fact that there were more fields of drakus seed somewhere.

"Re, what's this?" Teeg came in the following morning. I was exhausted since I'd gotten in late and then was unable to sleep afterward. I didn't bother with a jacket today and wore a stretchy, sleeveless shirt—it was summer on Campiaa and warm inside the kitchen, even early in the morning. My breasts, such as they were, were visible under my top. And when my nipples hardened at Teeg's appearance, it made me flush with embarrassment.

"I'm a girl. Master Arvil discovered that fact last night, even with my best disguise. There," I muttered, turning away to tend to something on the stove.

"He didn't touch you, did he?" Teeg was turning me back to face him, a look of concern on his face.

"No." My reply was sullen.

"I'll kill him if he does," Teeg's hands clenched. I stared at him in shock—where had that come from?

"Don't worry," Teeg said. "Go back to your cooking. The countertops will be delivered sometime today. They couldn't give me an exact time."

Neele chose that moment to wander in and he grinned at me. "Delvin told me," he laughed.

"Of course he did," I muttered.

"Nice black eye you gave him."

"He deserved it."

"Probably," Neele was still laughing. "I hear you're Master Arvil's new bodyguard, as well as his cook."

"I'm so lucky," I snapped.

"Re," Teeg warned.

"It's Reah," cruel-mouth walked in. He stared at me the whole time I fixed something for breakfast. Teeg checked the plumbing. He checked all the new appliances. Checked the new cabinets and made sure he had enough supplies to lay the new countertops. Cruel-mouth finally left.

"Neele, is there any furniture polish anywhere?" Teeg asked my assistant.

"I think the housekeeper has some," Neele replied. Arvil's housekeeper was likely in her twenties and looked as if she hopped into bed with Arvil whenever he snapped his fingers. Her long dark hair and pretty face hadn't gotten past Neele either. "I'll go ask," Neele trotted out of the kitchen.

"Reah, if that wizard so much as looks at you wrong," Teeg didn't finish his statement. I wasn't sure why Teeg would be concerned, or what he could do if cruel-mouth did look at me wrong.

Neele trotted back in with a bottle of furniture oil. "This will do nicely—do you have an old cloth or anything?" Neele found that, too, by going to ask the housekeeper. He was gone longer the second time. Teeg did a thorough job, oiling and polishing the wood cabinets. They were red wood, and the new countertops were supposed to be black stone. It would look very nice when finished.

When Neele walked out of the kitchen to go to the bathroom, Teeg spoke again. "Reah, meet me in front of the casino when you're done tonight," he said.

I wanted to ask him why, but my desire to meet him just about anywhere kept that question behind my teeth. "All right," I agreed. "But they'll watch me, I think."

"Arvil won't care—I work for him, too. He keeps me busy at all his casinos most of the time. He pulled me away from my current project to finish this. I'll go back to that, tomorrow."

"They'll still have an eye on me," I said softly. Teeg was kneeling on the floor, oiling a cabinet door next to the stove, which meant he was right beside me as I worked.

"Only until they see you're with me. Don't worry, Reah. All right?"

Asking me not to worry was like asking the sun not to rise. Not possible. Teeg had no idea who I was and why or how I'd gotten here. And he was quite handsome, turning heads wherever he went. What could he possibly see in a small, nearly flat-chested female with a shaved head? It made absolutely no sense at all.

CHAPTER 6

"There you are—I was beginning to think you'd changed your mind."

"Arvil wanted extra dessert," I mumbled as Teeg pulled me along beside him. We were walking down the street that ran between the casinos on the beach and the beach itself. I'd been right, too, about Arvil's guards watching me. They'd melted away as soon as they saw me with Teeg.

"Let's sit here." Teeg chose a spot with a nice view of the moon hovering over the water. I dropped beside him and sat cross-legged on the sand. That seemed to amuse Teeg for some reason. We didn't talk for several ticks.

"Reah, did you think I wouldn't know? I can't believe those idiots didn't see it sooner," Teeg turned to look at me. His face was in shadow, but I could see moonlight glinting in his dark eyes.

"I should have hit Delvin harder," I grumbled.

"He does have a nice black eye," Teeg agreed. "But I don't like the way Haral looks at you, now."

"Is that his name? I was calling him cruel-mouth."

"He has that, certainly," Teeg agreed. "You didn't call him that to his face, did you?"

"Do you think I'm that stupid? I watched him fry a man." The thought of that made me shudder.

"Reah, I think anyone else would have gone into fits over that," Teeg said, bumping his shoulder against mine. "Or fainted."

"I wish I had fainted."

"No, Reah. We don't need to hand them any more weapons than they have already."

"What do you mean?" I was concerned, now. And a little frightened.

"If he learns he can make you pass out, then he might do it, just so he can," Teeg shivered.

"Oh, gods," I dropped my face into my hands.

"But since he knows you can deliver a good right hook," Teeg smiled crookedly, "maybe he'll back off. Watch him, Reah. He likes the young ones—the smaller ones."

"Arvil told them they couldn't touch me unless I wanted them to touch me. I won't ever want them. Any of them. Ever."

"Then don't put yourself in any position to make it a he-said, she-said situation. Arvil may side with his wizards. They're valuable to him, I know."

"You seem to know a lot about them—for a contractor."

"Reah, I've been in and out of Arvil's palace and his casinos. I've heard all kinds of things. Trust me—burning that poor man to death was one of Arvil's quicker murders. He owns Campiaa, Reah. Don't ever forget that. The constabulary are for the others, when they murder, rape or steal. Arvil gets away with whatever he wants."

"Yet you work for him. My employment was involuntary."

"I heard that too," Teeg sighed. He didn't bother to explain how or why he worked for Arvil San Gerxon. "I know you don't belong here, Reah," Teeg went on. "You're like a lily standing in a patch of blackweed." His analogy was good; blackweed was a pernicious plant that choked out all other plants if allowed to grow unchecked.

"Let's go walk in the water," I suggested. Our conversation was only serving to frighten and depress me. We took off our shoes and waded in the water while the moon shone upon us. After a bit, I pulled the piece of pipe from my pocket—I'd been afraid to leave it in my room—and flung it far out into the water.

"What was that?" Teeg asked as we watched it curve over the ocean before dropping in with a soft plop.

"A piece of my former life," I sighed and walked on.

~

"That fool Delvin let the bull out of the barn." Norian felt like hissing, even if he wasn't currently in his lion snake form.

"So they know she's female now." Lendill raked a hand through his hair.

"On another note, we've managed to convince wizard Bel to work for us. He was so angry over being duped by Delvin that he wants to help us out any way he can. I think the fact that they grabbed Reah had something to do with it." Norian had Bel's signed conscription on the comp-vid lying on his desk.

"That serial number she gave us checked out—those fields are on Reliff. We can have a team in place by tomorrow."

"Do it," Norian nodded.

~

Anyone who was still in bed was pulled from their sleep early the following morning and hauled off to a huge media room inside Arvil's palace. We all watched as drakus seed fields burned on Reliff. A reporter was saying that two farmers from adjoining property had gotten suspicious after seeing what they thought were fire blasts two nights earlier. They had reported to the local constabulary, who'd done an initial investigation before calling the ASD. Arvil was so angry, he was ready to pull his hair out and kill someone.

"I told you your blasts were useless against those things!" Delvin was shouting at cruel-mouthed Haral. Haral looked as if he were about to send some of his blasts in Delvin's direction.

"Arvil's family is coming home today, too. Don't do anything to upset him." The gray-haired wizard was whispering to me while Delvin and Haral glared at each other and Arvil stared in disbelief at the huge vid screen. "My name is Milus," the gray-haired one continued. "I'm sorry we were never properly introduced."

I wanted to ask Milus about Arvil's family, but I didn't have to. Arvil told me himself. "My brother and his wife are coming home today, with my two cousins," Arvil announced as he rose from his chair. "Treat all of them as you'd treat me and watch them like a cat watches a bird. Reah, I'll be issuing a knife and a pistol to you. If any of my relatives threatens me—kill them."

"Yes, Lord Arvil," I nodded respectfully.

"See, that's how I should be treated. And I like the *Lord* Arvil. Much better than Master. Haral, since those blasts of yours cost us our fields on Reliff, perhaps you can go back there and find those two farmers. Make them dead for me, all right?"

"With pleasure," Haral stood and folded away.

That's how I ended up sending mindspeech while I cooked breakfast for the others. *Lendill, a wizard named Haral is coming to Reliff to kill those two fictional farmers*, I sent.

There really were two farmers, but the locals didn't report them to the ASD. We found the reports after we sent our team in. See, we do try to protect you where we can.

You're only protecting your information source. You don't give a damn about me. Yes, my last transmission was grumpy in the extreme and exactly how I felt. No doubt the ASD's esteemed Vice-Director would have something to say to me, or perhaps allow me to spend a day or two in a cell when I got back for getting snippy with him. At the moment, I didn't really care.

"Come with me." Arvil handed a knife and a pistol to me as soon as breakfast was over—Neele was expected to clean the kitchen. I was dressed in black leather again, with the knife clipped to the back of my belt and the pistol in a holster on the right side. Delvin was with us as we followed Arvil San Gerxon to his private transportation—a luxury hover-limo. Delvin and I sat in the back, across from Arvil as we made our way to the shuttle station.

"You could have gotten here sooner," Jazal San Gerxon snapped angrily as I lifted two of his bags. He wasn't saying it to Arvil, he was saying it to me, as if I'd had anything to do with it. It wasn't that uncommon—if you couldn't attack the one you were truly angry with, you found an alternate to vent your anger upon. Arvil was the head of the family; I wasn't sure Jazal had enough sense to run a sandwich kiosk. Jazal's wife, Anith, was only concerned about how she looked in public. She was applying lip color when we arrived, before smiling vapidly at Arvil. If she knew how Arvil truly felt about her and her husband, she hid it well.

Delvin pushed the overloaded cart filled with the other luggage, I carried Jazal's last two bags and still we were forced to hire a hover-taxi to carry the surplus. I rode next to Arvil on the way home; Delvin, since he took up more space, got to ride in the hover-taxi with the surplus luggage and Arvil's twin cousins, Kita and Lita.

Dinner that evening was strained—I cooked for Arvil, all the wizards except for Haral (who wasn't back yet) and Jazal, Anith, Kita and Lita. Kita and Lita weren't nearly as pretty as Anith, but then you can't choose family. You do choose your spouse. Anith was going on about their two moon-turn vacation while Arvil's eyes glazed over. I wanted to laugh several times as I served the soup course with Neele's help. Six more courses followed, including dessert.

"Your cook is now your bodyguard?" Jazal's voice sounded contemptuous.

"Reah is good at both," Arvil sounded bored.

"I find that difficult to believe, brother."

"She didn't miss a single thing she shot at the other night." Milus dipped into his cream cake dessert.

"Reah doesn't miss," Delvin agreed. "Cake's good, Reah."

"Thank you," I nodded stiffly at Delvin. If he thought I'd soften toward him over a compliment, then he was very wrong. I was polite, though. It always paid to be polite.

"I'll hire another assistant," Arvil sighed when dinner was over. Jazal and the relatives had gone off to the casino to play. They weren't held to the no-gambling resident's rule, it seemed. Arvil stayed behind to talk with his employees. I nodded at Arvil's words—Neele and I had been hard-pressed to serve that many people in Arvil's grand dining hall.

"Hire two, at least," the red-haired wizard agreed. "That way we can still get a meal if Reah has to go out and kill with us."

"Good enough. Reah, will it upset our cook to hire another?"

"No, and I think Xiri might like that job," I said. Xiri didn't like working with Kiasz very much.

"Good. Bring Xiri in and hire two more assistants." Arvil was feeling generous.

"Don't worry, I've already seen it. In the casino kitchen, no less," Xiri shuddered as I attempted to warn him about what he might see inside Arvil's palace. I wanted to ask Xiri how he'd come to Campiaa, but felt it might be a private matter. I left it alone. If he wanted me to know, he'd tell me. Xiri had brought two of his night assistants with him, which no doubt angered Kiasz. Kiasz was going to have to look for a new night cook and two others—Xiri had just wiped out a third of the night staff. Arvil didn't seem to care—he expected his people to fill in the gaps until replacements were found.

We were making dough for dinner rolls and setting it to rise when Teeg walked in, followed by three carpenters—they were bringing in the new island they'd built at their shop. The wood behemoth was hauled in on its side on a wheeled transport. Teeg grinned at me as I watched his three helpers lift the island into place. The doors were added next, and then the stone top was brought in and laid down. A small sink was going into the island too, for prep purposes. Teeg did that himself, after sending the others back to his shop.

It was pleasurable, watching Teeg's legs and lower torso twist and turn on the kitchen floor as he hooked the water lines up after dropping in the sink. I think I smiled at him several times as he installed the faucet.

"Reah, want to meet me out front again?" he asked quietly after he finished wiping the countertop and sink.

"Yes." I didn't hesitate for even a blink. I'd missed seeing him every day.

"Well, girlie, that's a fine specimen," Xiri sighed when Teeg walked out the door. Xiri had learned I was female; I learned that Xiri liked men. I think I knew that already, I just hadn't thought it yet. It made no difference to me. People were people. Why worry over who they loved?

"Let's get a drink." Teeg led me down the strip of casinos until we came to one not owned by Arvil San Gerxon. Only six of those existed on Campiaa. "There used to be a lot more that Arvil didn't own, but they hauled everything off to Le-Ath Veronis as soon as the permits were given." Teeg was giving me information as we sat at the bar inside the Sandstorm Casino. A huge, round aquarium had been constructed inside the circular bar, and fish of all kinds swam through it. A gaming screen was located at every seat at the bar, too. As employees on Campiaa, Teeg and I weren't allowed to play. A block was placed on our credit chips, preventing it. None of the casinos accepted any other currency.

"Reah, the servants' quarters are getting cramped at Arvil's. Move in with me. I have an extra bedroom. You won't be bothered. Unless you want to be, that is." Teeg offered a wry grin.

"Arvil won't allow it." I hunched my shoulders. If I had the choice between living with Teeg or taking the chance that someone else might die in front of me at Arvil's, well, Teeg would win every time. There were other reasons, but I wasn't ready to face them yet.

"He will, I've already asked him. He thought he'd be forced to move you onto the family floor—he didn't want any of the others up there.

I'm less than a quarter click walk from Arvil's palace. Come on, Reah. I'll feel better if I know you're safe while you're sleeping."

"It'll take five ticks to move," I ran a finger down the side of my wineglass, gathering up condensation—I'd asked for a chilled, white wine. "I think I have five outfits."

"And three pairs of shoes. Reah, eight-day is tomorrow. I'll help you move and then we'll find more clothes and shoes."

"Teeg, you don't have to run after me." I stared into warm, dark eyes.

"Reah, I've never found anyone else I wanted to run after." I watched his lips as he spoke—they were sensual and smiled crookedly at his statement.

My mouth was hanging open as I stared—Teeg reached over and lifted my jaw up with a finger.

❦

Teeg told me he'd come for me around nine bells, so I was standing in the kitchen the following morning, having a quick glass of juice and some toast when Xiri came to me. He'd been preparing breakfast with one of his assistants. "Reah, Neele's been sleeping with the housekeeper," Xiri whispered next to my ear. "You ought to say something to him—he'll get killed if Master Arvil finds out."

Mutely I nodded at Xiri—he was right. I only had a moment to ponder how Xiri had learned of Neele's indiscretion when Neele walked in, dressed only in pajama bottoms and looking rumpled. He snagged one of the breakfast pastries that Xiri's assistant had just pulled from the oven when Arvil walked in, dragging the housekeeper with him by her hair.

Neele died with a single ranos pistol shot to his forehead, a tart halfway to his mouth. The housekeeper, who'd started screaming, was flung on top of Neele's body and shot in the head as well. Blood gushed all over the new tiles when Xiri dropped to the floor in a dead faint. His assistant was curled up on the floor and shaking, a look of horror on his face. It most likely mirrored the expression on my face, to be truthful.

"You couldn't do this somewhere else?" Teeg drawled as he walked into the room. "I just had those tiles laid." Arvil lifted an eyebrow in Teeg's direction but didn't say a word. Instead, he stalked from the kitchen, shoving the ranos pistol into his belt.

⁓

"Reah, just grab your things and let's go," Teeg was herding me through my small bedroom as quickly as he could. "Let those wizards clean up the mess."

"But Xiri."

"Xiri will be fine—his assistant is helping him," Teeg hissed. "Come on, sweetheart. Let's go." Teeg wasn't waiting around for me to look for anything I might have left behind. He was hauling me out of there as fast as he could. I was shoved into a hover-taxi waiting outside Arvil's walls and Teeg ordered the driver to leave as quickly as he could.

"Reah, I'm sorry, but that was Arvil's lover, and he doesn't take that from his lovers. I don't want him looking in your direction next." We were already at Teeg's apartment complex and he was tapping on the window that separated us from the driver. The driver scanned Teeg's wrist for credit after we climbed out of the vehicle, loaded down with my few possessions. The cab driver left us standing there.

"Come on, Reah. You can't let Arvil do this to you. You have to act normally the next time you see him."

I think my teeth were chattering—shock was setting in. I hadn't hired Neele and I knew he had a wandering eye, but I never expected him to act that stupidly. Now he'd paid for that, as had Arvil's housekeeper. I realized I hadn't even known her name.

"Drink this." Teeg had dumped my clothing onto the floor the moment he got us inside his apartment and kicked the door shut. He'd poured out a very generous portion of bourbon in a glass and handed it to me. "Drink it all," he directed. Teeg watched as I swallowed the bourbon in only a few gulps. "Here, have more." He poured out half as much again. I drank that, too. He tilted up the bottle and drank what was left.

"Come on, love, we're going out in public." Teeg hauled me off the barstool; we left my clothing lying in the foyer and walked out the door.

Teeg lived on the ground floor of a three-story apartment building and we walked down cushioned walkways until we came to streets filled with shops of all kinds. Tourists were everywhere—Arvil owned most of the shops open for business, in addition to a majority of the casinos. Teeg told me that as we walked along.

"See, there are shops that cater to small women," Teeg pulled me inside a shop.

"Trust me, your chip will hold up," Teeg declared as the pile of clothing grew. I'd picked out mostly slacks or pants, with shirts and blouses to go with them. Teeg asked for skirts and dresses. He insisted on staying just outside the dressing rooms as I was fitted for underwear.

"See, this makes what you have much more appealing," the clerk informed me as I stared at the lacy underthing that now covered my breasts. Several of those went into the pile, as did panties that showed much more than they concealed. My face was burning when I got away from the salesclerk.

My credit chip did cover what I bought, and it was substantial. Teeg paid extra to have it packed up and delivered to his address later. Then we went shopping for shoes. Teeg was very fussy over dress shoes. "Just the right amount of heel," he said. "No sense in killing yourself or damaging your toes." I paid for twelve pairs—Teeg paid for another six. Those were the ones he liked and I didn't have any use for. Those would be delivered, too.

"Now, let's get the best food on Campiaa that doesn't come from Reah's kitchen," Teeg hugged me against him as we walked down more cushioned sidewalks.

The best food turned out to be a tiny restaurant that took your order at the counter and then shouted out your name when it was ready. Self-service, for the most part. I understood the logic—there wasn't any room to put tables and no room to place waitstaff—the outer area was filled with tourists waiting for their food or waiting to order.

"This is good," I lifted up my sandwich, wrapped in one of the best flat-breads I'd ever tasted. The sandwich was filled with beef, onions, sour cream and a sauce I liked very much.

"See?" Teeg grinned at me as we sat at a tiny table in a nearby courtyard to eat. I'd gotten fruit juice to go with my sandwich; Teeg had ordered a mixed drink.

"Thank you," I said. Teeg ducked his head and lifted a crisp he'd gotten with his sandwich. He knew what I meant—he'd worked hard to get the morning's horror out of my mind. We went back to Teeg's apartment when we finished eating.

The delivery van arrived almost when we did, and boxes and bags were hauled inside Teeg's spacious apartment. I got what we'd left on the floor out of the way and everything was placed on Teeg's kitchen island. He didn't have a table—the island served double duty.

"This is your bedroom," Teeg showed it to me after the deliveryman left. The suite was very nice—the bed was big enough for two or three people, the closet held everything with plenty of space left over and I had my own bath.

"The apartments are all built that way—in case tourists want to rent them instead of staying at one of the casinos," Teeg explained as we tucked the last of the shoeboxes inside my closet. "I stocked you with towels and sheets," Teeg smiled. "Let's get in the spa."

"You have a spa?"

"Out on the patio. All the upgraded apartments have one."

"I didn't know you had a patio."

"I do. Put that swimsuit on, Reah, so I can see how knobby your knees are." He was laughing at me. I swatted at him but he moved away easily.

The swimsuit had been Teeg's idea and he'd managed to get it into the pile of clothing even after I'd put it back. Twice. We carried a bottle of wine to the spa on Teeg's patio. A high fence surrounded the small patio and a few tropical plants placed in the corners kept it from appearing so empty and stark. Teeg looked more than fine in the small suit he wore. I had to keep myself from staring.

"Here," he poured a glass of wine for me after I slipped into the bubbling water. "Now, tell me where this came from." He touched the spot on my shoulder where Nods had shot me. The swimsuit he'd picked out was strapless—he could see my shoulders just fine.

"Got shot a little while back." I sipped my wine.

"Ah. Did it hurt?"

"More than you know." I wasn't about to tell him what happened *after* I got shot. That was between Tory and me.

I was wrapped in a towel later as I put something together for our dinner. Teeg had stocked a few things. I was going to the market as soon as I could to get everything else we needed.

"See, good things can come from nannas that are almost overripe," I said, slicing off a piece of the sweet bread I'd made. Teeg took my hand holding the piece of nannabread and ate it from my fingers. I think he sucked on the fingers, too, before he was finished. I stared at him.

"It is good," he agreed. He kissed my hand and gave it back to me with a smile.

I was ready to tell him it would be even better with a vanilla sauce I made and a particular type of wine, but that thought flew right out of my head, followed quickly by the breath from my body.

"I don't want to move too fast," Teeg murmured. "If you want more, let me know." I stared after him as he walked down the hall toward his bedroom. I heard his door close a few ticks later. I got my breath back and swallowed with difficulty.

First day, worst day went through my mind as I walked through the gate in the wall. One of the guards nodded to me—I'd worn new clothes today—a pair of slacks and a pretty blouse I'd gotten with Teeg's help the day before. New, comfortable shoes were on my feet, too. It never made sense to wear anything else while cooking. Teeg had given me a quick peck on the cheek before I'd gone out the door.

"Reah, I'd like something good for breakfast," Arvil plopped down on one of the barstools on the far side of the island. Who knew that killing people would work up an appetite? I made something good for Arvil's breakfast and set it in front of him. Delvin came in with Milus and they got the same thing.

"Why don't you check those fields on Twylec," Arvil told Milus as he sighed happily and pushed his plate toward me. Arvil was lying again. Did he think he was going to catch me that way? Did he test all his employees like that? I just placed his dishes in the dishwasher as if I hadn't heard anything.

"Is that carpenter doing you all right?" Delvin sounded snippy.

"The *contractor* is fine, thank you," I snapped right back.

"Just make sure he keeps on being fine." Delvin stalked out of the kitchen.

"Don't pay any mind to him," Milus said. "He doesn't know what he wants. Spends his nights with those twins, if they're here," he added. "Food was good, Reah." Milus handed his plate over and left.

"Reah, are you all right?" Xiri walked in and tied an apron around his waist.

"Yeah. I was going to ask you the same thing," I said, giving him a quick hug. I'd had to hug his middle—he was too tall for anything else.

"Dinner wasn't that good last night," Xiri muttered.

"Well, it never is if somebody dies in your kitchen."

"Two somebodies," Xiri nodded.

Two things happened that afternoon—Haral came back from his errand and Arvil received guests.

"I don't know what they are, but they're not all humanoid," Xiri hissed as we put dinner together for an extra eight guests. The housekeeping staff added leaves to the dining table, making it considerably longer. Xiri had seen at least two of the guests when he'd gone to relieve himself. He didn't describe them to me—Jazal had come into the kitchen demanding a snack be brought to him, Anith and the twins out by the pool. Must be nice to wave imperiously and get whatever you wanted.

Tiny sandwiches, fresh fruit and drinks were placed on trays and Xiri's two assistants and I hauled it out to the pool. I'd never seen Arvil's pool before—it was huge, with a wide flagstone patio around it, a waterfall at one end and a spa on the opposite side. Jazal had stripped down to a tiny suit, which he shouldn't have purchased. If you had that kind of paunch, then you were better off buying something a bit larger and more concealing. Anith looked quite good in the sea-green suit she wore—it went well with her blonde hair and eyes. Kita and Lita went for basic black and dark glasses. I served fruit drinks—all of which were liberally laced with rum. Snacks were placed by each lounge chair.

"Bring another round of these," Jazal demanded after sipping his drink. I nodded, lifted the drink tray and went back to mix another batch. They had three drinks each before they were done. Honestly, they were all better people when they were drunk.

"This ox-roast very good." Arvil's guests looked to be part reptile. That's what they looked like to me. Their faces were humanoid, but they had slitted eyes, just as a snake did. Their nostrils, too, were a bit on the narrow side and they sounded slightly short of breath when they spoke—as if they were hissing. The one who seemed to be in charge was complimenting my food.

"It is a pleasure to serve it to you," I gave a slight, respectful bow. I hadn't been introduced to any of the guests, so I couldn't give an honorific to his name. I'd served the ox roast wrapped in mushrooms, sauce and pastry, in addition to baby vegetables, the soup Arvil loved, crispy rolls, salad and dessert.

"Master Arvil, I like this served at my home," the same guest spoke again slowly, as if he were thinking carefully about each word before he spoke.

"Perhaps something might be arranged," Arvil smiled. Jazal was still drinking and didn't speak. It was probably better that way. Anith was talking animatedly with another guest, who was politely ignoring her. Lita and Kita sat on either side of Delvin. Well, he was making his bed. At least Arvil didn't get homicidal when somebody slept with his cousins.

"We'll bring two more assistants from The San Gerxon," Arvil told me inside the kitchen later. His guests had gone to Arvil's media room with Jazal and the others. Our current assistants were there pouring drinks. Xiri and I were doing our best to clean everything up.

"Thank you, Lord Arvil," I nodded to him. Xiri was doing the same.

"Next time, I'll try not to shoot the garbage inside your kitchen, Reah." Arvil walked out, heading toward the media room and his guests.

"He needs a new woman and fast," Xiri muttered. I agreed. I didn't want Arvil San Gerxon to come anywhere near me. At times, he was polite and congenial. Until he decided to kill you, that is.

"We have eight new houseguests, plus the brother and his crew," I sighed as I sat next to Teeg on the sofa. He'd been watching news vids —Campiaa had pirated feeds from the Alliance.

"Who are they?" Teeg casually stroked fingers against my temple.

"No idea—they look humanoid for the most part, but their eyes are slitted like a snake's and they have small nostrils and hiss a little when they talk," I closed my eyes; Teeg's fingers were sending me to sleep.

"Come to bed, baby." Teeg's voice was soft as he lifted me and carried me down the hall. I wasn't awake when he got me into bed.

The pounding on Teeg's door in the middle of the night had us both off the bed in less than a blink, only Teeg was growling as he pulled on his pants. I didn't have time to wonder or worry over being in his bed to begin with. I was right behind him when he flung his door open after checking the security camera on the wall. Delvin was outside, waiting for us to answer the door.

"Arvil wants both of you to come and come quick, we're getting away from Campiaa—tonight."

Teeg and I were flinging clothing, shoes and toiletries into bags that Teeg pulled out of his closet. Delvin was tight-lipped when Teeg asked him where we were going. A hover-limo waited for us outside; the driver helped Teeg fling bags into the back and we were at Arvil's palace in a fraction of a click. The other thing that surprised me, in addition to my being wakened like that, was that there were no less than six females I didn't recognize who were going with us.

"Arvil employs them—they service his best guests," Teeg whispered when nobody was listening to us. The amount of luggage for Arvil, his brother, wife and cousins, the wizards, all eight of them and the houseguests was staggering. Xiri's gear, with that of his two assistants, was much more modest.

"I wouldn't have taken you, Teeg, but we have to keep Reah happy," Arvil tapped the top of my head. My hair was growing back some—I no longer looked like I'd been shaved.

"I'll do my best to keep her happy," Teeg said. Arvil's wizards folded us away, bags included.

CHAPTER 7

"Welcome to my home." The guest who'd spoken the night before was giving us a formal greeting now. His home was a large single-story in a plantation style. Tile and wood floors were everywhere, and it was spotless. He had a good housekeeping staff, looked like.

"We not properly introduced," our host took my hand and bowed over it slightly. He had skipped over some of his words. I noticed that some of the others did the same, whenever they spoke. "Fine cook is rare. I am Farzinalek, but please to call me Farzi." That was easy to remember; it sounded a lot like Marzi—another person I would never forget. "Of course, Master Farzi." I nodded respectfully.

"Where are we staying?" Anith's voice was annoyingly whiny. Teeg was pulling me away from Farzi even as he thought to address the problem of his other guests. Arvil, his family and his wizards all got rooms inside the main house. Teeg and I were given a guest bungalow a few steps away. Xiri and his assistants got the bungalow next to ours. Farzi looked as if he'd prefer to send Jazal and Anith to a bungalow, but that would offend Arvil so he didn't.

"Reah, you and Xiri will be helping with the cooking here, since we are imposing on Farzi," Delvin informed me. I nodded before we were led out the door and shown to our bungalow.

"Baby, I wanted you in my bed before, but I wasn't going to do anything." I listened to Teeg's words as we both stared at the wide bed inside the only bedroom in our bungalow. "I'll sleep on the sofa if that's what you want," he added.

"No. Let's just go to bed—I'm tired and I don't know how much they'll expect me to do in the morning," I muttered.

"Come on," Teeg pulled me with him. Our bags had been left on the floor, Teeg and I stripped to our underwear and crawled into bed like that. When the aud-alarm went off in the morning, I found myself pulled tightly against Teeg and his body was angled over mine. He didn't want to let me up, either, but let me go after a few kisses and protests.

"We got moved because our guests got wind that the Alliance was tailing them on the last part of their trip to Campiaa. Arvil didn't want trouble, so he had his wizards move us here," Xiri hissed as we went through cabinets to see what we had to work with.

They must have been important for Arvil to come back with them, but I didn't tell Xiri that. He loved to gossip and could get more information out of anybody than anyone else I'd ever known. I got confirmation on Xiri's gossip a few ticks later when Lendill spoke in my mind. *Reah, where are you?* he asked.

No idea—we got moved in the middle of the night, I answered. Lendill cursed in several languages.

Are you with San Gerxon and several Reptanoids?

Is that what they are?

Yes.

I wanted to ask about reptanoids but didn't—I had no desire to get a mental slap on the head.

Reah, do you have any idea where you are now?

No. It looks like a jungle outside—lots of tropical trees and plants, and it's really humid. I only saw that this morning, while I was walking to the main house. Single level—looks like a plantation home. Huge.

Reah, we've been after those reptanoids for a while. If you can get any information on where you are, send it right away.

All right.

"Reah, what we have for breakfast today?" Farzi had come into the kitchen.

"What would you like, Master Farzi?"

"Whatever you make we welcome." I wondered why Lendill had been after these for so long. Was there an entire planet of these beings or were there only a few? What had they done that the ASD wanted them? "I dismiss my cooking staff, they not good anyway." His clipped common speech made me think that he had another language, although his words in the common tongue were precise.

Xiri gave me a look as Farzi settled himself onto a chair at the island and we cooked breakfast for him. Others wandered in, including more reptanoids, wizards and finally Arvil. Jazal and his crew were still in bed.

"You have carpenter with you?" Farzi turned to Arvil.

"He can do anything as far as building goes," Arvil replied.

"Perhaps he help me—we find a way to kill wood-chewing ants here. But much wood on south side of house needs replacing," Farzi said. "Ours here now not know much in way of building."

That told me that the reptanoids hadn't put up the house or anything around it. Had they bought this place or gotten it some other way?

"Reah, find Teeg and bring him in—we'll see if he can help Farzi out." Wiping my hands on a towel, I nodded at Xiri to keep up his inventory and went off toward our bungalow.

"Teeg, we can feed you at the house—I think they need help repairing termite damage and none of them know what to do," I said. Teeg was up, dressed and going through the tiny kitchenette we had, looking for something to eat. We didn't have anything there—I saw that right away.

Teeg got his breakfast inside the main kitchen later as he listened to Farzi describe his insect troubles.

"Not a surprise, they like moist, warm places," Teeg agreed. I took his empty plate and he followed Farzi toward the south end of the house.

"I am come to help with missing food." A reptanoid came silently through the wide door. Xiri stared at our new arrival, so I had to piece out what he meant.

"You mean you'll help us get what we need?"

"Yes—what is missing." He gestured toward the cabinets.

"Very good—where can we find missing food?" I was getting on board with this. He grinned at me, which transformed his face. I couldn't help but smile back at him. He and the others all had brown hair and golden-brown, slitted eyes. In the dim interior of the plantation's kitchen, his eyes rounded until they appeared almost humanoid. So far, too, I hadn't seen anything violent from any of the eight reptanoids and wondered again why the ASD hunted them.

"I drive," he was still smiling at me. He drove. The vehicle was an ancient hovercar, but it ran. I got the idea he was the one who kept the vehicle in good repair. Xiri and I learned he was called Nenzi. Nenzi took us to a thriving market about a click away. Solar power was in use, so meats and other items in need of refrigeration were kept cold or frozen.

"Buy missing food." Nenzi held up a necklace chip.

"How much?" I asked, unsure how much he wanted to spend.

"Whatever," Nenzi flung out an arm. Plants, dust and children seemed to be everywhere as we made our way through the market. The children were all wearing the least amount of clothing one might get away with. The native population was darker-skinned than the reptanoids—I saw that right away. The children were running and shouting as they played, using a language I didn't know.

Xiri and I made our choices, Nenzi right behind us. He paid for everything—we had to get quite a bit to feed the crowd at the plantation. Nenzi didn't seem to mind. I was thankful the plantation had several large keepers—we were going to need them. Tropical fruit was everywhere and freshly picked. I had a sauce recipe that required some of the fruit we found. That went into our purchases.

The hovercar was packed full for our return trip, so I paid more attention to the fields we passed on the way home. I was looking for drakus seed but didn't see any from the road. That didn't mean it wasn't there, though.

They have grapefruit, orange, nanna, mango, pineapple, avocado and round melons, I sent to Lendill. *All growing locally. They also had meat from a sheep they called Palaca,* I added. *I found green nuts too.*

Reah, I know that's important to you, but I'm not sure what good it will do us, Lendill replied. I'd have gotten out my comp-vid and gone looking to see where all those things were grown in one place. But then I wasn't Vice-Director of the ASD, either.

Then give it to Chash as a research assignment, I grumped and ended our communication.

"It would have worked perfectly, if somebody hadn't gotten wind of us," Norian wanted to shout or put his fist through a wall; he couldn't decide which. "When we caught that fool wizard Haral on Reliff, Aryn's compulsion worked flawlessly. Haral spilled the information that the reptanoids were in this up to their foreheads. We would have had all of them; we were an arm's length away from having them," Norian wanted to go to lion snake so badly it was almost painful. He wanted to bite something—kill something. Realizing it was very close to the full moon on Le-Ath Veronis, he did his best to calm down.

"If we'd known this wasn't going to work, we could have turned the wizard over to King Wylend. He has a death warrant out on that one, and probably most of San Gerxon's other wizards too." Lendill was nearly as frustrated as Norian was. They should have had Reah back by now. Both he and Norian had thought it would only be a matter of days. Now, they had no guess at a timeline—they didn't even know where Reah and the others were. Lendill didn't want to hand the information to Tory and Aurelius. Gavril, too, young as he was, wanted information and was begging his mother to ask Norian about Reah every day.

⁓

"Reah, do they expect you to do this every day? Work from dawn until they go to bed at night? What are those house servants for?" Teeg was hauling me inside the door. We'd been at the plantation for a week and there hadn't been anyone there to offer us a day off or give us a break. I fell in bed every night, asleep before my head hit the pillow most of the time. When the alarm went off, I dragged myself to the shower, cleaned up and went off to the house.

It took Xiri, Ande, Malin and me all day to serve three meals, drinks and snacks for all the people at the plantation. Arvil went off in a hovertruck a time or two with Farzi, Nenzi and several wizards. I wasn't invited along. I could only assume they were going to inspect the crops. Jazal, Anith, the twins, six courtesans and Delvin stayed behind, lazing around the pool and sipping drinks that we made for them. We were now serving forty-six people—that included the staff at the plantation. Nenzi had driven us to the market twice since we'd arrived. Now Teeg was seething over it.

"Teeg, just let it go, all right? I don't see anyone else with cooking skills, do you?"

"I don't see any one of them helping, and Arvil doesn't think you need more assistance?"

"Come on, I want to go to bed, not get into an argument." I pulled Teeg's arm, leading him away from the door.

"Reah, I get to knock off work before the evening meal." Teeg had been rebuilding walls and woodwork damaged by termites.

"That's nice." I was headed toward the bed.

"Reah, I want to love you. But I'm not about to take advantage of my girl when she's so tired she can't stay awake."

That stopped me where I stood. "Teeg, I'm sorry. I have to go to bed."

"Then I'll take you," he grumbled, lifting me right off the floor.

107

"I see we tire our cooks." Farzi walked into the kitchen the next morning as I was pulling the second pan of pastries from the oven. The kitchen was hot from the oven, heat—the plantation's solar air cooler could only do so much and the humidity inhibited its effectiveness. Xiri was already fanning himself and Ande and Malin looked like a bucket of water had been dumped over their heads. If my hair was longer, I imagined I'd look just the same.

I didn't really have time to talk with Master Farzi but I wasn't rude, even if I wanted to be. I drizzled glaze over the pastries as Xiri put plates of sliced fresh fruit out, and then added broiled strips of bacon. Eggs were difficult to find, so we saved those for sauces and baking most of the time.

Farzi followed us as we carried huge trays of breakfast plates into the dining room—it was cooler in there at least. Arvil was served first, as usual, and then Farzi, who sat down, still watching us. We went down the sides of the table after that, putting a plate in front of everyone. The staff's plates were left on the island in the kitchen—at least they came to get their own after it was cooked. Teeg did the same, only he usually took his breakfast outside where it was cooler.

When I got back to the kitchen, I broke with tradition and took my plate outdoors to eat beside Teeg. He sat on a low wall surrounding a flowerbed. I leaned against him while I ate, then set my plate aside after eating only half my food. I closed my eyes.

"Reah, wake up." The words were soft.

"Hmmh?" I moaned softly when I opened my eyes. Teeg had wakened me, but Arvil was standing in front of me when my eyelids lifted.

"Take her to the bungalow. I'll handle this," Arvil said and stalked off.

"What happened?" I was suddenly frightened.

"Farzi informed Arvil that there were too many people for four to wait on hand and foot," Teeg pulled me up. "Come on, sweetheart, we just got the day off."

I was happy to shuck my clothing, wash in a cool shower and climb into bed in clean pajamas. At least our bungalow had a clothes machine—it washed and dried. Teeg stripped down to his underwear and crawled in bed with me. I slept until late in the afternoon.

"Reah? Sweetheart, wake up." Teeg was nuzzling my chin and neck. He nipped my neck lightly, too. "Come on, baby, open your eyes."

I reached up to run fingers through his dark hair. It curled just a little. Teeg gave me a crooked grin before leaning down to kiss me.

The covers were on the floor, we were both naked and Teeg was giving me pleasure. "I know what my Reah wants," he whispered as his body stroked into mine. His kisses covered my moans as the waves of ecstasy came. I felt like a wanton, wrapping my arms and legs around his body and digging my nails into his back. He didn't seem to care.

"Want more?" Teeg's body was between my legs as I sat on the bar in our bungalow, eating a slice of melon with my fingers. He wiggled suggestively, letting me know he wasn't talking about the fruit. I fed him a chunk of melon. He let me finish the rest of it before he took what he and I both wanted.

I learned what course of action Arvil had taken the moment I walked into the kitchen the morning after my day off. The place was a complete mess.

"Those women not know how to cook," Farzi was there and shaking his head. "I and mine were forced to hunt."

"Sorry," I heaved a helpless sigh.

"None of your fault. You were tired. I have hope you are rested, now?"

"I am rested now." I started cleaning up the mess.

"Perhaps Master Arvil will bring those here yesterday and force them to learn?"

"I have no control over that," I said, wiping flour off the counter and into a waste bin. They'd wasted at least five pounds of flour—it was scattered across the flat surfaces in the kitchen.

"What you control, young cook?"

"Nothing." I ran water in the sink, preparing to wash dishes. Xiri walked in, yawning widely. He took one look at the state of the kitchen and moaned.

"I will find help for you—three days out of eight." Farzi nodded to me and walked out.

"How long are we going to be here?" Xiri hissed as soon as we were alone.

"No idea," I said and started washing plates.

"Thank goodness we get decent food, now." Haral was gazing angrily at the six courtesans—that let me know who it was that had been ordered into the kitchen while Xiri and I had been off. The women didn't take Haral's criticism well. If he'd been bedding any of them, his favors might have just dwindled. I didn't have any expression on my face as I handed out plates of food.

Farzi hired six locals to cook three days out of each eight-day. They went home at night, too. I thought that was a good thing. Teeg was overjoyed to have three days to spend with me. Things might have worked out, if spawn hadn't come.

"They killing my workers," Farzi moaned as he walked into my kitchen.

"What? Who?" Xiri and I were staring at Farzi immediately. Ande and Malin had also stopped peeling fruit to listen.

"Those creatures—we not know how bad they could be." Farzi was pretty upset, I could tell.

"Demons," Arvil snarled as he and his wizards came in, carrying crates of ranos rifles. I wanted to correct him but didn't. Arvil hadn't seen a demon. Yet.

"We'll go out tonight—Reah, go get some sleep."

"Why does Reah need sleep?" Farzi didn't understand.

"She's the best shot we have," Delvin said. "We have to get these charged up." He pulled a rifle from a crate, along with the solar charger.

"A cook can kill those things? I am puzzlement." Farzi went off, mumbling to himself.

"Reah, what are you doing back here?" Teeg was sanding wood in front of our bungalow.

"They found spawn out in the fields. I have to go shoot them tonight."

"Are you joking?"

"Teeg, that's one of the reasons they grabbed me to begin with. That and another thing I can do," I grumbled. I wished I was anywhere except where I was, and I wanted to take Teeg with me.

"What other thing?"

"Teeg, don't ask."

"Reah, we love each other. Tell me."

"Teeg."

"Reah."

I wanted to tell him. Everything. But he worked for Arvil San Gerxon for some reason. I kept forgetting that. Lendill hadn't gotten back with me either. What was I supposed to do—work for Arvil for the rest of my life?

"Reah, if Arvil already knows, what harm can it do?"

"I don't know that Arvil knows. Delvin knows." I walked inside the bungalow.

"And he's the one who snatched you. From where?"

"Teeg, I don't want to say that. I don't know what you know or what Arvil knows. I have to protect myself, Teeg."

"You don't trust me to protect you?"

How could I tell him that I could protect myself just as well as anyone else? How could I tell him that if it weren't for being enslaved by the ASD, I could skip away in a blink. "Reah, answer me." Teeg grabbed my arm.

"Teeg, would you trust anyone who worked for Arvil San Gerxon?"
I jerked my arm from his hand and stalked toward the bedroom.

Teeg didn't speak to me when I rose later and dressed in my black
leathers. I didn't know what to say to him—I'd pretty much said that I
didn't trust him. I wasn't treating him very well and I knew it.

"I'm sorry, I didn't mean it the way it sounded," I said before
walking away from him and heading toward the main house.

"Mine have some effectiveness, our others do not," Farzi and the other
reptanoids had come with us. I suppose what he meant was that he
and others like him could see spawn. The locals couldn't. I made a
mental note to ask Lendill about it. I was seeing the drakus seed fields
for the first time, too. I wondered if Farzi was completely aware of
what it was. I couldn't ask.

"All workers, missing." Nenzi used that word a lot.

"He means they've gone—they've been ordered out of the fields,"
Delvin walked up beside me. "Heard you and the carpenter had a little
fight."

"We're good," I muttered angrily. Did Delvin have eyes and ears
everywhere, or did Xiri have his gossip lines open? How was I to
know? I picked up my usual two rifles to start with. Arvil had come
with us again, but I had no idea why—he was only a target since he
couldn't see what we fought.

"Enemy not close—we can tell," Farzi said. I guessed that he could
scent them somehow.

"Then I want to inspect the crop," Arvil said.

"Reah, like to see our river? It is this way," Farzi pointed to our left
—I could see a line of trees there. He was probably directing me away
from his and Arvil's illegal cash crop, but I didn't want to see that
anyway.

"I'd like to see the river," I said. That's how Arvil and his wizards
went in one direction, Farzi, Nenzi, six other reptanoids that I had no

name for and I all headed toward the river. We were about halfway there, too, when the firebombing began.

The first blast blew everything high into the air and set the fields on fire. Farzi and the others ran. I stood and stared until I was jerked off the ground.

What do you do when you find yourself disembodied? That was the only explanation I had for it—I was flying over the tops of trees while more firebombs exploded behind me. If I could have screamed, I would have. I had no mouth, no limbs, no body, even, to struggle against what held me. More explosions sounded behind me and then I was flying over the plantation. I hit the water of the pool hard; it nearly knocked me unconscious. Struggling to rise to the top to catch my breath, I heard the firebombs hit the plantation with a muted boom. Someone landed in the water next to me, clamped a hand over my nose and mouth and pulled me back to the bottom.

CHAPTER 8

*R*ed was all I could see from the bottom of the pool. I struggled against the one holding me. I also struggled to take a breath, knowing that if I did I'd only draw in water. Things began to go dark and still there was red light—and heat.

"Reah?" Someone was calling my name. I coughed up water as I rolled over. Feeling was finally coming back to my arms and legs. I lay on a hard surface—I knew that much. "Sweetheart, open your eyes, please." Teeg was with me. I opened my eyes and every other part of me awoke and began to ache.

He helped me sit up; I blinked at my surroundings. Everything was gone—All of it burned to ash around us. The flagstones beneath us were cracked and blackened. The water in the pool had been vaporized —it only held a small amount of moisture in the bottom, now.

"It lasted long enough to keep us alive," Teeg muttered, holding me steady as I wavered beside him. He was covered in ash and soot, just as I was.

"Where are the others?" I asked. My voice was barely above a whisper and speaking made me cough again. Teeg waited for the fit to be over before he answered. "Everybody died, except us," he said. "At the plantation, I mean."

"Xiri?" I wanted to cry. I couldn't.

"Dead. Jazal, his wife and the cousins—dead too. The six women and Xiri's assistants are gone. I can't say whether any of the staff was here. I haven't gone searching for other bodies." I stared at Teeg. His face was covered in black smudges; his hair looked wild and stood on end.

"Love," I reached out to wipe a bit of black ash off his face.

"Reah, we almost didn't make it." Teeg sat next to me and pulled me close. That's where Farzi and his seven reptanoid brothers found us later.

"Our little cook lives. And the carpenter."

"Pool," Teeg jerked his head toward the nearly empty concrete hole.

"We take river—much thankful we are that current is slow at this time." Farzi knelt next to us. He was covered in ash and cinders. He and his people looked worse off than Teeg and I, but then they'd walked through blackened fields and burned jungle to get back to the plantation. What was left of it, anyway.

"What about the others?" Teeg asked.

"Not knowing. We not find any piece of them. We look, as soon as heat gone." Farzi's common speech was more garbled—I felt it was the aftereffects of nearly being killed. I knew, even if the others didn't, that the firebombs were courtesy of the Alliance. Regular Alliance Army, or RAA, used them to destroy drug fields. I wondered if it had been ordered by the ASD. Had Lendill learned where we were and sent in the bombers, thinking I was expendable? It wouldn't surprise me.

"I wasn't able to contact Reah last night, and now I learn that the RAA has firebombed Urdolus?" Lendill wanted to yank his hair out.

"They're not obligated to contact us if they find something and have the ships nearby," Norian snapped. He was nearly as frustrated at the news as Lendill was. "All our agents know the risks."

"Reah didn't."

"Well, there wasn't much time to tell her."

"We didn't because we're cowards."

"There's that." Norian raked a hand through his hair. "I can only handle that accusing look for so long."

"Aurelius will kill us."

"No. Aurelius will kill you. Tory will kill me. He's High Demon and immune to poison. Have you tried to reach Reah again?"

"I was afraid to."

"Try."

Nothing was left—of the plantation or anything around it. I'd heard that about firebombing—that only skeletons might be found, if that, and perhaps melted or twisted metal. Anything else flammable would be reduced to ash. It shocked me as I kicked ash aside in the ruins of Xiri's bungalow. His bones were there and I found them just as Lendill's mindspeech found me.

Reah? I thought for a moment about not answering.

What? I'm sure he read the sullenness in my mental voice.

Reah, thank the gods. I thought the RAA may have bombed where you were.

They did. A moment's silence followed my statement.

Reah, were you anywhere near that?

In the middle of it. Somebody shoved me into the pool. The whole thing went to steam before the heat abated. Just about everybody else died.

San Gerxon?

Not sure. He was surrounded by wizards.

Reptanoids?

Still here—all of them. They went into the river.

Reah, I know you're not happy with us right now, but we didn't order the firebombing. RAA moved without consulting us.

And I'm supposed to believe that?

Reah, you're being disrespectful with a superior. I didn't answer him. If he knew how disrespectful I wanted to be—I was staring at Xiri's bones, after all. I sobbed. *Reah? Reah, are you still there?*

You be respectful, Vice-Director, the next time a friend's bones lie beneath your hand. I cut off the communication. Lendill didn't try again.

~

"She's still alive, but didn't tell me what her condition is," Lendill looked at Norian. He didn't say that Reah had cut off the mindspeech. "She doesn't know about San Gerxon—the reptanoids are still alive—they jumped into the river when the bombing started.

"Who'd have guessed about Urdolus?" Norian sighed.

"I guessed about Urdolus." Gavril stood in the doorway to Norian's office inside the palace. "If you'd read the message I sent on your comp-vid two days ago, you'd have known, too." Gavril looked as if he were ready to cry. He ran down the hall.

"How did he?" Norian lifted his comp-vid and scrolled through unread messages. Selecting the one from Gavril, he opened it. "Fuck," Norian shouted.

"What?" Lendill came over to look. He found a list of all the fruit Lendill had given him, combining those elements with the green nuts and palaca meat, then listed all the planets where those items were available in the same location. Six held too much population to harbor drakus seed fields. That left only Urdolus. Gavril had sorted it out—Lendill had ignored it.

"Fuck," Lendill sighed.

~

"I don't have any tools to bury Xiri," Teeg knelt beside me. I nodded; I wasn't able to speak at the moment.

"Farzi, I'm so glad to see you're alive, my friend." Arvil's blustering voice came from behind. Teeg pulled me to my feet. Arvil's eyes widened as he saw we'd made it, too.

"The river, Master Arvil," Farzi stepped over piles of ash and rubble to reach Arvil, who was (no surprise) surrounded by all his wizards. "That one," Farzi indicated Teeg, "pool saves him." Farzi included me with the river jumpers. Just as well; I couldn't explain how I'd gotten to the pool the night before.

"My brother?" Arvil knew the answer before we told him. He didn't sound heartbroken.

"Reah, we'll find more help for you," Arvil was back to bluster. "We can go home, now—I hear the Alliance is looking elsewhere. Better to be away from here, anyway; they may come to inspect their work."

Arvil didn't even ask Farzi and the other reptanoids if they wanted to go back to Campiaa; his wizards took us there before we had time to think.

"Take two days off—we'll eat at the casino," Arvil told us. I nodded blankly, feeling numb. Teeg, who kept a hand and a close eye on me, herded me through the door. We got plenty of stares as we made our way to his apartment.

"Reah, we only frightened small dogs and babies on our walk here —they'll rebound." Teeg's head appeared above mine as I stared at myself in the mirror. "Come on, sweetheart, let's get cleaned up and go to bed."

I don't think I'd ever appreciated clean sheets and a soft bed so much in my life after spending the night on burned and cracked flagstones. I must have been unconscious most of that time—I couldn't remember anything other than pain and discomfort. My lungs still felt coated in soot, and I coughed at times. Teeg didn't—I suppose he'd gotten it all out of his system already.

"Go to sleep, baby," Teeg's words were whispered against my skin. My eyes closed immediately.

❧

"Sweetheart, your stomach is growling." That was such a romantic statement to wake to.

"Is it keeping you awake?" I stretched against Teeg—he was leaning on an elbow and looking down at me.

"Reah, I'm tempted to ignore our hunger and love you instead."

"I'll fix you something." I sat up in bed. It hit me, then. All those people. Still just as dead.

"Don't think about it," Teeg pulled my hand away from my forehead and slid me across the sheets until I was huddled against him. "It'll be all right," he soothed. I hoped he was right—even if I had no idea *when* everything might be all right. "You don't have knobby knees," he smoothed a large hand down my legs. "You lied to me."

"Teeg, I was trying to keep everybody from knowing I was a girl." I slid off the bed.

"I know." He was right behind me, running his hands beneath my sleeveless pajama top. We ate soup after thawing it in his zapper. With crackers. "We can go to the market later," I said. I felt too weary to move after we'd eaten.

"We'll go later." Teeg carried me back to bed.

❧

The eight-day that went by after I returned to cooking (and bodyguarding) for Arvil went without mishap. I found a flower shop in Campiaa City early one morning, bought a bouquet of blossoms and tossed them in the ocean. "For you, Xiri," I whispered. "Wherever you are." I wiped tears away while I walked to Arvil's palace.

❧

"Arvil wants to see you," Delvin came into the kitchen on seven-day afternoon. Almost asking what Arvil wanted, I decided not to put my worries into words and followed Delvin up two levels of stairs and into Arvil's private study. His private office was enormous and decorated with every luxury one might imagine or wish for. I wished at that moment that Teeg had mindspeech—I was worried about what Arvil wanted.

"Sit down, Reah." Arvil sat behind a desk large enough to serve as a bed for two people. Richly carved in dark wood and polished until it shone, the desk was still dwarfed by the size of the room. A comp-vid lay on one side; otherwise the desk was clean.

I sat on one of the chairs in front of the desk. "Her feet barely reach the floor," Arvil pointed. Delvin snickered at Arvil's attempted humor. I wanted to get up and hit him. He'd gotten me into this mess and I still owed him for that. Not in any good way, either.

"Reah, you know I lost my family," Arvil began.

"I'm very sorry about that, Lord Arvil." I was. Even if they weren't the best family, they were family. I'd feel sad if one of my brothers died. Well, actually they were my uncles and not my brothers. I'd still feel sad. Mostly for what could have been, but it would grieve me, just the same.

"I know you are. That's why I asked you here, Reah. Because you seem to care about things like that." Arvil rose from his chair and stared out a rather large window behind his desk. It overlooked the pool and gardens on the spacious grounds below. "Do you know how old I am, Reah?" Arvil's back was still turned toward me.

"No, Lord Arvil."

"I am more than two hundred. While I come from a race that lives to be three hundred or more, well, things happen." He was right about that—his brother and cousins had been wiped out in a blink. Even though he'd told me to kill them if they threatened him, he'd felt something, I suppose.

"I know how old you are, Reah Nilvas." He turned around, lifted the comp-vid in his hand and scrolled through information. "Conscripted by the Alliance. Fell in with the drug crowd—involved in a drug war—considered a traitor now. See, I have your information. You don't have to hide it anymore." He turned the comp-vid around so I could see that he did indeed have my records. The false ones. I still flushed and lowered my head.

In my entire life, I would never do what those records said I did. Lendill had done this to me. He and Norian Keef. I wanted to slap them. Call them names. That was childish. How was I going to get out of this? How? Even if my records were cleared when I returned, there were too many people who'd seen the newsfeeds and found these records. They'd still think I was criminal, even though I wasn't.

"Teeg is here as requested, Master Arvil." His new housekeeper—a male this time, showed Teeg through the door. I shrank back in my seat. Arvil was going to show that garbage to Teeg and he was going to think I'd done all those things, too. I wanted to weep.

"Teeg, sit down," Arvil nodded toward the seat next to me. "This is information on our little girl, here." Arvil handed the comp-vid to Teeg. His mouth was set in a frown as he read through the information. The comp-vid was handed back as soon as Teeg finished reading. He didn't look at me.

"Teeg, I no longer have family. They're dead now." Teeg lifted his eyes to stare at Arvil San Gerxon. "I've gone looking through the people I know. The ones who work for me. The ones who seem loyal. Tested all of them, at one time or another. Teeg, I want you to marry Reah here. This afternoon. I've had the papers pulled already. I'm naming you and Reah as my heirs. Don't cross me in this. I don't think either of you are greedy, as my brother was. I'm depending on you to help me in my business and treat me fairly and keep me alive. Be straight with me and I'll be straight with you. Deal?"

I must have been gasping like a fish. Teeg just looked grim. Well, he'd received two shocking pieces of news, one right after the other. He wouldn't want to marry me—not after what he'd seen on Arvil's comp-vid.

"When and where?" Were the only words that came from Teeg's mouth. I stared at him. He couldn't be serious.

"Right now if you're ready—I have the power to marry anyone on Campiaa."

"Do it," Teeg said. "Before I change my mind."

Arvil pulled papers out of a desk drawer and slid them across to us. "You're married. Just sign at the bottom." I looked over the standard marriage contract. I'd never seen one before, never having married anyone before.

"Reah, just sign," Teeg's voice was clipped. I accepted the pen from Arvil and signed my name.

"Now, for the adoption papers," Arvil slid another stack of papers toward each of us. Teeg and I scanned all of them. They stipulated that if we caused or attempted to cause Arvil's death in any way, the adoption would be voided. It also allowed for the adoption to void if we did anything untoward, like stealing from Arvil. That one I was pretty sure I could keep. The other one—not so much.

"Sign it, Reah," Teeg elbowed me after a while. I signed. What else could I do? I cursed Lendill Schaff and Norian Keef while I wrote my name and initialed many lines on many pages.

"Now, we'll have your things moved to the family wing," Arvil said when we'd handed the papers back to him. "Starting tomorrow, you'll both get your feet wet on running my businesses. Reah, you'll be in charge of all the restaurants in all my casinos. I think some of them are skimming off the top. Find that out for me, baby girl. Teeg," he turned to my new husband, "I want you to go through all the accounts for the casinos. Let me know if you find anything. You've never handed me any accounts from the construction side that weren't perfect and accounted for every penny you spent." Teeg nodded at Arvil. "You're my family, now. Reah, I hope you'll still cook for us occasionally. Hire somebody else for us, in the meantime."

"Of course, Lord Arvil." I ducked my head.

"You don't have to call me Lord Arvil, although I like it—I just adopted you, baby. You're only nineteen—I know that. On Campiaa, you won't truly come into adulthood until you're twenty-two. You're my little chick, Reah."

"I want to take Reah out for dinner," Teeg stood and pulled me up with him.

"The uh, new staff should be able to finish dinner—we got it started already," I said, pointing off in what I thought was the kitchen's direction.

"Don't worry about it—go have fun. We'll get going on this tomorrow," Arvil waved a hand. Delvin had stood by, his face expressionless as he absorbed the news. I wanted to fling him through the huge window behind Arvil's desk. Teeg hauled me out of the room instead.

"Reah, breathe, sweetheart." I was hyperventilating. I'd made it to the beach across the road, but then I was gasping for breath, hugging myself and going to my knees in the loose sand. Teeg was kneeling beside me, trying to get my breathing evened out. "Just breathe slow, baby, slooow." I realized I was crying when I did take shaky but more normal breaths after a while.

"Reah, I don't care anything about what that comp-vid said. I see what's in front of me. I'm not going to hold any of that stuff against you." I blinked at him—he'd said *stuff*. I sobbed.

"What's wrong, sweetheart?"

"You said stuff. Some old friends used to say that."

"You don't like that word?"

"I do, it was just," I flung out an arm, unable to say what I felt.

"Then I'll say it again—*stuff*. How's that?" I nodded mutely. "Come on, let's get drunk," he hauled me up.

We didn't get drunk but we did get tipsy. And then Teeg bought a ring. A really nice one. "I'd put Tiralian crystal on that finger, sweetheart, but they can't get any of it here." Teeg offered me a crooked grin. He had a beautiful mouth. He kissed me with that mouth after we got the ring sized and he slipped it on my finger. I hoped Aurelius and Tory were understanding. I didn't think I could give Teeg up. Not for any reason. We went to find something to eat after that, getting food to go and taking it to Teeg's apartment to eat.

"Last night here at my apartment," he muttered softly as we ate our dinner on Teeg's kitchen island. We'd gotten a decent pasta dish at one of the casinos Arvil didn't own. I wanted to check out the competition as much as I could. Edan used to do it for Desh's. I was never given enough money to check on the competition or I would have.

A hovertruck came for us and all our things the following day. I had some clothing left but half of what I'd bought with Teeg had been destroyed in the firebombing. I had mindspeech to send to Vice-Director Lendill Schaff, too. I wondered what he was going to say or do when I told him Arvil San Gerxon had adopted me. I wondered if Arvil could get his legal counsel to void the papers from his prison cell when the ASD came calling. What would I do, too—if Arvil asked me to kill someone for him? Someone like Neele that I had no desire to harm?

"What are we going to do?" I whispered as I grabbed Teeg's hand before we walked out his door.

"No idea," he leaned down to kiss me.

I fired three cooks, six assistants and eleven members of the waitstaff before the day was over. Either for theft, food safety issues or failure to report tips. I knew when they were lying. Too bad for them. They were escorted by Arvil's security to the shuttle station. A list of people waited to be interviewed—I sat in on the interviews. I knew when those people were lying or padding their resumes. Several of the head cook applicants made meals for the guards and me.

The guards loved it—they never got to eat like that. Arvil's kitchens and customers didn't suffer; we had replacements hired before the day was out. I also set up a rotating schedule with each of the security supervisors in every one of Arvil's casinos. Each member of the security team would get a voucher for one nice meal for two in

Arvil's casino of choice every eight-day. They could bring a date or a spouse on a day off and have an expensive dinner.

It never hurt to have security on your side—especially if you wanted their cooperation later. The guards loved it—they had to pay before and the nicer restaurants tended to be out of their price range. The best the casinos had wasn't inexpensive in any sense of the word. In return, they would be more likely not to turn their heads if they saw any of my staff taking liberties.

I sent mindspeech to Lendill while I was cleaning up before going to bed. Teeg was in Arvil's office, going over the books for several casinos. I was going to wait until I'd gone through everything on the restaurants before sitting down with Arvil.

Vice-Director? I sent.

Reah? I haven't heard from you for several days.

A lot has happened since I talked to you last.

Tell me.

Arvil's family—what there was of it—got killed during the firebombing.

Good news—what else?

Arvil adopted heirs.

Not good news. Who do we need to add to our lists of most-wanted people? Some of the reptanoids?

No.

Then who? Did you get names?

Yes.

Tell me.

Arvil San Gerxon adopted me and another person. That brought silence. Either Lendill was stunned or he was already putting my image on the comp-vid most wanted site. I waited. And waited some more. Finally, a response came.

I'm sorry, Reah, but the Director and I just laughed so hard we nearly cracked a rib. Arvil adopted you? I think he had to stop and laugh some more.

Yes. I am officially Reah Nilvas San Gerxon. The other person is Teeg San Gerxon. And you can't kill him. Arvil married us yesterday. Teeg is my husband. I don't think he's bad—in fact, the reason Arvil adopted him is because he's the one honest person, possibly, on all of Campiaa. He was a building contractor for Arvil before he was adopted.

A contractor?

That's what I said. And we're married. I sure hope Tory and Aurelius don't have a fit. I'm not giving this guy up.

Reah, you have been busy.

This wasn't my idea, Lendill Schaff. It was yours. What was I supposed to do—tell Arvil no, so he could shoot me in the head like I've seen him do with other people? Or watch while one of his wizards burns Teeg to death? You kept me here, Vice-Director.

I know. Do what you can to keep from breaking the law, but this is more than we ever expected. You are now in an even better position to hand him over to us. His contacts as well. Keep your eyes and ears open, Reah, and report back to me with whatever you learn.

Vice-Director, you are forcing me to live a bigger lie than I ever thought possible. Perhaps it will pay off for you, but it makes me feel cheap and dirty, even if Arvil is an evil that should be stopped.

Reah, lives will be saved in the long term, Lendill attempted to reassure me.

And how many deaths will I witness, before I can walk away? Or will my death be one of those? Honestly, I don't think you or the Director care about that, as long as you get what you want. I cut off the communication.

I was going over accounts on my newly acquired comp-vid when Teeg slouched into the bedroom. "Long day?" I asked.

"Bad day," Teeg pulled his shirt over his head. "Where does the laundry go?"

"I think the others just dropped it on the floor and expected the staff to pick it up. I have a pile going in the closet—I'll try to get a hamper or two tomorrow."

"What did you do today?" Teeg unbuckled his belt. Teeg has muscles—lots of muscles—that ripple when he moves. I can't seem to stop staring when he takes his clothes off like he does. His navel is like the center point in a hard, powerful body. I'd thought Bel and Delvin were well-put together. Tory and Aurelius might compete with this, but nobody else could.

"I, uh, fired people. For, uh, theft and stuff."

"You said stuff." He pointed a finger at me.

"I like that word. It's not in any dictionary I've ever seen, but I like it anyway. And I hired some people." The pants dropped. "And, uh, did my best to get security on my side, so they'd report future, uh, infractions," the underwear dropped to the floor.

"Reah, I love the look on your face right now."

"Uh, right." I turned back to my comp-vid, trying to make sense of something that now resembled gibberish.

"You think Arvil has cameras in this room?" That was something I hadn't considered before. What if he did?

"I don't know," I answered truthfully.

"If he does, we'll give him something to think about." Teeg climbed into bed. His comment had me worried, but his loving soon had it flying out of my head in favor of other things.

Head cook Kiasz grinned at me. I'd gotten rid of his troublemakers and hired better staff. Arvil's assistant, who'd hired the others, was the one Haral had fried in my kitchen. Now Kiasz was getting what he wanted from the kitchen help and waitstaff. "Wilffin actually didn't complain about his last visit, and normally he does," Kiasz said. "But I have to get you to show me how to make those oxberry tarts for next time—that's what he liked best. He said he hadn't gotten anything that good since he was on Tulgalan."

I schooled my face. "All right—we'll work on that. Are you expecting any oxberry shipments soon?"

"I have some frozen in the keeper inside my office," Kiasz whispered. "They're nearly as good as fresh if you cook with them."

"Then we'll work on that soon," I said. "Let me know when you have some time and we'll invite important guests for drinks and dessert."

"I like that idea." Kiasz traded his wide grin for a big smile.

~

"Little cook," Farzi nodded to me when I walked into the kitchen at Arvil's palace later. I was frazzled—keeping up with all of Arvil's casino restaurants was a tiring enterprise.

"Farzi—I am pleased to see you," I said.

"We have been out, searching for good place to replant," he said. "Many places have one thing but not another. Most have sufficient, but too many people. You understand?" He blinked golden-brown eyes at me.

"I do. Would you like something to eat?" It was late and the kitchen staff had already left. Nobody working in the kitchen lived in the palace now—Arvil had decided against it. Only the housekeeping staff stayed in the basement. The wizards had the first floor, since they were our defense if someone got past the guards surrounding the walls. Farzi was hungry, as were Nenzi and the others. They'd come in shortly before I did. I made a dish with fowl, mushrooms and sauce inside a flaky pastry. Farzi loved potatoes, so I made some for him in the zapper. Potatoes cook well there and it takes no time at all. All the reptanoids loved chocolate so a quick cake with a swirl of caramel and chocolate sauce running over it came for dessert.

"We not get food so good. Ever." Nenzi liked his dinner.

"Nenzi, I never had such a wonderful driver before." I sat next to him and gave him a hug. He looked at me in surprise for a moment before giving me a wide smile.

"Is there dessert left?" Arvil walked in. He got a plate.

"My restaurants are doing better and my head cooks don't grumble so much," Arvil said. "My new assistant that Teeg hired is also very good. He keeps me advised on this." Well, I expected Arvil to have eyes and ears everywhere. He probably watched everything on a vid screen somewhere. "My friend, did you have any luck on finding new fields?" He turned to Farzi.

"Not yet, friend Arvil. We go out again next eight-day." Farzi was tired—I could see that for myself.

"We ought to hurry—three plantings have been ruined."

"I know this. I do what I can." Farzi rose, causing the other reptanoids to rise with him. "We retire." Farzi nodded respectfully to Arvil.

I put the dishes into the dishwasher after Arvil left the kitchen right behind Farzi. I think he wanted a meeting with him, but I wasn't about to stick my nose into that.

CHAPTER 9

"We just have to get them away from the palace, separately or together, so Haral and one of the others can get rid of them. I'd prefer not to kill them, but we have to get them out of the way, somehow." Delvin held up a hand as he spoke to the other wizards. "Arvil should have designated one of us as the heir—if not more than one of us. We've done everything for him, including saving his worthless ass during the firebombing. Yet he gives everything away to those two."

"It was your idea to bring the girl along, if I recall." Milus snorted at Delvin's logic.

"Only to protect us from Wilffin's warlocks. We're dead if they figure out we want San Gerxon's stake in all this. They'll work with San Gerxon, because they have for years. As far as the girl and that carpenter go, we don't know how Wilffin will react to that. We'll have to get rid of those two, and then get San Gerxon to go with us, instead. We can take over quickly after that."

"You think San Gerxon will do this? I mean, we wanted the girl because we were afraid Jazal would find a way to kill his brother and we'd be forced out by Wilffin's warlocks. She was our insurance—you said she could protect us against their attacks." Haral spoke, now.

"She can. She has some kind of natural shield. It doesn't protect against physical attacks—just spells and magical castings," Delvin explained.

"I've only heard of a few races that had something like that," Carthin, the red-haired wizard, pointed out.

"She must have gotten some blood somewhere, from one of those, then." Delvin didn't want to get into an argument over this. He'd made a false promise to Reah—he knew that. It caused a bit of a twinge, but he'd betrayed a better friend in Bel. Reah and Bel had both saved his life, but that didn't matter now—Delvin was looking to his own future and he wanted it to be as a casino owner on Campiaa, with a firm stake in other moneymaking ventures.

He wanted everything that Arvil San Gerxon had. San Gerxon had initially convinced the High Commander to grow Drakus seed in the desert, and Delvin, Bel and the other Ranger wizards hadn't known at first that he was involved. When San Gerxon appeared on Mandil after the spawn were eliminated, he was looking for additional wizards anywhere he could find them. Delvin, forced by the High Commander to help guard San Gerxon, had leapt at the offer Arvil made. He'd known enough on Mandil—there was a wide universe out there, just waiting for him and his talent to conquer. Now it looked as if a small snip of a girl and a carpenter stood in his way.

"Wilffin isn't scheduled to be back for two eight-days at least. Plenty of time," another wizard spoke up. "Haral can fold our targets anywhere—all we have to do is make them unconscious, somehow."

"What about poison?" Haral liked poisoning people—he'd done it too many times to mention. With him, rape came first, death by poison next. It was a convenient way to get rid of any incriminating evidence. He'd fold his victim to a deserted planet and dump the body. Nobody ever knew.

"Fine—you get poison. Make sure it's a good one," Carthin grumbled.

"Oh, it will be," Haral grinned. Delvin watched those two—they'd be his biggest competition if he tried to take everything for himself.

~

"I know all of you used to be casino owners on Campiaa." Norian sat opposite Erland Morphis, Adam Chessman and Merrill Leopard.

"We no longer have any interests on Campiaa—you know that. We razed those buildings to the ground when we moved everything here —to Le-Ath Veronis." Erland sounded bored.

"I have information for you," Norian smiled.

~

"Are you saying that Reah and some guy are heirs to Arvil San Gerxon?" Ry and Tory were staring at Ry's father, Erland Morphis.

"That's right. Now, if Arvil somehow ends up dead and it doesn't void the adoption agreement, Reah will own half of Campiaa. This might be an opportunity to turn Campiaa into what it should have been—a legal gambling planet in that sector of the universes. We could expand if we wanted, with built-in clients. Norian says that the Founder and the Grand Alliance Council will consider bringing Campiaa in as an Alliance world if San Gerxon is gone and we can turn it around to make it legal."

"Holy crap," Ry mumbled. "Is Reah all right? She's in a dangerous position if San Gerxon learns she's ASD."

"He didn't say, one way or another, but she has to be worried." Erland sat on the edge of Lissa's desk.

"Why don't they let us go in?" Ry asked. "We could pose as new hires for Reah. Help her out with this."

"Wylend already suggested that," Erland said. Erland also knew why Wylend had suggested it—there were multiple reasons but Reah was at the center of it. "Lendill said he'd think about it—Norian is letting him have point on this one."

"There's something else." Rylend wasn't sure how to deliver this news.

"What's that?"

"Reah got a husband out of the deal—Arvil San Gerxon married her off to the other designated heir."

Tory was standing in a blink and breathing smoke. "If he's forcing her to," Tory was nearly at turning anger.

"That's not what I hear. She told Lendill that she wasn't giving him up."

"Bro, you can't be jealous, remember?" Ry was standing and attempting to calm his brother.

"I want to make sure she isn't being coerced." Tory was still breathing smoke. "Does Aurelius know?"

"Lendill told him. Aurelius' first reaction, after he almost choked Lendill to death, that is, was just about the same as yours—worried that she might have been forced into this. I get the idea that she really cares about this one—says his name is Teeg San Gerxon. San Gerxon being his adopted name." Erland watched Tory closely in case he needed to send mindspeech to Gardevik, Tory's father. While Tory was old enough, he was newly mated and might need Gardevik's help in calming the Thifilathi.

"I'm all right," Tory held up a hand. "But I would like to speak with Lendill. Quickly."

"I'm here." Lendill walked in, rubbing his neck as if it pained him. Ry was forced to hold back a snicker. Erland lifted an eyebrow at his son. "If I send both of you—and I want to—Reah will have to hire you to make you appear legitimate. I'm not sure how her new husband will take that, or San Gerxon, for that matter. We'll place you in the hiring pool on Campiaa and let Reah know you're there. She'll have to find a way to put you to work so you can help out with this. This is a delicate situation, and we don't need to ruin it—the possibilities are too good. And if we can find San Gerxon's allies and cronies in the drakus seed business, so much the better. Pack everything you need— you go tomorrow." Lendill was smiling—so was Erland.

"My King, Lendill is sending Ry and Tory. Will that ease your mind?"

Erland had been afraid that Ry might be sent and Tory held back, since he had a relationship with Reah. Lendill had cautioned Tory at length about showing any affection toward Reah—San Gerxon might be offended and attempt to kill Tory.

"That eases my mind somewhat. I do not like the fact that Haral, that perverted criminal of a warlock, is there with her. You know he likes small women and young girls. Reah is practically both."

"I think Haral's life will be on the line if he lays a hand on her—Tory's Thifilathi will tear him to pieces." Erland nodded to Wylend, who sat morosely behind the desk inside his private study. If Arvil San Gerxon could have seen the inside of the King of Karthia's study, he would have been eaten up with jealousy.

"I would like very much to go myself, but the risks are too great," Wylend sighed.

"Trust us to handle this for you, my King. Karathia is not an easy world to rule. You have your hands full."

"And yet I would still prefer to do this for Reah. Trapping that fool Haral would be a pleasure, too. We've tracked him for many years, my friend." Wylend nodded to Erland, who smiled. "This is the first time that we've known for sure where he is, and we are held back by the ASD, because of other concerns."

"I know you've sent Griffin to check on her a time or two."

"He was happy to do so—said he'd already considered it before I asked."

"Then he's seen something, too."

"Yes. It frightens me at times to know my son is the Oracle."

Reah, we'll be sending Ry and Tory tomorrow—you need to find an excuse to hire both of them; Lendill sent as I was pouring out a glass of wine. The day had been an exhausting one; it was very late, I had an appointment with Arvil the following morning to go over the accounts for all his restaurants and I hadn't taken time for dinner. Now things would be even more complicated with Tory coming. Yes,

I loved him and missed him, but there was Teeg. What would happen?

Did you tell Tory about Teeg?

Yes—he knows to be circumspect. Don't say anything to Ry or Tory that you don't want overheard. Send it to them in mindspeech only. They know not to push it, Reah. That was fine for him to say—what if I wanted to throw myself at Tory and weep? The stress from walking the tightrope between Arvil and the ASD was beginning to wear on me. I was tired of constantly feeling afraid. It interrupted my slumber and permeated my dreams, even with Teeg there to smooth things over and send me back to sleep. Now I was expected to produce a valid reason to hire Ry and Tory. And then stay away from Tory, as if he were a stranger or something. I blew out a breath, realizing as I did so that my hair was now long enough to stir a little if I blew a sigh upward. Resolving to pay more attention to my appearance in the mirror before going to bed, I asked Lendill what kind of work I ought to find for Ry and Tory.

Security or bodyguarding would be best but do what you can, he replied, cutting off our communication.

Haral handed a credit chip to the cocktail waitress. "Just make sure to tell her that one of our best customers has a complaint. Bring her to the office at the back of the casino around fourteen bells."

The cocktail waitress nodded. She'd taken others to Haral before, in exchange for a fat, non-identifying credit chip. Those were difficult to come by and untraceable. She had nearly enough money to leave Campiaa and set herself up elsewhere. She was still pretty but on Campiaa, cocktail waitresses were younger.

She'd turned her head when some of the girls she'd taken to Haral came up missing afterward. At least he was neat in his work—she'd never found signs of blood or other evidence of any crime. Besides, people came up missing on Campiaa all the time. The constabulary tended not to hunt for them unless they were paid very well to do so.

Even then, if Arvil San Gerxon was involved, nothing was ever done. He owned the constabulary, after all. If the waitress had known then that Haral's target was one of Arvil's new heirs, she never would have agreed, no matter the cost.

~

Teeg didn't come to bed until very late, and I was scheduled to get up in only a click or two. He pulled me against him and was asleep almost immediately. I left him in bed when I woke, bathing and dressing in our adjoining bath as quietly as I could. Tiptoeing out later, I scrounged something for breakfast in the kitchen, although the staff offered to make whatever I wanted. I got fruit and tea before going to my meeting with Arvil. That was the one thing I could say about Arvil—he was an early riser.

"Here are the accounts, Lord Arvil. I've fired everyone who had anything to do with the false billings and bad inventories." I pushed the comp-vid to Arvil, who slid his finger in a practiced manner down the screen, checking through everything I'd flagged.

"Did you recover any credits on this one?" One of the head cooks I'd fired had found a way to transfer a percentage of all income into his personal account.

"I had security help with that one—we went to the bank and took back what he'd funneled into his account—that record will be on the recovery file." I started to rise to show Arvil how to pull it up—he waved me back down—he'd already found it.

"Very good, Reah," Arvil nodded happily. He'd found the other accounts I'd recovered for him. Some think that stealing from a thief isn't stealing. Well, stealing is stealing. You might justify it now and then, but it's still theft. "What did you do with them afterward?"

"Made sure they were sent away and put their fingerprints and eyescans into the database of known criminals who can't return," I said. If Arvil expected me to murder them while they stood in front of me, he needed to find another heir.

"Good," he said and kept flipping through the accounts. I felt wrung out when I left his office about a click later. Arvil seemed satisfied with everything we were doing, including inviting some of his best guests to a reception to serve really good desserts, wine and cheese.

Kiasz and I had ordered cheeses the day before—the best that could be gotten. With the black market on Campiaa, that turned out to be quite a lot. We intended to serve salmon in small crusts too—normally it was served as a main dish, but we were making small ones for the limited number of guests we had, in addition to smaller versions of other, nicer dishes meant to lure them to the restaurants. Arvil promised to get some of his big name entertainers to attend so the attendees would be satisfied all the way around. We'd planned it for two nights later, so there was plenty to do. I hunched my shoulders as I walked out the side door to Arvil's palace, heading toward the side gate and the nearest employee entrance into *The San Gerxon* Casino.

"Reah, I think I'm in love." Kiasz had tasted the small salmon pastries. They had the lightest, flakiest crust surrounding the salmon with just a bit of butter, onion, herbs and creamy sauce.

"You wouldn't know love if it jumped up and bit you on the ass." Kiasz's assistant cook (and his lover, I'd learned) came by and swatted the ass in question. That made me laugh. Yindu, Kiasz's assistant, was short, brown-haired and loved Kiasz. I couldn't fault him—he was loyal to Kiasz. We'd had a talk about it, Kiasz and I. I told him that the relationship couldn't interfere with the running of the kitchen. He'd agreed. Yindu wasn't suffering any over his superior being his lover. "Where did you learn to make this pastry? I might be in love, too." Yindu tried one of the salmon-filled pastries.

"Pastry was the first thing I learned how to make," I said. "Followed by vegetables, pasta, sauces, desserts and main courses."

"Where did you learn?" Kiasz was interested. Arvil already had that information—the false records held a bit of truth—they said I'd worked in the kitchens at Desh's on Tulgalan. It never said my last name used to be Desh, though. "I worked in the kitchens at Desh's number two," I said. "On Tulgalan."

"I know where Desh's is," Yindu gave me a grin and sauntered off.

I was ready to visit the second casino kitchen on my list that day when a cocktail waitress caught up with me. "We have someone who is demanding to see you. I think he is very upset with the food order he received. He is waiting in the back office—he wants to speak with someone right away."

"Come with me," I said, motioning for the waitress to come along. Part of her statement was true, I just couldn't sort out which part. She hadn't given me a name, either, so I hoped she'd be able to make introductions since she'd been the one to carry the message. The girl seemed worried that I'd ordered her to come along, but she came with me anyway.

Haral had moved the desk aside—he wanted plenty of room in case the girl struggled while he was taking what he wanted. The poison was nearby, too—he'd force her to drink it afterward. Haral was strong physically and he usually chose his targets so they wouldn't be able to fight him. He sat on the side of the desk—it wouldn't be long now. That's why he was so surprised when his throat was slashed nearly to the bone. There wasn't anyone else in the room—he saw nothing. He might have shouted if his throat hadn't been severed—the wounds that appeared on his body after that made him want to shriek before he died.

"He's just inside here," The waitress led me inside the office and then began to scream. I stopped in horror at the sight of the blood splattered everywhere. Haral's body—what was left of it, was on the floor. His head was nearly severed from the body, his sightless eyes staring up at me as if he were silently begging for help. I pulled out my communicator to contact security.

"We need some help in the back office," I said curtly and waited for them to come running. The chief of security and three others showed up quickly. The chief cursed under his breath when he saw the body. "Get Arvil," he ordered. One of his staff had Arvil on a communicator immediately. Arvil and Teeg both showed up only a few minutes later. I'd backed up against the cleanest wall inside the office, pulling the waitress with me. She was still whimpering and sliding down the wall, huddling there and rocking her body in shock.

"Reah, what happened?" Teeg asked the question—Arvil looked as if he were about to explode. This was his most powerful wizard, after all.

"This one," I pointed downward at the waitress, "came and got me after I finished with Kiasz and his staff this afternoon. Told me there was an upset customer inside this office. Said he was angry about the food he'd gotten at the restaurant. I asked her to come with me, since she didn't give the customer's name."

Arvil and Teeg were both staring at the waitress now. "What do you know about this?" Teeg had the woman up, gripping her arm in his hand.

"He paid me—told me to get her here," the waitress sobbed.

"Why? Did he say?" Teeg's voice was hard as he pressed the waitress against the wall.

"No. He just said to bring her. And when we got here, he was like this," she wept. She was pretty—with long dark hair, brown eyes and plenty of cosmetics. I imagined that she thought she wasn't pretty enough so she wore too much makeup.

"Have you done this before? Brought girls to him?" I stared at Teeg —I'd never seen this side of him before. He was relentless. As surprised as I was at Teeg's behavior, I was more surprised at the waitress' answer.

"Yes," she quavered. "Many times. He paid me."

"What did he do with them? The girls you brought?"

"I never saw them again." The woman sobbed. Arvil still looked like a thundercloud, but he was staring at the waitress, now.

"So anybody who learned what he did to those women could have been out for revenge. Pull the vids," Arvil ordered. "Now. Teeg, hire bodyguards for Reah. Delvin?" Delvin and Milus had arrived and were surveying the murder scene.

"Master Arvil?"

"Did you know anything about Haral? What he was doing?" All of us turned toward Delvin.

"No, Master Arvil. I never guessed." I knew right then, even if Arvil and the others didn't. Delvin was lying.

"It looks like a warlock's work. Or a powerful wizard's." Arvil ran the vid over and over again. It went blurry at the same point every time. When it cleared—Haral was lying on the floor and there was blood everywhere. "Look into the disappearances for the last full turn—see if any of the missing women had a wealthy family. Someone who might have been able to afford this," Arvil ordered.

I watched Arvil as he fretted. Something had slipped past him and he didn't like it. It had been right under his nose, too. Now, not only had women been disappearing, but his pet wizard had been responsible. The waitress had been handed to the constabulary—at Arvil's insistence. She'd be charged on Campiaa. Perhaps sentenced to lengthy jail time—if Arvil didn't order her death. It wouldn't surprise me if he chose to do so.

Haral had been waiting to do the same with me. The chief of security had found the vial of poison, handing it to Arvil after it was analyzed. Arvil pocketed it. Delvin had remained silent while all this was happening. Milus hadn't said a word. Teeg ordered a security team and a special housekeeping detail to get rid of the body and clean up the mess.

"I'm going to contact Wilffin—I think I need his warlocks," Arvil muttered after a while. "Reah, Teeg, have you had anything to eat? Come with me."

I didn't want to eat and picked at my food. Arvil and Teeg managed to eat. Delvin and Milus also ate a meal inside Kiasz's restaurant, but I hadn't failed to notice the brief look of dismay on Delvin's face when Arvil mention Wilffin's name.

"Reah, sweetheart, I'll hire security for you tomorrow. Until then, I don't want you going anywhere without me, all right?" Teeg pulled me against him the moment we shut the door of our bedroom.

"Teeg, I'm just shaken up," I said. Teeg wasn't satisfied with that. "Come on, let's use that spa tub in our bath," he coaxed. I wanted to tell Teeg that Delvin had been lying to Arvil earlier while I leaned against his wide chest in our tub. How could I tell him that? How could I explain that I knew when people were lying? There wasn't any good explanation for it. It was just something that was.

I worried, too, over Teeg's interrogation of the waitress—it looked as if he'd done that sort of thing before. He'd known what questions to ask. It made me want to ask him about his background. Why he'd come to Campiaa—what he'd done before. I didn't. That might open up questions about my life before—questions not covered by the information on Arvil's comp-vid. I didn't want to lie to Teeg. I loved him. That's what I ended up saying instead.

"Teeg, I love you." I twisted in his arms so I could look up at his face. His lips curled into a heart-twisting smile as he leaned down to kiss me.

I had to use the vid-communicator to talk to Kiasz the following day —he was beginning to make preparations for the wine, cheese and dessert gathering. I was fretting—I wanted to be there to make the oxberry tarts. Instead, I was held captive inside the palace—neither Teeg nor Arvil wanted me to go out unless someone was with me. Teeg said absolutely not unless *he* was with me. He'd gone off to interview potential guards. Hoping he'd come back soon so I could go make tarts, I sent mindspeech to Lendill instead.

I can't leave the house, Vice-Director, until I have guards. That idiot wizard Haral wanted to kill me yesterday. Somebody else got to him first. Nearly took his head off and sliced him up pretty good. They must have used a really sharp knife to do that kind of damage.

Reah, I'll inform Erland Morphis—I know the King of Karathia had a price on that one's head—he was a warlock, not your garden-variety wizard, Lendill informed me. Well, that explained a lot. Warlocks tended to be worse than wizards if they went bad. It made me wonder about Milus and Carthin. They were the wizards, in addition to Haral, whom Bel said weren't native to Mandil.

Does Wylend have a bounty on anyone named Milus or Carthin? I asked.

You know Wylend? Well enough to call him by his first name?

Probably not to call him Wylend, but we did meet—I cooked for him when Ry, Tory and I were on Tulgalan. He came to check on Wyatt.

I forgot about that, Lendill said. It sounded as if he were mentally chastising himself. *I'll ask about those two. That may not be their real names, Reah. Many of them have so many aliases we can't keep track of them. If you meet with Ry soon, perhaps he can get a look at them. He's aware of those wanted by Wylend Arden, just as well as his father Erland is. In the meantime, don't trust your bodyguards. Don't trust anyone there except Tory and Ry.*

Don't worry, Vice-Director. There aren't that many anywhere who deserve my trust.

Slamming things around in the kitchen helped with my frustration, and that's where Teeg found me later. My new bodyguards were right behind him. He'd hired two. Those two were Tory and Ry.

Consciously closing my mouth (it hung open for several ticks, I just knew it) I listened while Teeg introduced my new bodyguards. At least they'd kept the Ry and Tory part. Ry was now Ry Nolin and Tory was Tory Lathif. I wondered if Lathif was Tory's bending of the term Thifilathi, but I sure didn't want to ask. Not out loud, anyway. Teeg grinned at my discomfort. Ry and Tory were disguised, but I could see right through that. A bit of shimmer lay about them, just as there had been when they'd been on Mandil. I'd learned that meant that Ry had used the ability he had to create the disguise.

"Don't go anywhere without at least one of them," Teeg gave his instructions to me. "Don't let her out of your sight unless she's with me," Teeg handed orders to Ry and Tory. Both nodded. "Now, go make those tarts, I know you can't stand it," Teeg gave me a quick grin and stalked out of the kitchen.

"He thinks this is funny," I muttered, crossing arms over my chest.

Avilepha, if I could, I'd be kissing you breathless right now, Tory sent.

I love you, too, I returned. *The kissing will have to wait.* Tory grinned. Ry was watching Tory and grinned when his brother did. "Come on," I sighed. "Let's go to the restaurant. We have oxberry tarts to bake." I led them downstairs and out the side door to get to The San Gerxon.

The private party was very successful. Arvil came, as did his hired celebrities. I stayed in the kitchen, making sure we had enough of everything. The salmon pastries went over very well, as did all the other samples of entrees. We'd pulled out the best wine we had in stock, and when the desserts came, I was baking more oxberry tarts quickly. Everybody loved them and wanted more. Arvil brought people into the kitchen after the third batch went out.

"Reah, this is Wilffin and Wilffox, the brothers Hardlow," Arvil smiled as he introduced the two most notorious criminals in and out of the Alliance. Now I knew who Arvil's partners in the drakus seed enterprise were. Tory and Ry, both of whom stood against a wall and out of the way, never blinked when those two names were announced. It was my bet, though, that one or the other was sending mindspeech to Lendill just as fast as he could.

"A pleasure to meet you, Lord Wilffox, Lord Wilffin." I nodded respectfully to both of them. I knew, as did almost everyone, that Wilffox was older and even more murderous than his murdering younger brother, Wilffin.

"You're the one who made these wonderful tarts for me last time. And that bit of chocolate cake with the cream center and the caramel," Wilffin was smiling. I'd unwittingly pleased one of the worst criminals, ever.

"Yes, Lord Wilffin," I nodded to him again. "I'm glad to hear you liked them."

"It's the best thing I've ever gotten here. Might I hope you'll cook for me again while I and my brother are here? I don't wish to impose —Arvil tells me you're one of his heirs."

"Yes, Lord Arvil has been very kind. With his permission, I will be happy to cook for you again."

"They'll be staying at the palace," Arvil was smiling again. "We can make dinner arrangements, most certainly. Have whatever you need brought from the restaurant, Reah. We'll make sure our guests are served only the best."

"Of course." I smiled at the brothers Hardlow. It wasn't until I watched them walk out of the kitchen with Arvil that I noticed the four—*yes, four*—warlocks that closed in and walked out behind them. Each Hardlow was protected by two warlocks. I'm not sure how I knew what they were, I just did.

Holy crap, Tory's voice sounded in my mind as I busied myself at the prep table.

Did you send mindspeech to the Vice-Director? I returned.

In less than a heartbeat, Ry's voice sounded in my head.

Don't worry, baby, we'll do our best to keep all of us safe, Tory said. I shivered slightly—mothers frightened their children into obedience by telling them the Hardlows would come get them if they didn't behave. We'd all heard horror stories and seen vids of horrible crime scenes, on and off Alliance worlds. No place was safe against them. They'd even been accused of starting wars on non-Alliance worlds. This worried me. Were they attempting to take the Alliance down with drakus seed? Prove that the Alliance army and the ASD were powerless against them, so it should be every planet for itself?

That would be an effective way to annihilate all of us. Divide and destroy. The Hardlows might be the biggest master strategists ever. I hadn't seen Farzi and the other reptanoids recently, either. Arvil must have sent them out to look for new planting grounds again. The ground suddenly felt shaky beneath my feet—this was a game too big and too deep for me to be playing. I had no experience with this sort of thing. Why had Lendill demanded I stay here? I was completely out of my element.

Steady, Reah. Tory knew. Must have read the emotions crossing my face. I deliberately didn't look at him, although I wanted to. There was nothing I wanted to do more at that moment than to run to him and fling myself into his arms. Ask him to take me away from Campiaa. Anywhere would do, as long as people didn't want me dead and I wasn't surrounded by criminals who might kill me on a whim.

Was Teeg in on this somehow? Did he know about the Hardlows? Another question I was afraid to ask, since I might not like the answer. I folded pastry around oxberries in creamy filling, preparing them for the oven. My automatic navigator worked that night. I couldn't depend on my brain to form any thought that wasn't wrapped in fear.

Tory and Ry escorted me back to the palace after the party was over. I was never so thankful to get out of a kitchen in my life. Ry must have placed a shield around us—Tory nodded to his brother first before pulling me against him and leaning down to give the promised kiss. Several kisses, actually. I clung to him before he pulled away. Someone could be wondering why it took so long for us to walk the distance between The San Gerxon and Arvil's palace.

"Sweetheart, you look ready to drop." Teeg was there waiting for us in the kitchen. I still hadn't eaten anything. He was having a sandwich. Ry waved all of us into our seats and proceeded to make good sandwiches for Tory, himself and me. I was nearly too tired to eat. Teeg did a little coaxing and Ry set a glass of wine in front of me. I just wanted to sleep where I sat. Tory was watchful, too, while Teeg massaged my neck. I'd forgotten about Tory's claiming marks there. Teeg hadn't even asked about them. I had no hair to cover them, even though it was growing out. I probably had three finger-widths of hair, now. Perhaps I should get it styled.

"Reah, you look fine," Teeg assured me. I didn't even notice that he'd known what I was thinking.

Teeg showed Ry and Tory to their bedrooms down the hall in our wing. They'd be sleeping on the same floor, at least, and I figured Ry would be putting a shield around all of us while we slept. That's what I would do if I had the ability.

"Reah, come here, baby." Teeg lifted me and carried me after we'd left Ry and Tory in their rooms. I wrapped my arms around his neck and buried my head against his shoulder. He helped me in the shower, holding me up when I wanted to huddle in a corner on the expensive tiles.

"Don't let them do this to you, sweetheart." Teeg rubbed a soft, fluffy towel over me, making sure I was dry before putting me to bed. He didn't bother with pajamas for either of us, just settled me under the covers and crawled in next to me. His nearness soothed me so I closed my eyes to sleep.

CHAPTER 10

*D*elvin didn't know what to do—Haral had mucked up the plan. Delvin still didn't understand how Haral had been killed—the wizard had a shield around him at all times. It could only have been a more powerful wizard, but there weren't any on Campiaa. Not that he didn't know about. He and the others had gotten word the moment the Hardlows arrived at the shuttle station. Both of them had come, bringing all four warlocks with them.

Delvin didn't have enough power to fight one of those warlocks, let alone four. Even with all eight of Arvil's wizards fighting, they'd still be out-powered. Reah should have been off the planet at the very least and he and the others could have plotted to remove Teeg. Arvil was extremely angry that Haral had betrayed him. He hadn't spoken five words to any of his wizards after the incident. Arvil hadn't wasted any time bringing in his allies, however, and the Hardlows had shown up in less time than it took to blink. At least Farzi and his bunch were off hunting new fields for drakus seed plantings. Farzi gave Delvin the shivers and Delvin couldn't explain why.

"Perhaps you should amass your wealth in a more conventional manner," Milus sat down at the bar next to Delvin. Delvin had chosen a bar at one of the casinos Arvil didn't own. Milus had tracked him down.

"We're this close," Delvin held up a thumb and forefinger.

"Perhaps you're that close. I am considering retirement, friend. I don't like the Hardlows or their warlocks. They could kill all of us with barely a thought."

Delvin gave a quick nod—they didn't want to say that name too loudly anywhere. The Hardlows were unforgiving if they felt slighted in any way. Bodies tended to pile up in their wake if the rumors were true. Not that the Hardlows would stoop to dirty their hands in a killing—that was what their hired warlocks were for. Milus wasn't being completely honest with Delvin—he'd already made up his mind to leave Campiaa the following morning. He wanted no part in killing the girl, and if he were honest with himself—he liked Teeg.

Milus was old as a warlock. Very old. The King of Karathia had hunted him for thousands of years. Milus was headed for a small, non-Alliance world where he could sell his smaller spells for enough to eat and buy a small home. Riches no longer called to him. Carthin had persuaded him to take this job since Arvil needed as many warlocks as he could get—insurance against the Hardlows' four. Milus smiled wryly. If Arvil only knew how ineffective his wizards and warlocks would be against *those* four if they decided to attack.

"Something funny, friend Milus?" Delvin swallowed the last of his drink and called for another.

"Just thinking about the Hardlows' warlocks," Milus said. "Have fun, friend Delvin." Milus slid off his barstool and clapped Delvin on the back. "I'm going to bed." Milus walked out of the casino. He'd made up his mind suddenly. He wasn't waiting for the morning. He could fold himself away easily, and he didn't want to take time to pack. Milus disappeared the moment he was away from prying eyes.

"Yes, I met him at the bar in the Sandstorm Casino last night," Delvin raked a hand through his hair. "He said he was thinking about retiring. How am I supposed to know whether he decided to go right then or if the same one who took Haral got him, too?" Arvil discovered that Milus was gone when he woke. All his wizards always gathered to learn what Arvil wanted from them during the day. Milus failed to appear. His room was searched—nothing was missing and all appeared untouched. Reah and Teeg had been called in, as had Reah's new bodyguards so Arvil could give them information on Milus' disappearance.

Delvin looked as if he were about to have a meltdown. Things were definitely not going as planned, somehow. I wondered just what it was that Delvin had been plotting. He wasn't lying about Milus—at least I knew that much. The Hardlows came in, warlocks in tow as Delvin was telling about his meeting with Milus the evening before. I got as much information as I could by snatching quick glimpses at the warlocks. All four looked similar—with dark hair and dark eyes. Close to the same height, but there were minor differences. It made me wonder if they were brothers. Ry answered my mental question.

They're brothers. Wylend has been hunting them for a while now. Very powerful, too. Only the Hardlows could afford all of them together, I think.

I thought about asking for names, but held back. Maybe it was better if I didn't know. It didn't matter—I ended up cooking breakfast for everyone as soon as the meeting was over. Arvil was going to investigate Milus' disappearance, but I could tell he didn't have much hope of finding anything. I was hoping Milus was far away; I found him to be the least offensive of all of Arvil's wizards. It made me sad, too—I'd liked and trusted Delvin at one time—when he'd been working with Bel.

"This is very good," one of the warlocks told me. I'd made coddled eggs for him and the others—with sauce and a few other specialties.

"I'm glad you like it," I nodded respectfully to him.

"My name is Astralan," he held out his hand. I took it politely. He already knew who I was. Stellan, Astralan's brother, introduced himself next, followed by Celestan and Galaxsan. Somebody's parents had been star-struck, it seemed. The table in the dining room looked like a hurricane had hit it when Arvil, his wizards, the Hardlows and all four warlocks finished their meal and left to tend to business. Teeg shrugged at me—he had to go with Arvil. That left me, the kitchen staff, Ry and Tory.

I helped the staff carry dishes into the kitchen, but they washed and cleaned everything for me. Tory, Ry and I went to The San Gerxon to order supplies and have some of them delivered to the palace. I was going to supervise the menu served to the Hardlows personally, if I didn't cook it myself.

What do you think happened to Haral? Ry asked mentally while I went over food orders.

Ry, when I saw him, his head had nearly been severed from the body and there were long, deep cuts across his chest and torso. There was also—I hesitated for a moment, trying to choose the proper words—*a cut around his groin. Blood was everywhere. It was hard to determine the extent of the injuries, there was so much blood.* I didn't want to tell Ry that it looked as if the genitals had been removed and destroyed—males seemed sensitive about that and I was embarrassed to say it.

I just wanted to know so I could pass the information off to Dad and Wylend. We also need to understand what we're dealing with here—in case whoever did this comes after any of us.

Bro, that's such a comforting thought, Tory broke into our mental conversation.

You can make the cameras go fuzzy if you want—with your talent? I asked Ry but included Tory in the conversation.

It's one of the easiest things to do—interfere with electronic signals. That's one of the first things Dad taught me. And then he told me he'd mute my power for years to come if I ever did it within Mom's palace. Ry ducked his head to hide the grin.

So, you did it elsewhere, didn't you?

Oh, man, Tory's laugh came through the mindspeech.

How's Aurelius? I changed the subject.

Aurelius is fine. Why don't you send him mindspeech? I think he's about to go crazy without you, and I think the Vice-Director still may have Auri's fingerprints on his throat. Ry was laughing mentally this time.

I took Ry's advice. I was still going through the kitchen comp-vid, ordering food and supplies. *Aurelius?* I sent.

Reah? Thank goodness. When Torevik sent the message saying that someone had attempted to attack you, I nearly took the house apart. Aurelius' voice was warm inside my mind.

Love, I'm sorry I didn't contact you sooner—I didn't know whether you were busy or not.

Reah, my beautiful love, I am never too busy for you. Even if I am in combat, I will get back to you as swiftly as possible.

Auri, I wish I were with you. Right now. I did—I hadn't ever been so worried in my life. Even when Edan was beating me, at least I knew it would stop for a while after he hit me. This was constant and completely over my head. Aurelius always seemed so confident. I wished for a little of that, right then.

Reah, you sound lost, love. Is there no way we can see one another?

Auri, I'm afraid. I don't know what I'm doing and Lendill wants me to stay here. Now, Arvil San Gerxon has named me one of his heirs and I'm a target for his enemies or those who want to take what he has. What am I supposed to do? I was wiping tears off my face even as I entered amounts of stock items into my comp-vid. Tory almost got up but Ry grabbed his arm and dragged him back to his seat.

Reah, don't cry, love. We'll see one another soon. Aurelius broke off the mindspeech.

"Reah?" Kiasz's voice broke into my concentration. I think everyone in the kitchen knew I was crying by that time. I hadn't meant for that to happen—I should have waited until later to contact Aurelius.

Avilepha, hold your head up. We'll take care of this later. Tory's mindspeech had me wiping my eyes. "She's all right," Yindu was shooing the others away. "Go on, you'd do worse if somebody tried to poison you." Well, that had gotten around fast. I wiped my cheeks and went back to work.

~

"I heard you worked in Desh's kitchen, but I never thought I'd get their yaris fish outside any of their restaurants. This is even better than I remember." Wilffox Hardlow certainly liked what he'd been served for dinner. Teeg hadn't said a word when he came in with Arvil and the Hardlows—I had no idea what they'd been doing or what poor Teeg might have done or witnessed. The warlocks were enjoying their meal, too. Arvil was smiling—his heir was making everybody happy tonight, except herself.

I still felt depressed after my conversation with Aurelius. Tory had done his best to reassure me with mindspeech, but Ry was keeping watch on him—there would be no more touching, I think. It was too dangerous. I made a point not to look at Ry and Tory as they stood guard in the kitchen; I knew there was a gossip mill now and didn't want to feed it. Tory and Ry were served in the kitchen; I got my dinner at the table with the others while my staff served wine, plates of food and desserts.

"Sweetheart, no more crying in the kitchens, all right?" Teeg pulled me against him after we made it to our bedroom and closed the door. Honestly, I wanted to cry again, but I held the tears back. If Teeg knew, then Arvil and the others knew. He'd think I was weak.

"Will he try to get rid of me?" I asked, looking up at Teeg. I meant Arvil. Teeg knew what I meant. He led me to the side of the bed and settled me on the edge.

"Reah, I know you're young. So young." His hands cupped my face. "I know that not long ago, you didn't worry this much about getting killed. Don't let that homicidal rapist hurt you like this." He leaned in to kiss me. How could I tell him it wasn't just Haral that upset me? All of it was weighing on me and closing in, like a windowless room. "Baby," he murmured, "I promise you, I'm not without resources. I'll protect you as well as I can."

I knew Tory would do the same, only Tory probably had more resources than Teeg could possibly imagine. So did I, but I always worried I'd be caught unawares. Lendill had told me not to change.

What was I supposed to do, wait until they killed me to decide otherwise? Ry was strong as a warlock, but could he stand against any one of those working for the Hardlows? I was afraid to ask, in case the answer was no.

≁

Lendill's hand automatically went to his throat when he saw Aurelius coming. Aurelius didn't look happy. "Now what?" Lendill decided to be practical about it and lowered his hands.

"Reah sent me mindspeech. She was crying before it was all over. That girl is frightened out of her wits, Lendill Schaff. And you're forcing her to stay there."

"She's in a unique position to hand over the biggest criminals in and outside the Alliance," Lendill pointed out the logic.

"She told me she's too inexperienced for this, Lendill." Aurelius' golden-brown eyes were hard as they raked Lendill's face.

"That's why I sent Ry and Tory. They'll take care of her."

Aurelius eyed Lendill's throat. Lendill put his hand there again. Aurelius snorted and walked away.

≁

Farzi, Nenzi and the others came in the following day. Nenzi came to me expectantly, so I gave him the best hug I could. Farzi nodded to me and smiled.

The moment Nenzi moved away, however, another reptanoid sidled up. I hugged him. Eventually, they'd all gotten a hug, including Farzi. They were hungry too; they'd come straight from the shuttle station. I had the kitchen staff put a light meal together for them. They went to rest for a little while before meeting with Arvil and the Hardlows. I got the idea that Farzi had found something for Arvil. Teeg and I ended up in the meeting.

"We return from Zephili," Farzi nodded to Arvil and both Hardlows. I'd arranged for snacks and drinks to be served during the meeting. Arvil seemed to like that very much. "Grish has crops being harvested now. He say we can have those fields, for part of profits." Farzi continued.

"Did he say how much?" Arvil frowned.

"He not tell me." Farzi was upset over that, I could tell. This Grish probably didn't think Farzi was smart enough or important enough. "He want to speak with you." Farzi nodded toward Arvil. "He want to see you." Whenever Farzi was upset, his speech deteriorated dramatically.

"Perhaps we should all pay Grish a visit." Wilffox lifted a tiny seafood salad appetizer and ate it, smiling maliciously. I wondered if he and Grish had some history. Wilffin agreed with his brother. "We can be there tomorrow if you'd like, friend Arvil."

"I'll have my assistant send the communication," Arvil smiled. "If we're lucky, Grish will die of old age while we're there and we can take over. Zephili will be ideal for our enterprise, I think. Fields are available there to replace all three of our lost crops."

"Reah, just pack your things." Teeg was frustrated, I could tell. I'd grumbled when Arvil informed me I had to go. Teeg was staying behind to run things for Arvil. At least Ry and Tory were coming with me. It might have been ideal if Arvil had left me on Campiaa. Wilffox and Wilffin had requested that I go with them—they liked the cooking.

"Sweetheart, you'll be able to talk with me anytime—by comp-vid communicator," Teeg watched me throw clothing into a bag a bit harder than was warranted. I wanted to scream, if I were honest. At Lendill Schaff. At Arvil San Gerxon. At Haral, Edan, the Hardlows, Delvin and just about anyone else who came to mind. "Ry and Tory will watch out for you," Teeg went on. "Besides, this will get you away from all the gossipmongers on Campiaa."

"Of course it will," I snapped sarcastically. "What are they saying about me now?"

"Reah, it's not important. Just finish packing. All right?"

I stood there, staring at Teeg. "Tell me," I said. He'd started this, saying what he did. Now he was going to explain it to me.

"Reah, ever since your hair started growing out and everybody recognized you as a woman, the rumors have been flying. Especially after Arvil got rid of his mistress housekeeper. At first they said you were sleeping with Arvil. That upset me until I found out differently. Now they're saying you're sleeping with the Hardlows or their warlocks. Reah, you're beautiful. They see that now. People are even placing bets on who you're sleeping with besides me."

"That's it, I'm leaving." I dumped the armload of clothing I held in the bag that lay open on the bed. I turned around and stalked out the door, Teeg right behind me.

"Reah, where are you going?" Teeg grabbed my arm.

"Anywhere but here. All I have to do is make it to the shuttle station. Tell Arvil I said no, thank you." I jerked my arm out of Teeg's grasp.

"Reah!" Teeg was almost running after me, hauling me off the floor while I flailed against him. I think a few blows actually landed on his chest and shoulders as he carried me back to the bedroom. After tossing me onto the pillows scattered across the top of the bed, Teeg growled and turned away from me. I attempted to slide off the bed, but he caught me and threw me right back. "Reah, listen to me!" Teeg was nearly shouting.

Too angry to say anything that made any sense at all, I folded my arms stiffly across my chest and refused to look at Teeg. "Reah, I shouldn't have told you that, but maybe it's better to hear it from me instead of getting blindsided by it when you're working at one of Arvil's casinos. People here gossip, Reah, and they gamble. The two go hand-in-hand most of the time. They get bored with the regular games, so they'll bet on anything."

"So they all think I'm going to bed with Arvil. Or the Hardlows." I was shaking now, I was so angry and upset.

"Reah, they're even betting that you're sleeping with your new guards." Those words hit too close to the truth. Tory and I hadn't coupled—we'd only had direct contact during the claiming and that had been unwilling on my part. Now, though, Tory and I—well, we were mated just as much as Aurelius and I were. I loved him, just as I loved Aurelius and Teeg. Multiple mates were recognized by the Alliance. I didn't know what the rules were on Campiaa and didn't want to ask Teeg—if he were fishing for information, I wasn't about to hand it to him. I did give him what I had, though.

"I'm not sleeping with my guards." And I wasn't. Not yet, anyway, and it would only be one of them if I did. My voice was now sullen.

"I know you're not," Teeg dropped onto the bed next to me. "Reah, I don't care if you sleep with someone else, as long as you love them and they aren't taking advantage of you. I just want to protect you, sweetheart. Gods, you're so young." He pulled me against him.

"If I'm too young, why did you marry me?"

"Now see, you're already learning to twist my words." He lifted my face for a quick kiss. "You're not too young for me to love you."

"Sounds like contempt to me." I struggled to escape his grip.

"Reah, hush." Teeg's arms tightened about me. "Trust me, there is nothing I have for you except love. I wish there was some way I could get that message through so you'd understand it."

"Sure." I struggled in his arms again. Teeg was strong—more so than he looked, and he looked quite strong. There were things that he still didn't know about me. Things that I didn't know how to tell him, if the time ever came when I could tell him.

"Shhhh," Teeg gathered both my hands in one of his, kissing them before holding them against me to keep me still. "Now is a perfect moment, Reah. We're together, and nobody is asking us to do anything. You're safe in my arms, my love." The teardrop fell before I could stop it or wipe it away. Safe? Even in Teeg's arms I didn't feel safe. I didn't feel safe anywhere. Not as long as I belonged to the ASD. Vice-Director Lendill Schaff would use me as much as he could, even when I didn't have the background or experience to be where I was, doing what I was. I shuddered and wept.

⁓

Alcohol didn't have as much of an effect on Teeg as it might on others. He sat at the kitchen island and drank anyway. "Mind if I join you?" Tory walked into the kitchen.

"Glasses are over there," Teeg jerked his head toward a cabinet. Tory pulled one out and sat down nearby. Teeg poured out the bourbon. Tory downed his glass in one swallow. Teeg poured more bourbon. "Any advice on how to deal with women?" Teeg asked, topping off his glass.

"None," Tory replied, downing his second glass.

"We'll be back before you know it," Arvil blustered. I don't know why he even bothered. Heaving a frustrated sigh, I turned away from Teeg, knowing I'd probably start crying again if I looked at him. Ry and Tory flanked me as Astralan and his brothers prepared to fold the rest of us to Zephili.

Folding is always so fast, and I knew as soon as my feet landed on a polished wood floor that it might be a while before I got to see Teeg again. I had my comp-vid communicator in my bags, but that was small consolation. *Avilepha, I will be with you,* Tory reassured me. I knew that, but how closely would Arvil be watching us? A servant came and bowed to Arvil and the Hardlows. The rest of us barely got a glance. He was small, pale-skinned and dressed in white linen, this servant. He was also dangerously close to blending with the wall color.

"I am Master Grish's private assistant," he informed us. "Master Grish is waiting—please follow me." Farzi was beside me, Nenzi on the other side while Ry and Tory came behind. I didn't miss the frown that tugged at Farzi's mouth as we followed Grish's assistant.

Were the others prepared for Grish? I know I wasn't, but I was hidden behind taller people, so the widening of my eyes wasn't seen. Grish was pale, ancient and shrunken. Every bit of exposed skin was wrinkled beyond imagining. Staring was rude, so I turned to Farzi.

His face was set in a frown—he didn't like Grish at all. If Farzi had problems with this one, it was probably a good idea to be wary.

I also saw why Grish hadn't come to greet us himself—he sat on a wheeled chair with a high back. It was motorized and heavy—I couldn't see his personal assistant pushing Grish around in it. Wispy strands of colorless hair were combed away from Grish's face, and he appeared cadaverous to me. A monkey-like creature sat on the arm of Grish's chair, and the creature operated the controls, moving Grish's chair from one place to another.

"So, Arvil San Gerxon, you bring your business partners with you? Don't think I fail to recognize Wilffox and Wilffin Hardlow," Grish spoke. "If you think I will charge less for the use of my fields because they present a danger to me, then think again. You are on my world and I am not without resources." Grish's voice was breathless with the effort to speak and his eyes were nearly lost in his face, they were so sunken. Those eyes darted back and forth, now, watching Arvil and the Hardlows closely. He should have been watching the warlocks instead. The moment three more men folded into the room, attempting to throw some wizardry or other around us, Astralan and Stellan had them fried to a crisp. They screamed as they died; I watched in horror as their bodies turned to ash and disintegrated before us.

"Don't send threats against us—I assure you we've survived for a very long time with the help of our warlocks," Wilffox informed a cowering Grish. "Now, we can have a civilized meeting and perhaps come to some arrangement, or we can fry you where you sit and take what we want instead. Personally, I have no desire to run Zephili—I just need the use of your fields for a few full turns."

"I expect to be compensated well," Grish whined. As first meetings went, this might be the worst I'd ever seen or been a part of. Farzi was as close to me as he could get on my left, Nenzi was hugged up against my right side and Tory was nearly holding me up from behind. Ry stood close enough that he'd be included in our shield, as would the other reptanoids, I noticed. A small question niggled at me, but I didn't have time to dwell on it right then—Arvil and the Hardlows were engaged in a standoff with Grish of Zephili.

"We will inspect your fields tomorrow, to see if they are suitable. We will compensate you if we find them so, Grish." Arvil waved a hand as if that would make his words true. I didn't hold much hope that Grish might survive if Arvil found the fields too much to his liking. "May we hope you still have your bribes in place with the Alliance?"

Arvil's question stunned me and Tory put a hand on my shoulder. Warning me, no doubt, not to make a sound. I didn't—I knew better. We were in a dangerous game and the stakes had just been raised. I hoped Ry or Tory were busy sending mindspeech to Lendill. My brain had gone into frozen overload and I wasn't sure I could have sent anything at that moment.

Lendill? The Vice-Director was receiving mindspeech from Rylend Morphis in the middle of the night.

Ry, this had better be good, Lendill opened one eye, determining that it was still three clicks before dawn.

Maybe—Arvil San Gerxon just asked Grish of Zephili if he still had his bribes in place with the Alliance.

Ry, if you'd thrown ice water in my face, I might have wakened more slowly. Lendill was now sitting straight up in bed.

Yeah—it got our attention too. I think Reah is catatonic, right now.

Do you have any names?

Not yet, Lendill, but we'll send information if we get it.

Ry—do your best, you and Tory—make sure Reah isn't too scared to speak. Aurelius said she was crying, she was so scared when he talked to her. That isn't what I meant to happen.

Lendill, what were you doing when you were nineteen?

Raising hell in school—why?

Reah wasn't prepared for this. She worked in a kitchen all her life until now. And just because she managed to kill off a few spawn on Mandil, you put her in the middle of this. Tory complains about it every day. At least that man she married isn't bad—he seems to care about her. If he didn't, I don't think he'd live long after this is over. Ry wasn't mincing words with the Vice-Director.

I know. Look, I'll try to make it up to her, somehow. Just—do your best to smooth things over, all right?

I'll do what I can, but Grampa Wylend already asked me to look out for her. You don't turn down Grampa Wylend.

I would imagine not. Lendill's sending was dry. He didn't think too many people managed to defy a request from the King of Karathia. Ry cut off the communication and Lendill, now wide-awake, stood up and went to turn the light on over his desk. He'd received a message from his father three days earlier. He hadn't heard from Kaldill Schaff in years. Wondering why he was getting a message now, Lendill punched in the private code to contact his only living parent.

~

Kaldill stood in his kitchen on Wyyld. Not long ago he'd learned to bake bread. He enjoyed it now—getting out of bed early to set the dough to rise. He hadn't needed much sleep in a long while. If Lendill hoped to wake him, he'd failed. Kaldill smiled brightly as his son's face appeared on the comp-vid screen. "Lendill, you finally choose to return my call?"

"Father." Lendill nodded respectfully.

"I suppose you want to know what I want?" Kaldill was still smiling.

"Yes, father, that's why I contacted you." Lendill knew not to trust the smile; Kaldill could have the worst news and would still be smiling at his son.

"Ah, well," Kaldill employed power to settled the comp-vid on the wall before his face so he could keep working and still speak with his son.

"Well, what?" Lendill had never had the patience the others of his race did. He was only half-elven, after all. He'd wondered through the years just what it was that convinced his father to have a child with a humanoid. Lendill looked human, but his father had pronounced him immortal the moment he was born. Another of Kaldill's talents, Lendill now knew. Lendill would have died long ago if he hadn't been immortal. He just didn't get any other gifts from his father's race. Lissa, who was very powerful, had given him mindspeech. He still hadn't told Kaldill about that, else his father would be contacting him that way quite often, more than likely.

"I know you are attracted to someone—I saw it while I was working not long ago," Kaldill pounded dough onto the smooth, floured surface of his wood countertop.

"So? I have been attracted to several, over the years."

"Not like this."

"I still don't understand why you contacted me about it." Lendill was feeling grumpy with his father, who treated all matters as if they might be trivial. As a general rule, anyway.

"I contacted you because, in the words of some of your mother's race—I still love her, even though she is gone from me—you are fucking this up." Kaldill's cursing was legendary among his race, but he seldom used Alliance Common during profanity-laced outbursts.

It was early and Lendill had a difficult time following Kaldill's convoluted speech for a moment. "You're saying I'm fucking this up? Father, I'm not sure I've ever heard you use that humanoid term before."

"It exists; therefore I will use it if it applies. It does not alter the fact that you may be ruining any chance you might have with the woman who is your breath, your heart and your soul."

Lendill's eyes widened. *Breah-mul, Cheah-mul* and *Deah-mul* were popular phrases on Wyyld. Few knew that those words were Elvish in origin. Many Elf words permeated the native language of Wyyld. "You can't know she is those things," Lendill scoffed, although he felt worried. His father was seldom wrong about these things. Actually, his father had never been wrong about these things.

"You are fucking this up," Kaldill repeated, shaking a flour-coated finger at Lendill. "Make it right or make your peace with being alone for the rest of your life."

"Father, what are you doing?" Lendill directed the conversation away from himself.

"Making bread. It is my new hobby. I like it. Go back to bed." Kaldill punched the button on the comp-vid, terminating the call.

Lendill cursed. One never won an argument with Kaldill Schaff. Kaldill was right all the time and he knew it.

CHAPTER 11

Grish had a battalion of cooks, kitchen helpers and medical assistants, all busier than ants when something attacks their nest. It made sense—Grish being in as poor health as he was. We'd been awakened by servants—Ry and Tory had spent the night in my suite but in an adjoining bedroom. Grish's plantation palace was quite large, but my suite was one of the smaller ones. The reptanoids were quartered nearby—Farzi, Nenzi and two others slept in Farzi's suite, the rest of them inside a second suite. My suite was squeezed between both. I would have welcomed Tory in my bed the night before, I think—I felt cold, although the air was warm on that portion of Zephili. Sleep hadn't come easily, either.

Ry says there aren't any cameras, I'll be there tonight, baby. Tory was sending mindspeech as we sat down at a huge table, waiting for breakfast. Breakfast was almost intolerable—the food was bland and unseasoned, likely prepared so Grish could digest it. He hadn't made any accommodations for his guests—we all received the same meal he was having. At least the juice was good—freshly squeezed. The citrus must have been grown on Grish's plantations. We appeared to be near the equator again, just as we'd been on Urdolus. Grish didn't feed himself, either, he depended upon the monkey-like creature to lift the spoon and drop mushy food in his mouth. Much of it dribbled down his chin. An assistant stood by to regularly wipe Grish's face with a napkin. I'd seen Grish move his hands and arms to gesture while he spoke, so I failed to understand why he refused to feed himself.

I didn't want to watch Grish eat lunch later, so I asked for a sandwich and went outside on Grish's patio. He had a beautiful pool, but I had my doubts that he ever used it. Plenty of comfortable chairs sat beneath umbrellas, with small tables sitting nearby. Farzi, Nenzi and the others came out to join Ry, Tory and me.

"I am Darzi," one of the reptanoids sat at the foot of my chaise. Chazi, Perzi, Yanzi, Bekzi and Hirzi introduced themselves as they sat nearby. Ry was smiling. The last six had never given me their names before. Now we were all sitting around Grish's pool, having lunch together.

"Master Arvil wishes to see fields this afternoon," Farzi frowned as he stared into the distance. "We all go."

"Then we'll all go." I gave Farzi a small smile.

"Yes, we all go," Farzi nodded to me. I didn't know if Arvil wanted me along, but Farzi did. A hoverbus took us after lunch—one of Grish's staff drove but I could see Nenzi clenching his hands—he wanted to drive. I rubbed his back in consolation as we got off the bus. The fields around us had been harvested, but the plowing hadn't been done for the next crop. Arvil hadn't failed to notice that. Grish didn't come with us—a lesser assistant held a comp-vid with Grish in constant contact on the other end.

"How long will it take to plow this field?" Wilffox asked Grish's image.

"Two days for this one, two to three days for similar fields," the assistant relayed the message.

"And how many do you have that are this size?" I looked around at the field—I could see trees marking the boundaries far off in the distance.

"More than a hundred," the assistant smiled.

"How many fields can we plow at once?"

"We have the equipment to plow fifteen fields simultaneously,"

Grish's voice came over the comp-vid. "This allows for planting and harvesting the same fields at the same time. It is a rotating schedule—as soon as the crops planted first are harvested, the next fifteen fields are ready. We get optimum use out of the employees and the machinery. I have a repair staff to take care of any breakdowns. The only thing that might slow us down is the weather."

"We could have these fields plowed and planted in a moon-turn or less," Arvil was smiling at Wilffox and Wilffin.

"We'll give you fifteen percent of the take," Wilffox offered.

"Twenty-five," Grish counter-offered. I listened, wanting to sigh at the haggling going on via comp-vid. They were discussing lives and the future of the Alliance, while we stood on a field that should be planted with legitimate crops to feed hungry people. The most deadly drug known to the Alliance would be raised there instead. I schooled my face into non-expression and kicked at the clods of dirt beneath my feet.

"Farzi—how often does it rain here—do you know?" I asked him. He turned his brown, slitted eyes to me.

"It rain often here. Perhaps once or twice each eight-day. Seldom do sprinklers need use."

"The nearest village or city?"

"Two clicks that way," Farzi pointed to the north. "By hovercar. Large city—find what you need there."

"Reah is missing something?" Nenzi looked hopeful.

"Not yet, but if I do, I want you to drive me," I grinned at him.

We flew the hoverbus over many other fields—I saw them stretching out as far as I could see. More fields beyond that, even, with citrus groves and nut trees interspersed. It made me wonder how much of the fruit and vegetables Grish supplied to non-Alliance worlds and if there would be a shortage as a result of the fields being used to grow drakus seed instead. I posed my question mentally to Ry and Tory on the way back to Grish's plantation.

No idea, Tory replied. Ry didn't know either.

Ask somebody to get Chash to work it out for me, I suggested. Tory sent the mindspeech to his mother.

Mom says it's a good problem for him to focus on, Tory lowered his head to hide the smile. *Gav misses you.*

We had dinner with Grish, and once again the food was bland and certainly not what we were used to. Grish wasn't concerned for his guests; we were served what he would eat and nothing more. That's why I answered the knock on my bedroom door later in my pajamas; Ry and Tory right behind me. Thankfully, they were still dressed. Wilffox, Astralan and Stellan stood outside my suite.

"Reah, we would very much like for you to prepare dinner for our party tomorrow evening," Wilffox said.

"I'll be happy to, but I don't want to offend our host."

"As long as he gets what he wants, I don't believe Grish *can* be offended." I covered my mouth—I didn't want the snicker to escape at Wilffox's words. "His kitchen staff, however, may be a different story."

"Yes, if they're anything like his personal assistant, then there could be a problem," I agreed. "I get the idea that they are running things— Grish is kept around as a figurehead only—he has the contacts. He no longer runs his business, I think."

"Interesting concept—I'll have my people work on that," Wilffox nodded to me. Astralan winked at me before he turned to follow Wilffox. I closed the door and put my back to it, staring at Tory and Ry.

What was that about? I sent.

I think they like your food, Ry returned.

Baby, can we get in bed now? Tory was a little impatient, I think.

"Let's go." I took Tory's hand and pulled him toward my bedroom. Ry was muffling laughter when we closed the door.

"Avilepha, I don't know how patient I can be," Tory was busy unbuttoning my blouse. "The first time after the claiming is the linking. My mind links with yours. You feel my desire and vice-versa." Tory was kissing whatever he uncovered, paying special attention to my neck. He kissed the back of it, where his claiming marks were and I began to feel flushed. It wasn't hot in the house—Grish had the best air-conditioning anyone could hope for. Either he or his staff liked the temperature to be much cooler than most people preferred.

"It's starting," Tory whispered against my mouth. It was; whatever it was. I was on fire, suddenly, and Tory couldn't get my clothes off fast enough. I couldn't get *his* clothes off fast enough. I wanted him—was ready for him—right then. Tory was frantically kissing me and pushing me back on the bed at the same time. He used his hands. He used his mouth, his teeth, his body—I wanted everything. I was almost begging him there at the end, until we were joined. If I'd thought the fire had come earlier, I was very wrong. I was clawing him and that only served to make him more frenzied. I wanted him to thrust himself into me. Hard. I learned later that Ry had to throw a sound-dampening shield around our bedroom; otherwise, everyone might have known what we were doing. It was very, very late—or early, depending upon your perspective, when we finally wore ourselves out and fell asleep.

I'd just gotten out of the shower and dressed the following morning, when I suddenly felt ill. I knew someone was in trouble and I knew who it was. Danger and terror were clouding my brain, almost preventing my ability to think rationally. I threw good sense to the winds. Snatching up my knife and pistol, I skipped away before Tory could stop me. I was so angry by what I found I wanted to kill.

Nenzi was shrieking—three of Grish's assistants were tying him to a table while Farzi and the other reptanoids were shouting at them to stop. Grish was in his chair nearby, watching the entire episode while another man I hadn't met was putting on gloves and a surgical mask. A huge surgical robot stood in the corner, ready to go to work. I had no idea where I'd landed, I'd just followed the trouble. That trouble was about to get complicated.

"What is going on here?" I shouted.

"It is time for Master Grish's transference." I stared at the surgeon —he was prepared to take Nenzi? I was furious in the time it took to blink.

"Don't be so surprised, young woman," Grish's voice was

whispered malevolence. "I've been alive for more than a thousand years by employing this technique. I'm surprised Master San Gerxon failed to mention it to you." Grish laughed at my shock—he'd done the same thing—committed murder many, many times, in order to stay alive.

"This one seems simple, so we chose his body," Grish continued.

"Is everything prepared?" That was gloves and mask speaking, as he jerked his head toward the shrieking Nenzi. Well, he'd just told me everything I needed to know. He was about to transplant Grish's brain into Nenzi's body. That wasn't going to happen. There was a reason this procedure had been outlawed across the Alliance—it was murder.

The surgeon's three assistants got cut when I freed Nenzi, pushing him toward Farzi. When the physician decided he wanted in on the conflict, I had the knife to his throat in very little time. I imagine that none of them expected me to move as swiftly as I did. Faster than a blink, actually. The physician was gurgling as I held him, the knife pressing into his flesh.

"Now," I said to Grish, who was staring at me in surprise. "If you touch one of my people again, I will flay the wrinkled skin from your bones and scatter it across your fields for the crows to eat. Do you understand?"

"But it's time for my transference," Grish whined.

"I don't think so," I said. "How many people have you murdered for a new body? How many times did you do it for him?" I jerked the physician around and slammed him into a wall. His eyes were huge as he mumbled "Three." Now I was learning that Grish did this regularly, with the help of a homicidal physician and his assistants. Who knew how old Grish really was, or what else he'd done through the centuries to stay alive?

"You disgust me." I slammed the physician's head against the wall so hard it knocked him unconscious. "And you," I pointed my knife at the three assistants who began to back away from me. "If you want to die, lay a hand on any of mine. Do you hear me?" All of them were bleeding from some sort of wound. One I'd gotten across the chest—he'd been tying Nenzi to the table. The other two had been holding Nenzi down. Both had slashes on their arms and hands.

"You cannot kill us," one of them was brave enough to say.

"She can and she will." Tory and Ry walked into the room—I had no idea where we were inside Grish's plantation home, since I'd skipped to where the trouble was. Tory and Ry were followed by Arvil, Wilffox, Wilffin and all four warlocks.

"I'll save her the trouble." Astralan had all three assistants turned to ash in a blink. It wasn't what I wanted, but this time I wasn't going to argue. I wanted Grish to be fried too, but that wasn't on the agenda. At least not yet.

"Grish, I hope you can live with that body for a while; I don't think my heir appreciates the idea of your stealing anyone else's." Arvil was smiling nastily at Grish. "And I like the idea of her flaying you. Hold onto that thought, Grish and don't cross me or mine again." Arvil stalked out of the room.

"Nenzi, are you all right?" I slid my knife into the sheath at my waist and went to hug him. Nenzi was gabbling in some language I didn't understand and holding onto me as if his life depended on it. Ry and Tory herded me and the reptanoids from the room. Astralan wasn't finished, though.

"Offend our cook again and I'll make sure there isn't enough of you left to scatter for the crows," he pointed a finger at Grish. As threats went, I'd take it seriously. The warlocks must have folded the Hardlows out of the room—I heard Grish whining pitifully for servants to come and attend him.

"Farzi, what happened?" I asked, as soon as we got the reptanoids outside. I learned that we'd been in Grish's private quarters—they took up a good third of the entire plantation.

"Three came," Farzi said, meaning the three assistants. "Say Grish wishes to see Nenzi. I not invited, but go along behind." Farzi's speech was worried and less intelligible, just as Nenzi's or the others' was when they were upset. I nodded—Farzi had sneaked along behind the others. I might have gone, too—there wasn't any reason for Grish to want Nenzi alone. There was no logical purpose I could think of—

none at all. "They attack Nenzi near room. He fight back. I shout at him. We not knowing what Grish want. Then physician tell what he want. I yell. They not listen. Then Reah comes." Farzi was nodding respectfully to me.

"I can't tell you how happy I am that I did come," I muttered. If they'd killed Nenzi, I would have killed them all. Lendill Schaff or no, I'd have turned and razed the plantation to the ground. Grish was counting on Arvil not wishing to kill Nenzi, even after the transference, I think. Grish was more dangerous than I'd believed possible.

I'll put a shield around their rooms, Ry offered mentally.

Good, I replied. "Nenzi, can we get you tea or something?" He was still shivering over his ordeal.

"Tea." He nodded. I think he just wanted the comfort and safety of others around him. I wasn't about to say no. We walked into Grish's kitchen and I put tea together for all of us, then proceeded to make breakfast. Grish's kitchen help had backed away from us the moment we appeared—word traveled fast, I suppose. They weren't going to argue with any one of us. The others started trickling in and got breakfast too. I left the kitchen cleaning with Grish's bunch. Grish and his animal driver wheeled in just as I was leaving with my four. Farzi hissed at him as Grish drove past. Grish pretended not to hear. Well, I hoped he remembered Astralan's words. I'd still flay him if he so much as stared at Nenzi again—if the warlocks didn't get him first.

"And there I thought you'd named her one of your heirs because you liked her cooking." Wilffox grinned at Arvil as they sat inside Wilffox's expansive suite, drinking.

"You've never seen her handle a ranos rifle," Arvil lifted his glass to drink. "We've dealt with demons on several worlds. Most people can't see the fuckers coming in the dark. The wizards can. Reah can, too. And she doesn't miss when she shoots, like some of my wizards." Arvil was tipsy or he'd never have revealed that information. He generally didn't want anyone to know that his wizards had weaknesses. "She saved my life the first time we took her out—the demons stepped up their attack and headed right for me. Her gun was empty so she kicked one, hit another in the head with the butt of her gun and punched a third. She moved so fast I couldn't even follow it."

"I wouldn't have believed it if we hadn't seen her throw the good physician against the wall," Wilffin snorted at the mental image.

"I think I chose well, and she and Teeg will work beside me for years to come," Arvil drained his glass. "You've seen how fiercely she protects me and mine."

"Full moon tonight. Please to come with us," Farzi said later, after dinner had been served. I'd cooked, adding enough for ten extra plates —in case Grish's appetite hadn't disappeared. He was glowering as he was driven to the table, but the moment he tasted the fowl I'd prepared, I think he forgot everything else in favor of the food.

"Now you see what a master cook can do," Wilffox had raised his glass to me. I wasn't a master cook—hadn't taken the exams to qualify. Wilffox didn't seem to mind.

"Where are we going?" Ry and Tory lifted eyebrows at my words. They hadn't been invited.

"Out—near fields," Farzi flung out an arm.

"I'll come," I nodded. Farzi was trusting me with something. I was going to find out what it was. *I'll be fine*, I sent to Tory, who looked a bit concerned. That's how I ended up dressing in the black leathers I'd brought with me and trooping toward the fields with Farzi, Nenzi and the six other reptanoids.

"We tell our story, then show you. We hope to keep trust," Farzi settled on the ground underneath some citrus trees. They'd been harvested already and the new fruit hadn't begun to grow yet.

"All right," I nodded to Farzi. This was important to him, I could tell.

"We were made. Not born—made," Farzi began. "DNA with egg."

He gestured with his hands. I nodded—his birth had been manipulated. Probably grown in a pod—some parents chose that if they didn't or couldn't birth a child the normal way. "We have one father." Well, one sperm donor, I think was what he was saying.

"He was shapeshifter." That I hadn't really guessed at—I thought perhaps the eggs had been from reptiles of some sort. Now I was learning that wasn't the case. I nodded, though—Farzi hadn't lost me yet, or upset me in any way.

"Did you know him—your father?"

"No. Others take his seed to make us. They want someone like him. We not exact," Farzi explained. "Eyes different. Other things—different. Some things are same. Many of us, in beginning. Now, only eight." Farzi looked sad at that statement.

"You lost some of your brothers." I rubbed his back.

"And all sisters. Only seven of those in beginning. All gone, now."

"I'm sorry, Farzi."

"The ones who make us become afraid. Someone hunting them. And us. They sell us to Master Arvil. He place chips." Farzi pointed to a spot on his chest. Arvil had implanted location chips on the reptanoids, just as others did for their pets or children. Farzi could never escape Arvil San Gerxon. No wonder Arvil sent them off with barely a thought. He could find them again if they ever thought to run.

"So, they used you. Then sold you to Arvil, so he could do the same."

"Yes. You are exact. But on full moon, we do as our father did. He have to turn, Reah. We have to turn. But we still know who is friend when we turn. We do not harm. Enemy—we know them, too." I blinked at Farzi. I knew what he was saying and I wasn't about to argue. I nodded my understanding.

"We like Reah to come," Nenzi spoke up.

"I'll come along for you, Nenzi." I might not have for any of the rest of Arvil's crew, but I would for these. There was an honor of some sort that the reptanoids held, and I had no problem going with them.

We all stood, and one by one, with moonlight shining down upon them, each reptanoid became what their father had been before them, a lion snake shapeshifter. I wondered if Norian Keef knew what they were. Somehow, I knew he wasn't their parent—that one had knowingly allowed their creation, even if he'd not given his children any of his time afterward. I think they missed that—having a parent. I knew that feeling. Perhaps that's why I felt close to them. The largest —Farzi—was around fourteen hands in length, the others varying in size with Nenzi being the shortest at around eleven hands. I gathered their clothing, placed it in a neat pile and followed behind them as they slithered toward Grish's plantation.

The house was quiet—there was only one guard posted outside Grish's suite. Seven lion snakes and I held back, watching as Nenzi crawled up the door facing until he looped himself around the first of a series of light fixtures hanging from the ceiling. All was dark inside the hallway; the guard might have thought to look upward, otherwise. An open transom window lay above Grish's bedroom door; Nenzi used that to crawl inside.

We waited. Nenzi came back half a click later, retracing his path. His lion snake dropped silently onto the floor and we crept outside again. I followed the reptanoids that night as they hunted prey— capturing rodents, sleeping birds and other snakes. I didn't turn my head away while they swallowed their meal whole. I thought it was important that they knew I didn't find them repulsive. A few clicks before dawn, they returned to our original gathering place, regained their humanoid shape and dressed.

The same physician I'd tossed against the wall the day before pronounced heart failure as the cause of Grish's death and got away from the plantation as quickly as he could. He probably thought the warlocks had done it and didn't want to tangle with any of them. Nenzi had been discreet—when I went in with the others to check on Grish, I didn't see any sign of bite marks anywhere.

Several more of Grish's assistants died before the morning was out, after they attempted to argue with Arvil over who now owned Grish's lands. Arvil and the warlocks won. Arvil shot two, three others were fried by Celestan, I think. Ry, Tory, the reptanoids and I took a long walk while that argument took place. When we returned, it was to see Grish's remaining servants driving away in one of the hoverbuses kept at the plantation.

"I'll need staff here—we must plow and plant quickly," Arvil didn't seem daunted by the task. That's how Ry, Tory and I, along with Farzi and two other reptanoids, ended up in the nearest city, looking to hire workers. Nenzi drove.

"We made sure they could do as they said," I told Arvil later. I didn't tell him I knew if they were lying. We found experienced workers who knew how to operate the equipment. Tory sent mindspeech, joking over the fact that Lendill might have, in his words, *a cow*, if he could see what we were doing right then. I just shrugged, smiled at the inexplicable cow statement and went on. The fields were plowed two eight-days later—rain had come three of those days, which held things up a little. Arvil sent Carthin somewhere to get the drakus seed to plant—I suppose it was a secret location only he and the Hardlows knew. Ry said he could follow the signature path and sent the information to Lendill when Carthin returned.

Delvin feels power signatures from wizards and warlocks. How are you getting around that? I sent to Ry. We were having an after-dinner drink around the pool. Farzi and the others had been out in the fields, supervising the work. Nenzi headed the machinery repair detail. He was happiest, I think, when he came home covered in grease and muck.

Mom, Ry answered my mental question. *She has a shield around me that no wizard or warlock can crack.* When I lifted an eyebrow, he explained. *She's mated to Kifirin, remember? She's what he is.*

And I didn't bow to her?

She doesn't like it.

Thank the stars. I thought I'd messed up somehow.

◦~◦

"I haven't heard from Reah since I sent Ry and Tory. I get all the reports from them, now." Lendill flopped onto Norian's sofa. "Why do you have a bigger office than I do?"

"Because I'm your boss." Norian knew Lendill was teasing. "Why are you worried that Reah isn't giving you the reports? Ry and Tory have more experience at this."

"They didn't know how Grish died, but Ry thinks Reah knows something. He says she was out half the night. Grish was dead the next morning."

"Did she kill him?"

"Tory says no—there was a guard posted outside all night."

"Doesn't matter—we may find out who the Alliance double agent is this way. They'll have to contact San Gerxon if they want to keep getting paid."

"True. And I didn't shed a tear over Grish—he's been smuggling drugs and contraband with his fruit and vegetable shipments for years. That's probably how he met up with his Alliance contact."

"More than likely."

"I still want to hear from Reah."

"Then send her mindspeech."

"She doesn't like talking with me."

"You just don't like feeling guilty."

"Neither do you."

"That's why I put you on this." Norian was grinning at his oldest friend.

"Do you think she'll ever get over this—all of it?" Lendill leaned back on the sofa and closed his eyes.

"No idea. Why are you worried about it?"

"No reason." Lendill's lie had Norian frowning.

◦~◦

"Have you heard from that son of yours?" Wylend Arden asked Erland as soon as Wylend's guards left his study.

"Yes, Reah is fine. Ry said she almost knifed somebody because they grabbed one of her people."

"Well, I can't blame her. Can you?"

"I would have put a spell on them, but the intent would be the same."

~

Reah? I hadn't gotten mindspeech from Lendill in a long time.

Vice-Director? I wanted to keep this formal if I could. I was cleaning up in the bathroom before getting into bed with Tory.

Reah, Ry says that you were out half the night when Grish died. He says he doesn't think you had anything to do with his death, but that you might know how he died. I'd like that information, please, to put in the case file.

I stood rooted to the bathroom floor for ticks, trying to form words to tell Lendill Schaff how Grish had died without getting the reptanoids into more trouble. *He died of snakebite,* I finally handed Lendill the truth. I just wasn't going to give the complete truth.

And you know it was a snake bite because? Lendill left the question hanging.

Because I saw the snake that bit him. Watched it crawl in and then crawl out. Satisfied?

What kind of snake?

No idea. What kind of snakes are local?

Three that I can tell—that are poisonous, anyway. Field vipers, white-mouthed adders and lion snakes, Lendill replied. *I think he was looking the information up on his comp-vid.*

Do any of those have a black pattern on their scales?

Only the lion snake.

Then it must be that one, I said. *Black, teardrop patterns, one end to the other.*

That's a lion snake all right. Lendill sent a mental sigh. *And the death* is quick—*you only have a few ticks to administer antivenin. Grish probably didn't live long.*

So, no pain or thrashing about in terror?

No—it happens too quickly, Reah.

Too bad, I returned.

I see you didn't like Grish.

He was a murderer of innocents, Lendill.

Reah, I have a question for you.

What is it, Vice-Director?

Will you marry me?

hat's wrong with her? Lendill demanded. Tory had heard Reah hit the bathroom floor. Lendill was sending mindspeech to both Tory and Ry the moment he failed to get a response from Reah.

Out cold, Tory replied, slapping Reah's cheek lightly. "Reah? Reah baby, what's wrong?" Ry stood over Tory, unsure what to do. He didn't want to ask for a physician—that could be trouble.

Let me know if I should send someone, Lendill instructed his operatives. Lendill considered contacting Karzac—the healer could get in and out without raising any suspicion. Lendill just didn't want the tongue-lashing Karzac was likely to hand out afterward.

She's coming around, Tory sent. Lendill breathed a relieved sigh.

*Tell her—*Lendill began—*tell her that I'm serious. About what I said to her. Tell her I want to talk to her about it when she gets back. Tell her that it's making me crazy.*

I'll give her the message. Tory cut off the communication.

~

Tory was washing my face with a cloth that Ry had handed to him when I came around. Had I truly fainted when Lendill Schaff had—no. He couldn't have asked that. Couldn't have. Not with the way he'd treated me.

"Back, now, avilepha?" Tory was brushing back what little hair I had with the washcloth.

Ry knelt to take a look for himself. I felt embarrassed.

"Lendill says to tell you he was serious," Tory said. "What did he ask you?"

"Nothing," I said, trying to rise. Tory got to his feet first, then pulled me up. Ry stood, too.

"Whatever it was, he said it was driving him crazy," Tory went on. "And he wants to talk to you about it as soon as you get back."

"Is there any way to not go back?" I asked sarcastically.

"Reah, he gets on my nerves too, sometimes," Tory soothed. "But he's good at his job. He has to be."

"Don't ask her to let some of that go—not yet anyway," Ry countered. "We haven't been treated like that. Em-pah is still in a snit over it."

"Em-pah?" I didn't understand who Ry was talking about.

"Grampa Wylend," Ry gave one of his heart-stopping grins.

"Oh." What did Wylend have to do with all this? He'd been there when I woke after the whole shooting and claiming incident. Karzac had sent him away.

My comp-vid was beeping when Tory herded me back to the bedroom. Teeg was calling. Tory and Ry left the bedroom.

"Teeg?" I saw his face and wanted to cry. Only then did I realize how much I missed him. Lendill's Schaff's words had unsettled me, too—how was I supposed to react to a marriage proposal from someone who probably didn't care anything about me? Where had that come from? And I couldn't say a word to anyone, least of all Teeg. I wanted to, though. I wanted to skip away to where he was, wrap my arms around his neck and tell him all my troubles. Instead, we were worlds apart, speaking through a comp-vid.

"Reah, sweetheart." The half-smile Teeg offered was doing funny things to my insides. We talked about Grish and his death. We talked about the planting and pending harvest in six eight-days. We talked about a lot of things. Teeg brought up something that I hadn't considered, though. I knew I hadn't seen Delvin and a couple of Arvil's other wizards for a few days. Arvil hadn't told me what they were doing.

"They've been here, gathering several courtesans to take there," Teeg informed me. "Reah, don't trust any of them." My eyebrows lifted in alarm at his comment. I knew not to trust Delvin or the others—was this a ploy to get rid of us, just as Arvil was getting close to harvesting his dream?

"Arvil had me send out invitations, too, Reah—to all his business associates. It'll coincide with the harvest. Do I need to tell you to be careful?"

"No." I ducked my head. I had to be careful every moment. I was going to go to Farzi, too, and tell him what Teeg had told me. He and his brothers could help me keep watch.

Teeg terminated the call after saying he loved me. Well, I loved him, too.

Arvil's holding a formal meeting here with his business associates—Teeg told me he sent out invitations, I sent the mindspeech to Tory and Ry when I was finished talking with Teeg.

Does that mean we're staying here until the harvest? Ry asked.

I don't know, I returned. *Arvil hasn't said anything to me, but then he didn't tell me about the big meeting either. He's bringing several courtesans—Delvin and two other wizards went to pick them out. Teeg told me to watch all of them.*

Something's up, Tory agreed.

Delvin wants what Arvil has—he was lying when he said that he didn't know what Haral was up to. I was pouting as I sent the mindspeech.

You can tell when somebody's lying? Tory was staring at me.

Yes. I crossed my arms over my chest and the pout got bigger. *I think he's bringing those girls to help him get what he wants. Those other wizards—I don't think they understand how ambitious Delvin has become. He'll do just about anything to get what he wants, including sacrificing his best friends.* Bel came to mind.

He doesn't have the intelligence or experience to run Arvil's empire, Ry snorted aloud. *He has no idea about the business end of things. If all he can do is sneak around trying to undermine people, with the occasional murder here and there, the best he'll become is somebody's underling—which is exactly what he is. Even if he kills Arvil, there are too many others out there who would have his liver for breakfast. The Hardlows would kill him without thinking about it.*

I shook my head, still trying to reconcile the wizard I'd met on Mandil with the wizard I knew now. It was as if he were two different people. *That doesn't mean he can't do damage along the way,* I said. *He'll come after me and he may go after Teeg, to see if he can worm his way into Arvil's good graces.*

Now's the time I wish I had compulsion, Tory grumbled mentally.

Delvin and his two wizard buddies returned the following day with six courtesans. Arvil took two of the women with him when he went to bed, the other four went with the Hardlows and their warlocks. Farzi wasn't happy at all with those arrangements.

"We hear from workers in fields—they say that Grish staff-those that left, are talking about returning to cause trouble," he grumbled to me as I poured out juice for both of us.

"Does Arvil or the Hardlows know about this?" I stared at Farzi.

"Do the Hardlows know about what?" Astralan walked into the kitchen.

"There's a rumor going around that Grish's old staff wants to organize and cause trouble," I said. "I don't know what kind of trouble, or if it's anything more than rumor."

"Why don't you check on that? Tell me if you find anything," Astralan got out a glass and waited for me to pour juice for him, too.

"I will." I nodded. "But I'll probably have to go into town to do it—those people are there unless I miss my guess."

Astralan shrugged and grinned. I shrugged right back.

"Farzi," I jerked my head toward the kitchen door that led to the patio outside. Farzi came with me, carrying his glass of juice.

"Farzi, I talked to Teeg last night—he says to keep an eye on the women that came in today. I don't know what he suspects, but he suspects something," I whispered as we walked along the cobbled stone trail that led to the barns. "I think we should watch Delvin and the others, too. Delvin was lying when he said that he didn't know what Haral was up to."

"I suspect this as well," Farzi said. We came to a wood fence, so we climbed to the top of it and sat down. "I think wizard Delvin wants more than he can handle. Not smart," Farzi added. I nodded at his assessment. "My brothers and I—poison has no effect. We live many times because of this." Farzi snorted and looked away.

"Somebody tried to poison you in the past?" I was shocked, although I shouldn't have been.

"Many times. We make poison. Others have no effect on us. I tell you this because Haral had poison. Poison also woman's weapon of choice if she is not strong."

"You think Delvin and those women look to poison us? What would be the easiest way to do that?"

"In food or drink, our Reah." Farzi had called me *our Reah*. I think he meant his and the other reptanoids. I didn't mind the title. I nodded. The same thing had occurred to me. I sent mindspeech to Ry.

Reah? His question came back.

Ry, can you put a shield or a guard or something on the kitchen, so we'll know if anybody tries to poison the food or drinks?

Ry didn't answer for several ticks. When he did, he shocked me.

Em-pah Wylend is on his way with Dad.

What? I almost shrieked my question aloud.

Meet us in the pantry, Ry ordered. I hauled Farzi along with me and met Ry in the pantry. Wylend Arden and Erland Morphis appeared only ticks later.

"Here." Wylend handed a fine gold necklace to me, one to Ry and smiled when he handed one to Farzi. Farzi stared at Wylend.

"Farzi," I cautioned, "you may not tell this tale to any except yours."

Farzi was nodding, struck speechless, I think. Wylend looked as if he'd been at High Court or something, he was dressed so finely. He also had a gold band settled around his head, with jewels winking in it. He was King of Karathia and looked the part.

"These," Erland explained, "will tell you whether your food has been poisoned. Here's an extra for Tory, just in case." Erland handed another necklace to Ry.

"That must be extremely helpful," I muttered, slipping the chain over my head and settling the small, jeweled charm inside my shirt. Farzi watched and did the same.

"I would do this and many other things for you, my darling." Wylend leaned down to kiss me. Now I was the one struck speechless. Wylend and Erland disappeared just as quickly as they came.

When I regained some of my sense, I discovered that Ry was grinning widely. I wanted to smack him. "Who was that?" Farzi mumbled.

"Farzi, that was the King of Karathia," I whispered. Farzi's eyes grew even wider.

I learned just how effective the jewels were the next day—someone had poisoned the flour during the night, causing my jewel to send a slight jolt to my skin the moment I touched the canister in the kitchen. I dumped the flour, then went to the pantry to look for more. There wasn't any, so I skipped from there to the city, bought more and was back before anyone suspected. If Delvin wanted to pin the poisonings on me, then he needed to think again. I just wanted to catch whoever had done this and turn them over to Astralan or one of the others. I did pay close attention though, to anyone not eating the hotcakes I served for breakfast. Delvin, Carthin, all six women and the rest of Arvil's wizards refused. They were all in on it. Tory, Ry and I had a brief mental conversation over that.

Arvil wanted to inspect the fields after breakfast, so he and a few others went. Farzi, becoming even more helpful, asked Darzi and

Chazi to follow Delvin and Arvil's other wizards. Yanzi and Hirzi were discreetly following the women. All reptanoids were going as lion snakes. Farzi appeared grimly determined—he was familiar with poison. I think if anyone his brothers followed made a wrong turn, they'd get poisoned in a more conventional manner.

Nenzi went to his repair shop—he loved that. I made a mental note to put him in charge of Arvil's vehicles on Campiaa—if any of us ever made it back there. I think I knew even then that if Norian Keef or Lendill Schaff wanted to lock up the reptanoids, they'd have to go through me first.

"Tell us what you know." Ry tossed Grish's former assistant onto the floor at Arvil's feet. We'd gone looking for a conspiracy among Grish's former employees. It wasn't difficult to find.

"You'll pay," the assistant hissed. "We've got more people behind us than you can possibly handle."

"You want to die, don't you?" Astralan was there with his brothers, which meant that Wilffox and Wilffin were also there. They'd taken comfortable chairs in a corner of what used to be Grish's study. It was large, just as Grish's ego had been.

"We will see that you die, instead," the assistant whined. Arvil now had him gripped by the shoulder. The shorter assistant didn't struggle —Delvin, Carthin and Arvil's four other wizards had arrived. I wasn't sure I wanted to watch Delvin and the others kill this one—they might not be as neat about their killing as the warlocks.

"We need to get the information first!" Ry shouted but it was already too late—Carthin had attempted to do what Haral had done for Arvil before—setting the assistant on fire. I walked out before it was all over, it apparently took a while for the man to burn to death and his screams echoed throughout the plantation for almost a quarter click.

"So, what do you think, cook Reah?" Astralan climbed onto the top of the wood rail fence where I sat, gazing toward the fields of newly planted drakus seed. I would have to go back in a very short time—dinner would have to be started soon.

"I think Arvil's wizards got ahead of themselves for a reason, killing that man so fast," I said.

"We think this too—the Hardlows and my brothers."

"Those six women have already tried to poison everybody." My statement made Astralan jerk his head around to stare at me. "Did you notice that none of them ate the hotcakes the other morning?" I asked. "They poisoned the flour. I replaced the tainted flour in the canister before I cooked breakfast. If I find evidence that anyone has tampered with our food or supplies, I won't use it."

"They're not only trying to poison us, but attempting to blame you for it, perhaps?" I looked up at Astralan's face. Did I think he could actually be kind? That answer was no. I'd seen him kill too many times in the short time I'd known him.

"I hadn't thought that far, I guess," I muttered, lowering my gaze.

"Wilffox had his doubts, when Arvil told him that he'd named a young woman and her husband as his heirs. We came to check that out as much as anything else," Astralan informed me. "Honestly, I haven't seen the Hardlows this impressed in a very long time."

"I'm a good cook," I replied stiffly.

"Oh, it's not just that. And if they worried whether Teeg was competent, well, their fears are unfounded. I'll get with my employers. We can make arrangements not to get poisoned again, I think." Astralan hopped off the fence.

"I'll be there in a bit to start dinner," I said, watching the tall warlock walk away from me. I'd listened carefully to everything Astralan said. He hadn't lied. Now, something else was worrying me.

Dinner was roast pork with a glaze, potatoes and new vegetables.

Farzi loves potatoes. I made them with him in mind. He smiled at me when his plate was laid in front of him.

"So, Delvin, I want you and Carthin to go to the city tomorrow and find the other conspirators," Arvil pointed a fork at the two wizards who sat near each other. One of the courtesans sat between them; the other women were scattered along the table. I saw one try to feed Wilffin. He brushed her hand away, much like sending an annoying insect flying off in another direction. Astralan had already had his talk with the Hardlows, looked like.

"More than happy to," Delvin nodded respectfully at Arvil. I wondered then how long Delvin had been working with Grish's former employees, convincing them that they could walk right in and take the plantation back. Even with his and Arvil's other wizards backing them, they still didn't have the firepower the Hardlows' warlocks had. In fact, one or two of them would likely be more than enough. It made me wonder when Delvin was planning to attack.

"Reah can come with us," Delvin grinned. Well, there was the insect in the sugar bowl. Tory cut into his meat more vigorously than necessary—he knew what Delvin was planning just as well as I did, although we hadn't discussed it.

"Reah will stay with me, I am expecting visitors tomorrow," Arvil snapped. Well, the Hardlows had told Arvil what they suspected as well.

"You didn't tell me you were expecting visitors." Delvin was walking a dangerous path, arguing with Arvil. How stupid did he think Arvil was?

"When did you start thinking that I would include you in all my business?" Arvil was very close to killing, I think. His hands weren't on the table or anywhere near it. I had the feeling that a ranos pistol might have been in the waistband of his tailored pants.

"My apologies, Master Arvil." Delvin went back to his food.

"Good. Go to the city tomorrow as I asked—I don't need any of those fools thinking they can become an irritation to me." Arvil went back to his dinner as well.

"Of course, Master Arvil." Carthin's reply was smoother than Delvin's had been.

~

Delvin and Carthin took off right after breakfast the following morning. The same woman who'd sat between them at dinner the night before was going with them. I was worried that they'd ask Nenzi to drive them, but Nenzi had conveniently disappeared. I think Farzi knew something was up, too and sent his youngest brother off to the equipment sheds in record time. If he hadn't, I'd been about to make up some excuse that I needed him for something around the plantation. We still had a few of Grish's old employees around to clean and maintain the lawns. Plus, we had the new workers out in the fields. But I wasn't foolish enough to ask any of them to assist me with anything.

Arvil wasn't lying, either, when he said he was expecting guests. Two men came in by hovercar shortly after Delvin and Carthin left. I was watching Arvil's remaining wizards carefully. Tory and Ry were close behind me wherever I went, but I was invited to a meeting with the two arrivals, Arvil, the Hardlows and Astralan. Ry and Tory were excluded. It didn't matter, I had mindspeech. Anything I heard I could relay immediately if necessary. I did learn, however, that Celestan and Galaxsan had been sent off on an errand of their own by the Hardlows.

Arvil had asked for the rum and fruit drinks I made—he was just as fond of them as his brother had been, I think. I'd mixed a batch before the meeting started. Ry had given me a sly grin as he helped carry them into Grish's old study before hurrying out. I sat in a chair near Arvil, the Hardlows took the sofa nearby, leaving two chairs for our guests.

"This is Berthias and Windelin," Arvil introduced the two men to me. Both shook my hand before taking their seats. Berthias was short and thin—not much taller than I, with watery brown eyes and a thatch of black hair. His nose and lips were thin as well, giving me the image of a burrowing animal. Windelin was taller and heavier, although he wasn't fat. Windelin looked as if he got regular exercise. He had light-brown hair and green eyes that darted nervously, as if he wanted to know about everything going on around him. His features were more regular than Berthias', too.

"These gentlemen are our contacts from the Alliance," Arvil was nearly beaming. Well, he'd managed to break into Grish's records to find their names. I expected no less, in all honesty. And contact was a mild term. I had no doubt that these men had made it possible for Grish to smuggle contraband and who knew what else, straight into the Alliance.

It gave me the idea that they worked together, somehow. One was likely an official at the nearest Alliance distribution center, the other had to work in shipping and receiving. Everything had to be inspected before heading anywhere into the Alliance. Zephili was an Alliance world—the Alliance didn't do business outside the Alliance. Zephili had only belonged for around a hundred fifty turns or so. Long enough for Grish to get his claws into these two and bribe them to keep his illicit activities quiet.

We spent the morning hammering out the amount of payment Berthias and Windelin would receive for allowing the drakus seed to get sent through their station. Only Arvil never mentioned it was drakus seed. I had a feeling that Berthias and Windelin thought it was more of what Grish had been sending through—the poppy drugs and such. Neither Arvil nor the Hardlows led them to believe otherwise, merely telling the two Alliance employees that Grish had died of heart failure (Arvil even provided a copy of the physician's statement). Arvil made them believe that he and the Hardlows were Grish's named heirs and that was the end of it. An agreement was reached and Arvil made both happy by upping their percentage. The meeting was almost over when I received mindspeech from Tory.

Reah?

What?

Reah, it looks like half the city is burning to the ground.

~

If Arvil wanted to send a warning to his remaining wizards, this was the way to do it. Delvin and Carthin's crisped bodies were dumped on Grish's wide front porch. "Well, that ends our little takeover problem, now doesn't it?" Arvil sounded positively gleeful. I felt ill. Tory was trying to calm me down through mindspeech—I wanted to find a powder room and heave. The sight and accompanying stench made my stomach churn.

Farzi, Perzi and Yanzi came to stand beside me—Tory couldn't put his hands on me. Farzi did, instead. He even came with me when Celestan delivered information in the meeting we attended later. Delvin had been behind the impending revolt. The woman who'd gone with him had been killed right away; Celestan and Galaxsan just hadn't bothered to transport her body back with Delvin and Carthin's. None of the other women said a word.

"It has been brought to my attention," Arvil was now looking at the women who sat together on a sofa, "that someone tried to poison us. I have the vids." Arvil held up a chip. "Care to see it, or do you want to confess now and save me the trouble?"

I'd never bothered to learn any of their names. I also hadn't realized that there were cameras inside the kitchen. Thank goodness there weren't any in the pantry, and those in the kitchen were vid only, with no sound. Grish hadn't bothered with upgrades. When the women refused to admit to anything, Arvil played the vid. I saw at least three of the women, one of whom was their dead co-conspirator, placing a powdery substance inside the flour canister. I was more than thankful it showed me dumping out the flour and then walking into the pantry to get more. If I'd skipped away to buy flour while still inside the kitchen, Arvil might have tried to kill me, too. I'd skipped from inside the pantry, after learning there wasn't any more flour inside it. I schooled my face into the best non-expression I could.

Reah, you have to stay or Arvil will think you're weak, Tory sent mindspeech later. Arvil had tied all five women to the rail fence Astralan and I had sat on only the day before, and then blindfolded them. He'd then accepted a ranos pistol from one of the warlocks and shot each of the women in the head from close range. A ranos pistol from only a hand or two away will blow a large melon into microscopic fragments. Every one of those bodies was slumped against the fence, headless and bloody, when Arvil was done.

If his remaining wizards had any thought as to their potential sentence if Arvil found them guilty of conspiracy with Delvin, they were all gulping nervously now. I knew they knew about it, I just didn't know how much they knew or how far they'd gotten involved. Even if Arvil didn't know, I think the Hardlows and their warlocks did.

"Reah, baby," Tory's hand was cool against the back of my neck as I vomited the contents of my stomach in my bathroom shortly after the executions. Ry was standing nearby, handing me a cold, wet cloth. Of course, my comp-vid was going off right at that moment. Tory moved back and Ry handed it to me. Teeg was calling again.

"Teeg, I'm a little busy right now," I managed to gasp before dry heaving again.

"Reah, I've gotten communication from Arvil so I know what happened."

"You didn't see it happen, I did," I muttered.

"Sweetheart, come on. Wash your face and stand up. You can't show them any weakness."

"Teeg, go away," I moaned.

"Reah, get up and walk out of there now. You can't do this."

"Teeg, someday we'll have a talk about this, all right?" I hit the terminate call button and the screen went blank.

"Come on, he's right." Tory came back and lifted me off the floor.

I'm going to slap Lendill Schaff into next eight-day, I sent the mental grumble to Ry and Tory before rinsing out my mouth and stalking out of my suite.

I cooked dinner as if nothing had happened. The only good thing to come from all this was there were fewer to cook for. Farzi was watching me closely, however. Nenzi, too, as were their brothers. Arvil wanted another sit-down with me after dinner. I wanted to huddle in my room. Even though the courtesans had all been trying to kill me, their deaths were too horrible to contemplate.

"Reah, I haven't failed to see how Farzi and the others act around you." That had me jerking my head up to stare at Arvil. What was he getting at? Was he accusing me of something?

"Reah, what I'm saying is that I want Farzi and the others to act as your bodyguards. I'm taking Tory and Ry."

"That's fine," I said. It was, although I'd miss Tory at night. Tory and Ry could watch out for Arvil and listen for his deepest secrets. Honestly, if Lendill Schaff and the ASD didn't have an inescapable grip on me, I'd have skipped away and Arvil would never have found me after the killings earlier.

Tory and Ry replaced Delvin and Carthin in Arvil's suite later. He had three bedrooms inside his suite. Tory and Ry got the rooms leading up to the nice, large one belonging to Arvil. Farzi, Nenzi and the other reptanoids moved into the two smaller bedrooms inside my suite. If I worried about spending my nights alone, I shouldn't have. Farzi and Nenzi crawled into bed with me as lion snakes.

"You should not worry that we try to couple," Farzi told me the second night. "When we were made, we were neutered."

"When we not turn out like they want," Nenzi added sadly.

"Nenzi, I am so sorry." I pulled his head against mine.

"We learn to deal with this," Chazi said. He never talked much, like most of his brothers.

"I still love Reah." Nenzi had his arms wrapped around me.

"And I still love you." I kissed Nenzi's cheek. "I think we have a lot in common, don't you?"

"Yes. We know Reah different when we see her first time," Perzi nodded his head.

"And we keep secrets," Farzi said.

"I know." I placed a hand around the back of Farzi's neck and bumped his forehead with mine.

∾

Two days later, Nenzi drove me to the city, accompanied by Farzi, Yanzi and Perzi. We saw what the two warlocks had done when we arrived. Entire housing districts had been burned to the ground. The warlocks had hit a centralized natural gas station that still supplied fuel to an ancient portion of the city, none of which had been upgraded to solar power. The resulting fire had spread swiftly, and some residents hadn't made it out before the fire swept through. So many homes burned at the same time that the outdated fire departments nearby had been unable to handle it.

I'd heard some of the news vids—they were blaming the fire on a huge gas explosion, with no explanation as to the cause. If Celestan and his brother had found a way to do that so that fingers wouldn't be pointed in their direction, I had to marvel at their efficiency. Just because Zephili belonged to the Alliance didn't mean they couldn't have crime or uprisings. I was surprised that Lendill hadn't sent anyone in to investigate. Or perhaps he had and left me out of that loop.

"They knew where to hit this, didn't they?" Lendill examined the crater that formerly housed the hub where natural gas was pumped in and then sent through smaller pipelines into an older housing district. This one still had natural gas lines instead of the upgraded solar power relays. The pipes were insulated well—they should have been impervious to anything short of a very large bomb blast. Of course, nobody had factored in powerful warlocks when the thing had been designed.

"Yes." Norian crunched over blackened rubble. Surprisingly, only fifteen people died in the explosion and subsequent fires. *But we'll hold off on the true cause of all this until we finish this with San Gerxon and the Hardlows,* he added mentally. *We'll just say our findings are inconclusive and we're still investigating.*

Lendill nodded, not sending a reply. He considered sending mindspeech to Reah but held back. His last communication with her hadn't gone very well. Had he known it, Reah was less than half a tick away from him at that very moment.

❧

"We worry about two fields," Farzi informed me as we selected fruits and vegetables to buy for the plantation.

"Why?" I turned to him while sniffing a melon. I could always tell the ripe ones if I did that.

"They dry out—plants look brown though we water often," he said.

"You don't know why it's happening?" I placed the melon in a basket Nenzi held out.

"We have not the explanation." Farzi was eyeing the potatoes. I gathered several large ones and added those to the basket.

"I'll bake these for you," I promised, getting a smile from Farzi. We picked up butter and plenty of sour cream, all the vegetables and fruit we needed, plus several kinds of meats. The only thing truly missing here was good, fresh fish. Frozen could be had readily, but what they passed off as fresh fish wasn't. I bought some frozen shrimp, though. It was probably a good idea to keep Arvil as happy as we could and the soup he liked might be a good start.

"Can I come to the fields with you tomorrow?" I asked Farzi. He seemed to be Arvil's expert on growing crops.

"Of course," Farzi seemed pleased that I'd asked. I wanted to see these plants for myself. Perhaps there was some sort of blight, insect or animal that was responsible. If nature could give a helping hand in taking out the drakus seed crop, all the better.

"Farzi, what do you know about what we're growing?" The time had come to find out.

"Powerful drug. Should not be used," Farzi muttered. "Arvil wants, so we do. He give me home on Urdolus after first successful crop. I hope then he leave us there to live. Not to be," Farzi sighed. "Now, all gone."

"I'm sorry you lost your home, Farzi," I hugged him. We'd lost more than that. Xiri had died there, as had Arvil's remaining family.

We were unloading our purchases into the kitchen later when I learned that Arvil had been folded to Campiaa to take care of business. Astralan, who'd moved Arvil, Ry and Tory to Campiaa, had brought Teeg back with him as Arvil's replacement.

You didn't even give me a warning? I sent mindspeech to Tory. I could feel his mental shrug.

No time, it just happened, Tory replied. Teeg stood in the doorway to the kitchen, a huge grin on his face as I cut off the mindspeech with Tory. Honestly, multiple mates definitely had its downside.

Farzi, Nenzi and my other reptanoid bodyguards stood aside as Teeg swept me up in his arms and kissed me breathless. I wrapped my arms around his neck and buried my head against his shoulder. Farzi and Nenzi would have to sleep in the rooms with their brothers while Teeg was there.

CHAPTER 13

"This steak sauce is exceptional." Stellan was fond of steak, it appeared. I'd found some thick cuts at the market that looked fresh and tender, so we were serving those with a sauce and Farzi's baked potatoes, plus a green vegetable and a nice dessert.

"I'm glad you like it," I said, cutting into my steak. I'd cooked a smaller portion for myself. Teeg was busy eating—I think his mind was on what he intended to do as soon as he could get me away from the table.

"Planning to get me drunk?" I asked. Teeg held a bottle of wine and two glasses in his hands when he slipped into my bedroom later. I think the kitchen had been cleaned in record time. I'd showered and dressed in my nicest lingerie while I waited for Teeg to have a brief meeting with the Hardlows and their warlocks.

"Absolutely," he gave me a heart-stopping grin.

"This is nice," he trailed a finger along the black lace covering my breasts.

"You picked it out."

"I have exceptional taste." We didn't even open the wine, it wasn't needed. Teeg's hands are strong and firm and he takes his time at first until he makes me crazy. After a certain point, I want him so badly that he could do anything he wanted with me and it would be all right, including nipping my inner thighs. That gave me a climax, all by itself.

"I know what my Reah wants," Teeg whispered against my mouth as his body slid over mine. He did. As much or more than Aurelius or Tory.

~

Teeg had to worry with Wilffox, Wilffin and the warlocks while Farzi, Nenzi and the others took me to the drakus seed fields the following morning. "See?" Farzi lifted a branch of one of the plants. The leaves were dry, just as if they hadn't been watered. Except they had. In fact, the ground was still damp from the watering earlier.

"None of the other fields are like this?" I peered into the distance—it would take half a click just to walk to the opposite end of this field.

"One more on other side," Farzi pointed in front of us. I started walking through the field with Nenzi, Farzi and six other reptanoids following me. It wasn't particularly hot this early in the morning, but the farther I walked along, the hotter I felt until I thought my insides would melt. What did this mean? I stopped still and looked at Farzi. "Farzi, do you feel hot right now?" I asked, my voice sounding breathless.

"No, our Reah. Are you not well?" Farzi came and put a hand to my forehead. "Your forehead does not feel like fever."

"I don't feel like a fever either—not there, anyway," I said. "I feel it, here." I pointed to my chest. "There's no pain," I was holding Farzi off; I think he was about to fling me inside Nenzi's hovercar and rush me back to the plantation. "It just feels really warm." More than anything, I wanted to contact Gavril and ask him what he thought. Bouncing ideas around with him often led to better conclusions. He never looked at me as if I were crazy when I said something, and this was definitely sounding crazy.

"I want to walk a little farther," I said. Farzi didn't want me to; I could see that right away. He didn't argue with me, moving along beside me silently as I strode farther and farther into a field of drakus seed that stretched as far as the eye could see. I knew immediately when I reached the warmest spot inside the field. The plants were almost completely brown around me, but even without that visual confirmation, I would have known. Closing my eyes, I concentrated on the heat itself.

"Our Reah, are you well?" Farzi eventually reached me from where I'd gone.

"Farzi," I smiled at him, curling my hand around his neck and drawing him close.

"Reah, I say again, are you well?"

"Yes, Farzi, I am well," I assured him. "Now, you said before that you knew I was different when you met me."

"Yes. We not know how, but we know." Nenzi had come up beside me to give me a hug.

"Then I ask you not to be frightened when I show you what I am. I promise that I also recognize my friends and enemies when I turn."

"I'll be big," I warned before undressing and concentrating on the turn. I sat on the ground to make the change so I wouldn't tower over my friends.

Eight faces were turned upward as my larger Thifilatha loomed over them, even sitting down. "Our Reah," Nenzi was breathless as he gazed at me in wonder.

"I won't hurt you," I promised. "Ever," I added.

"Stretch out wings?" That was Hirzi asking. I stretched out my wings. The sun glinted off the gold of my scales and the membranes of my jointed wings.

"What is our Reah?" Yanzi knelt down before me.

"High Demon," I said. "Those things that come and attack us are not demons. They are the young of a monster. I would know if they were demons." I concentrated on turning back to myself. Nenzi helped me dress. "Were you afraid?" I asked him.

"No," he said. "Our Reah is a queen."

"No, Nenzi. I'm not a queen," I shook my head. "But I thank you for the compliment."

"Your skin scaled—like ours." Farzi seemed happy about that.

"Yes it is." I smiled at him.

"We are kin." Perzi wanted that to be more than anything, I think.

"We are kin," I tapped his chest. "Here, if nowhere else."

～

"What did you learn?" Teeg asked as soon as we walked inside the kitchen. He'd been waiting on us. I barely had time to put lunch together.

"Some of the plants look like they're dying, as if they're not getting enough water," I said. "But they are. The fields around those two are doing fine. The ground is damp and still the plants are brown."

"Only two fields, not a lot to worry about unless it spreads," Teeg brushed it off. I left it at that. I didn't tell him about my other feelings regarding the dying fields I'd wandered through earlier. I hadn't even told Farzi and the others what I was thinking. That was a secret I was holding onto as long as I could.

～

Berthias Tayde swallowed hard as the Director and Vice-Director of the ASD sat watching him squirm in his seat. "So," Norian Keef finally said, "you weren't aware that drakus seed was about to be funneled through your station?"

"N-no. Not at all," Berthias was shaking his head violently. Berthias knew if he were convicted of transporting drakus seed, he'd never see freedom again. They'd pulled Berthias in first, but Windelin was waiting outside, chained to a steel bar. Nothing would get either of them out of this.

"But you admit to allowing the poppy drug to go through, in addition to a few other illegal items, such as wizard's charms, stolen artifacts and such?"

"Y-yes."

"So, you thought that was all right, did you, allowing illegal substances to spread across the Alliance?" Norian's arms were crossed angrily over his chest.

"I th-thought it was harmless."

"Poppy drug harmless?" Lendill Schaff asked.

"W-well, mostly harmless."

"Ah. And how much were you paid to think it was mostly harmless?"

"Not enough." Berthias wished he'd never heard of Grish or any of his heirs.

"The first truth he's given us so far," Lendill observed.

"What are you going to do with me? Or Windelin? He has a family."

"Not anymore," Lendill pointed out.

"Unless," Norian stroked his chin a little, watching Berthias with a speculative expression on his face.

"Unless what?" Berthias pleaded. "Please tell me there's a way out of this."

"Well, a lighter sentence might be arranged, as long as you do everything we say." Lendill grinned nastily at Berthias.

"Reah?" Astralan came into the kitchen as I was preparing breakfast.

"Lord Astralan?" The honorific made him smile. He was handsome when he smiled, but I wasn't going to say that. I didn't know what to think about the warlocks most of the time. After all, Celestan and Galaxsan had gone to the city nearby and placed a well-aimed power blast at a natural-gas junction, killing fifteen people. Maybe they'd hit most of the traitors Delvin rounded up for his revolt, but I had no way to determine whether that was true or not. Either way, I didn't understand it.

"Reah, it's too bad Arvil found you first. Wilffox would have paid you whatever you asked if you'd come to work for him."

Wanting to ask him if that's what it took—a really big payday to do what he did, I just stared at the warlock for a few moments instead.

"Well, what is it they say about being in the wrong place at the wrong time?" I shrugged.

"Or the right one at the right time." Astralan was still smiling.

"I suppose it's all a matter of perspective," I said. "What do you want for breakfast?" Breakfast had turned into an informal affair, with people wandering in whenever they rose for the day. I was thankful the servants had their own quarters and took care of their own meals.

"Astralan." Teeg walked in, nodding to the warlock.

"I'm glad you're here, Teeg—I was thinking about going to the slopes somewhere. Want to come along?"

"That sounds good. Reah?"

I looked at Teeg before heaving a sigh. I didn't want to leave the reptanoids alone. Not with the Hardlows and any one of their warlocks.

"I can tell by looking at you that you won't even consider it," Teeg said.

"You should go, I know you like snowboarding," I said. "I need to get some things done around here."

"She won't go without Farzi and the others," Teeg said, making me want to throw the stack of hotcakes I'd just placed on the bar at him.

"Bring them," Astralan was laughing now.

"Only if they want to come," I had my hands on my hips. That made him laugh harder. That's how we ended up on a ski slope somewhere, Teeg, Astralan, Stellan, all eight reptanoids and me.

"I never do anything like this before," Farzi was watching Teeg go down the slope on his board. The two warlocks had skis and they were adept at going down the hill.

"I've only done it once before and I fell more often than I stayed on my feet," I said. "But you're really quick and limber—I think you can do this," I encouraged Farzi. The poor man had probably never had fun in his life. I'd seen him smile only a few times since I'd met him. Nenzi and the others, too. Actually, Nenzi was watching all the other skiers and snowboarders in fascination.

"Just watch your ankles—that's what gave me the most trouble," I said. Farzi nodded, hopped his skis to the edge like an expert and then dropped over it. I watched in amazement as Farzi went down the hill —he didn't fall once and before he got to the bottom, he looked like a professional. Well, something to be said for snake shapeshifters, I suppose. Nenzi and the others followed Farzi down, with almost the same results. They were all good, right from the start. I was learning all over again and Teeg was laughing after I fell the second time just before I reached the bottom.

"Very funny," I smacked him on the arm when I got up and slid the last few blocks down.

Before the day was out, Farzi and his brothers were all talking about buying ski equipment. They knew there was an artificial slope on Campiaa and they wanted to do this again. I just shook my head in wonder. Teeg got my neck in the crook of his elbow and was pulling me close to kiss the top of my head when I turned my equipment in.

"I'm glad you had fun," I was laughing at Nenzi; he was talking as fast as he could while helping me carry plates to the dining hall.

When we arrived, Teeg was talking with someone on his comp-vid. It was Arvil, asking Teeg to help him deal with a situation. Someone had killed Arvil's assistant and things were looking grim on Campiaa for the moment. I think my heart stopped momentarily and Nenzi stopped talking in midsentence. Stellan was planning to take Teeg away immediately, and then stay on Campiaa in case Teeg and Arvil needed someone with power. Somehow, I got the idea that Arvil's four remaining wizards were implicated in all of this. I should have known better, thinking that they'd be too frightened to do anything after Delvin and Carthin were killed.

"Reah, everything will be fine, sweetheart." Teeg rose from his seat, as did Stellan when Teeg finished talking with Arvil. Both of them disappeared right before my eyes.

"Reah, sit down and eat," Astralan ordered as soon as his brother had taken Teeg away. Nenzi gave me a swift look and he and I sat down to eat. The reptanoids and I were stuck on Zephili with Wilffox and Wilffin Hardlow, plus three of their four warlocks. I had no idea how that was going to end, which left me frightened and feeling cold.

~

Vice-Director, Tory and I are on Campiaa with Arvil San Gerxon. Teeg, Reah's other mate is here too, since those four idiot wizards belonging to Arvil killed his assistant and tried to get into Arvil's main command-computer. Tory got one of them when he tried to come after us; the other three got away. Ry was sending mindspeech to Lendill after a very busy and stressful afternoon.

Where are the other three wizards and where is Reah? Lendill's voice seemed more concerned than usual.

We think the other three are holed up in one of Arvil's casinos down the street—the situation is somewhat grim I believe, since they're holding guests hostage. When Teeg gets here, we're supposed to go down there and take care of this. Reah is still on Zephili with the Hardlows and three of their warlocks.

Reah is with the Hardlows? Alone?

Yes.

I'll send mindspeech to her. Lendill cut off communication with Ry.

What did he say, bro? Tory was fretting over Reah, that's why Ry had contacted Lendill to begin with. Ry and Tory both were belting on an assortment of weapons, preparing to go with Arvil and his army of guards to do battle with Arvil's three remaining wizards.

He said he'd send mindspeech to Reah. Come on, bro, Teeg just got here with Stellan. Ry led the way out of his and Tory's quarters.

"If you'll provide the distraction; none of these can carry themselves away, they don't hold the skills," Stellan said to those gathered around the kitchen island in Arvil's palace, "then I can get in there and take care of them while they're looking elsewhere."

"They can throw blasts at us," Arvil looked grim and angry. "So we should stay just outside their range while we shoot."

"What about the guests?" Ry asked.

"Fuck the guests," Arvil growled. "They know Campiaa is dangerous. They come here anyway."

"Let me try to get inside from the roof," Teeg suggested. "Stellan can get in his way, I'll go through the hatch in the roof. I have a key, after all," Teeg pulled an electronic key from his pocket and dangled it in his fingers. "This fits all the emergency exits in Arvil's buildings, in case the builders and maintenance workers have to get in. Those three only think they have all the keys." Teeg's smile was grimly determined. He also patted the ranos pistol he had stuck in his belt. "Between Stellan and me, I think we can take them out if they're focused on your frontal assault."

"They stole the keys to the emergency exits?" Tory was amazed there was enough brain cells between the three wizards to even think of that. Of course, the one he'd killed couldn't fathom why his wizardry hadn't worked when Tory grabbed him by the throat and tossed him through a plate-glass window from Arvil's office on the third floor.

"All of them, except the one Teeg holds, when they broke into my office," Arvil growled. "They also got the codes to all the accounts from my casinos and were about to empty all my funds. I got that stopped before they could get too much out; I have the overriding code, after all. They were hoping I wouldn't discover this treachery until they were far from here. They had a shuttle waiting at the station. It's too bad Tory, Ry and I got back sooner than they expected from our trip up the mountain. No doubt that little emergency was hatched out by them as well." Arvil checked the charge on his ranos pistol before jamming it into his gun belt.

"Everybody ready?" Teeg asked. They nodded. "Let's go," he said and Stellan folded them to the casino down the street.

Reah? Lendill's voice came to me as I was preparing for bed.

Vice-Director? I know, my mental voice sounded sullen. I wasn't in the best of moods and frightened didn't begin to describe how I felt.

I hear you're there by yourself, with the Hardlows and three of their warlocks.

I am. It's such a happy place to be, I returned.

Reah, I don't think they'll hurt you, they're still too far into this with Arvil San Gerxon. I think you'll be safe, breah-mul. Don't do anything foolish, but stand up for yourself. These people will exploit any weakness they see. Don't show it to them.

I wanted to tell him it was easy for him to say that, he was light-years away and most likely in a safe place at the moment. I had no idea what the Hardlows might be like with nobody else around. *Fine,* I sent instead. *Anything else you want, Vice-Director?*

Nothing for now, keep me informed. Lendill cut off the communication. I finished brushing my teeth and walked out of my bathroom. Farzi and Nenzi were already in my bed as lion snakes. Their brothers were guarding the door into my suite. I think if anyone had walked in that first night while I was so frightened, they would have been bitten first and questioned later, while they were dying, of course.

~

"Come out and I may let you live!" Arvil shouted from behind the barrier in front of *The Moontide Casino.*

"You're crazy if you think we'll believe anything you say," one of the wizards shouted back. "We have hostages. We'll let them live if you'll stand back and give us safe passage to the space station."

"No deal," Arvil shouted back. "You think I care about any of them?"

True to his word, Teeg went through the emergency exit on top of The Moontide while Arvil shouted at the wizards below. Pocketing the electronic key, Teeg stealthily made his way through the crawlspace next to the electrical conduits. He knew where all the connections were. If he wanted to plunge the entire casino into darkness, it would only take the flip of a few switches. He was heading there now to do exactly that.

~

Stellan folded inside one of the casino restrooms. Any remaining security inside the casino had moved the guests toward the back of the building. The doors all over the casino were electronically locked, thanks to the keys the wizards held. The windows couldn't be penetrated by the weapons the guards held either—Arvil had ordered special glass because he didn't want attacks from rivals to come in that way.

"No casualties if you can prevent it," Teeg had instructed Stellan. Stellan nodded at Teeg and went to do his job.

Teeg held the knife he'd brought with him—it was the best he could find and quite sharp. He still could hear Arvil shouting at the wizards from outside as he crept toward the overturned gaming table that the wizards hid behind, holding three female hostages. Teeg knew Arvil didn't give a damn about the hostages, male or female. He would attempt to get them out alive. Teeg could see Stellan on the other side—the warlock had taken short folding jumps from place to place, in order to sneak up on their prey. Teeg nodded to Stellan to stay where he was. Teeg was about to take care of this himself.

"I'm about to start shooting," Arvil shouted. "You think those glass windows will hold up against a ranos pistol? Do you?" Arvil knew they wouldn't, just as the wizards did. Their hostages would only survive one direct blast and then they'd be useless. "Fuck you, answer me!" Arvil screamed.

"Stand down!" Teeg yelled from inside the casino. "We've got them, they're all dead." To prove his point, Teeg walked out of the casino, dragging one of the dead wizards one-handed. The wizard had been nearly decapitated. Teeg carried a bloody hunting knife in his other hand. Stellan followed, dragging the burned and blackened corpses of the other two wizards, dumping them on the decorative flagstones that fronted The Moontide. Teeg dropped his burden and wiped his brow with a sleeve.

"How is everything inside?" Arvil almost hissed the words as he kicked the body Teeg had dropped outside.

"There's a blood trail on the marble, but that should clean up," Teeg said. "All the guests are alive. They killed four guards before the others got out of the way. I've called for medical personnel to come and tend to the hostages."

"How did you manage to do this?" Arvil was quite pleased with Teeg and the warlock.

"They were too occupied with you, Master San Gerxon," Stellan nodded toward Arvil. "That allowed us to sneak up on them. It was easy."

"They were too stupid for words," Arvil muttered, aiming another kick at the dead wizard. "Well, Teeg, this means I need a few more personal guards. We'll put out notices tomorrow. Send my apologies to Reah, but I'll be keeping Tory and Ry as my personal guards. Tory managed to get one of those fuckers by himself. I like that kind of fearlessness."

"I'll let Reah know," Teeg nodded. "Now, with your permission, I think I'd like to clean up. Stellan may want to do the same." Teeg nodded toward Stellan.

"You're right, I would. I'll take us back to Arvil's palace." Stellan disappeared with Teeg, when Arvil gave his approval.

"Well, young man, you'll be getting a raise in pay after tonight." Arvil nodded to Tory. "Now, if you two will help me wrangle my security and get rid of these bodies." Arvil swept inside his casino. Tory and Ry exchanged a look and followed him.

"I know they were hired for you, sweetheart, but we'll find other bodyguards for you." Teeg had wakened me early after I'd spent a restless night. I worried that I'd kept Farzi and Nenzi awake with my tossing and turning. They'd plopped off the bed and went into the other room the minute I answered the comp-vid call.

"Teeg, if I can keep Farzi and some of his brothers, I'll be fine." I raked a hand through my short but growing hair.

"Baby, your hair is growing out, I can see it."

"Teeg, my hair looks like shit right now. Admit it." He was up and freshly washed and dressed; I'd seen that the moment his image appeared on my screen.

"Sweetheart, you always look good to me in the morning." Well, I didn't want to go there. With my limited experience with males, I think any woman would look good to them in the morning.

"You'll be all right where you are for a couple of days. I think Arvil will come back by then. Ry and Tory can be extra security for you when they get back. In the meantime, tell Farzi and the others they have permission to use any force necessary to keep you safe."

"I'll let them know," I sighed, feeling defeated.

"Reah, hold your head up, baby. We're counting on you."

I wanted to tell him that his statement sounded foolish to me. I didn't. "Good-bye, Teeg," I said instead and shut off the transmission.

"Farzi, you and your brothers just got assigned as my bodyguards, since Master Arvil took Tory and Ry," I told them after I'd dressed and brushed my teeth.

"Then we will protect Reah," Farzi nodded.

"Farzi," I went to put my arms around him. I wanted to cry, actually, but I was working hard to hold the tears back.

"Reah, not take this so badly," Farzi's arms were around me and Nenzi was rubbing my back. The others crowded around to touch me somehow.

Later, when I got myself in hand, we went to the kitchen to start breakfast. The reptanoids were served first, and they ate in the kitchen. Astralan wandered in. I gave him a cup of tea while I fixed his plate. He settled down at the island to eat just as the others had.

"I like this—having breakfast made to order when I get up," Astralan sipped his tea with pleasure. I made it just the way he liked it, with milk and honey. "Reah, I know how young you are," he went on, causing me to jerk upright after pulling rolls from the oven. "You don't need to wear that frightened look. None of my brothers are about to jump you because you're here alone."

"Farzi and his brothers are here." I went back to pulling trays of rolls from the oven. I served two to Astralan with some fruit spread. He'd already had his eggs and sliced pork.

"I know. I just don't want to see that look on your face, like we're about to jump out of your closet and attack you."

I wanted to ask him why he was bothering to tell me this. After all, I'd seen him and his brothers operate. Frying people in the middle of the floor wasn't a good way to reassure anyone, in my estimation. And the Hardlows? They'd just as soon kill someone as look at them, from what I'd heard. They liked my cooking. That had kept me safe so far. And Astralan had said that Wilffox would have hired me. Well, Arvil had adopted me. Not the same thing. Not by a long way. I still got shaky every time I remembered how caught in the middle of this I was. I was ASD and the ASD was looking to either kill or imprison all these people. Astralan would do his best to kill me where I stood if I told him that right then.

Wilffox, Wilffin and the other two warlocks wandered in while Astralan was finishing his second cup of tea. They sat down at the island while I handed out plates of food. Talk began about the impending harvest and the reception that Arvil planned. With everything else that had happened, that event had completely escaped my thoughts.

"I think we want a menu with perhaps three items offered," Wilffox said. "I want the yaris fish as one of the choices. Perhaps that special ox roast you make for another and a fowl selection, maybe?"

"Yes, that would be a good cross-section," I agreed. "Will there be any vegetarians?" I had a few things I could put together if that was the case.

"I don't think so," Wilffox looked to his brother. Wilffin was shaking his head. Well, they knew the crime kingpins from their part of the galaxy, I didn't.

"What do you have planned for today?" Wilffox asked.

"I was thinking about going back to those two fields that we were having trouble with—make sure it wasn't spreading to any of the others," I said.

"Sounds good. We'll come along," Wilffin announced.

Nenzi drove us. The fields were the same as before. The plants stunted and brown-leaved, but outside a swath in those two fields, nothing else was affected.

"We might get a partial harvest from these," Wilffox was examining the branch of the plant Farzi showed him. Farzi knew a lot about growing things, as did most of his brothers. Nenzi, though, was the one who was mechanically inclined.

"Yes, and harvest starts on first fields next eight-day," Farzi agreed. I still felt the heat I'd experienced the last time I'd come, I just chose to keep it to myself. No need to alert the Hardlows or their warlocks to that little anomaly.

"Let's go to the barns, then, and check on the shipments of crates and packaging materials," Wilffox suggested. Nenzi was quite happy to drive us everywhere. We went to the barns, a place I hadn't been as yet and looked over pallets and pallets of crates, in addition to boxes and boxes of sealable, waterproof packing material. They weren't concerned with the expense involved to make sure the drug got to its intended recipients. That drug was worth countless Alliance credits when it reached its destination, after all.

"Reah, don't ever touch this shit." Astralan's hand dropped to my shoulder as I gazed at the barn filled with shipping supplies.

"Don't worry," I replied. Farzi gave a quick look at Astralan's hand on my shoulder, but he didn't say anything. That wasn't Farzi's way. If he or any of his brothers wanted someone dead, they'd do it later in the stealthiest and quietest way possible. I wasn't worried about Astralan any longer, and I couldn't say why that was.

We stopped by one of the fields to check on the workers we'd hired. They were spraying weedkill when we arrived. I think they knew not to aggravate any one of us. Farzi spoke to the ones in charge, asking them about the upcoming harvests.

"We have everything ready—the equipment is in good repair," the man nodded toward Nenzi. If I knew Nenzi, that had been a labor of love.

"You'll get a bonus if it's brought in ahead of schedule," Wilffox promised. The man nodded respectfully to both Hardlows. We left shortly after. Time had gotten away from us, so I served lunch by the pool while the plantation staff went about their duties.

"I love these drinks," Wilffin settled on his chaise with a sigh of pleasure. "Too bad I don't have anybody to give me a massage."

If he were hinting, I wasn't about to take that bait. Wilffin could afford the most expensive courtesan anywhere. He was welcome to ask his warlocks to pick one up for him. Astralan offered to find a masseuse.

"Make sure she's pretty," Wilffin waved a hand. He went back to sipping his drink in the early afternoon sun.

Astralan came back later with three women, one of whom was short with pale blonde hair. He sent her in Wilffin's direction. I faded from the pool area, Farzi right behind me. He'd already sent his brothers away earlier.

"They will be having relations out there," Farzi hissed as we walked into the kitchen.

"That's all right, Farzi," I gave him a quick hug. "We'll just stay away."

The courtesans stayed for dinner, playing with Wilffox, Wilffin and the warlocks. "Sweetie," one of them said when I served her food, "You'd be stunning if you let your hair grow out."

"The haircut wasn't my idea," I told her and went on.

"How are things going?" Teeg asked when he called later. He always seemed to catch me when I was brushing my teeth. I'd had to rinse really quick to answer his call.

"Fine," I sighed. "We checked the fields today, and then Astralan brought in three women to keep everybody happy."

"Wilffin didn't bother you, did he?" That question had me raising an eyebrow.

"Only an obscure invitation to give him a backrub," I said. "Astralan brought in the courtesans after that."

"Good. Anything else?"

"Not really. How about you? What happened to the last of Delvin's bunch?"

"Dead. Easy kill. No tourists were hurt. Only lost four security guards."

"Well, it could have been worse," I mumbled, hoping I didn't know any of the dead.

"Definitely," Teeg acknowledged. "I'm going to interview people tomorrow; Arvil wants to replace his entire stable of wizards. You wouldn't believe how many applications we received."

"I'm not surprised—I hear the money's good," I said.

"Want me to buy you something, baby? Since we left you alone?"

"Teeg, I don't need anything."

"Sure you do. You need a dress and some jewelry for that fiasco Arvil has planned. I'll see about getting something for that."

"We're not going to match, are we?" I teased him a little.

"No. Who would do that?" He was grinning at me.

"You'd be surprised," I said. People used to come into Desh's all the time, looking exactly alike. It frightened me.

"Well, I can't give any guarantees over what the others will look like, but I'll make sure we don't match." Teeg ended the call shortly after.

"Ready, our Reah?" Farzi stuck his head inside my door.

"I'm ready," I nodded. He and Nenzi crawled into my bed only a few moments later. I hugged Nenzi's length against me as Farzi coiled up at my back. It made me feel safer to know they were with me.

The crash woke me an hour before dawn. Terrified, I reached over to turn on my bedside lamp. The image that greeted me will perhaps be burned on my brain forever. Wilffin was standing in my doorway with a ranos pistol in one hand, his other arm draped around the blonde courtesan.

CHAPTER 14

illffin and the blonde were barely dressed; Wilffin was waving the pistol and giving me a drunken leer. The woman, however, had a hand clapped over her mouth in terror. All eight lion snake shapeshifters had their heads raised high, prepared to strike if Wilffin and the woman came any closer. The courtesan wasn't the only terrified person there. How was I going to get out of this? I didn't want Wilffin to shoot any of my lion snake protectors, and if Farzi or his brothers bit either of my uninvited guests, then Wilffox would see that they were killed if Wilffin didn't get them first. If Wilffin were allowed to come in as he wanted, I was terrified of what he intended to do. "Farzi, please stay back," my voice shook. Fear for my own safety took a back seat to my fear for the lives of the shapeshifters. At least Wilffin might leave me alive after all it was over.

"Wilffin, you will go back to your bedroom now and make love to this fine woman." Teeg and Astralan were there behind Wilffin somehow. Wilffin blinked at Teeg for only a moment before nodding and pulling the woman away with him. Farzi and the others relaxed visibly the moment Wilffin walked out the door.

"Thank the stars," I muttered, realizing only then I had a death grip on my sheet and blanket.

"Farzi, I'll take things from here," Teeg nodded to the proper lion snake, even. Farzi and his brothers slipped out of my room. "Thank you, Astralan," Teeg nodded toward the warlock.

"No trouble," Astralan said and disappeared.

"Sweetheart, that shouldn't have happened," Teeg settled on the side of my bed. I realized I was trembling uncontrollably when I let go of my covers. "Here, just slide over a little," Teeg scooted me over in the bed. "Now, just lie here with me," Teeg kissed my forehead and pulled me against him. My heart was still pounding when he reached over and turned off the light.

"Reah, just act like it never happened," Teeg told me the following morning. He'd let me sleep late and woke me with a kiss around mid-morning. It made me wonder what the others had done for breakfast.

"They got something from the staff," Teeg murmured against my throat—he was placing kisses there.

"Are you going back to Campiaa?" I was trying to fend him off so I could ask questions.

"Reah, I have to," Teeg nipped my neck. It caused my entire body to flush when he did that.

"But I'm afraid to stay here with them." I was whining, but I was terrified, too.

"Reah, sweetheart, they won't bother you again—I promise." How could he say that? He wasn't the one in the bed the night before, faced with a drunken crime kingpin waving a pistol. "I know you're worried, but I've alerted Astralan and his brothers. They'll watch out for you."

That was fine for him to say—I wasn't paying the warlocks, the Hardlows were. I think they'd do what their employers said, rather than choosing to protect an unimportant woman.

"Let Farzi and his brothers do their job. They and the warlocks will take care of you, sweetheart."

"Fine." Teeg realized he was finally getting what he wanted—my cooperation—both in and out of bed. Still, when Teeg left—Astralan took him back to Campiaa before returning—I watched my back and made sure I was never alone near Wilffin. The three women did stay several days, even after Arvil came back to plan his drakus seed harvest party.

"Here's the menu, pending your approval," I handed my comp-vid to Arvil. He was using Grish's old study, staying in close contact with Teeg and his newly hired assistant. Arvil had brought three new wizards back with him to Zephili—he'd hired them in record time. I was wary of all of them. The bad news was he'd left Ry and Tory with Teeg for the time being. "The wine choices are attached, but we don't have what we need here. Is there any way I can get to Campiaa to buy it?"

"This looks good, Reah. I'll see if Wilffox will lend Astralan to you for a day, just so you can pick up all of this. Bring a full staff of cooks and assistants back with you—as many as you need." Arvil was giving me permission to do whatever I wanted with this. "Will you serve the soup I like?"

"It's there, with the fish choice," I nodded toward the comp-vid.

"I see it. It'll be a good night. I just know it. We'll have a victory out of this, Reah. The Alliance is within our grasp and we will crush it from existence." I watched as Arvil's fist closed around an imaginary enemy. I nodded and ducked my head. I felt ill when I left Arvil's temporary study.

Vice-Director? I must have sounded shaky when I sent the mindspeech to Lendill Schaff.

Reah, what's wrong? Lendill got back with me right away.

Has Ry or Tory told you about the big party that Arvil is planning shortly after the first few fields are harvested?

I only have sketchy information. What do you know?

That Arvil is inviting the biggest and the worst, I sent. *This party will coincide with the first shipments going out. I'm supervising the menu and the meal preparations. Arvil just admitted to me that he intends to crush the Alliance.*

Is the party all he plans?

No, he's going to take all of them out to the seed fields and show them how extensive the crop is.

Before or after?

The party is set for early afternoon, with the visit to the seed fields immediately after. They're bringing in luxury hoverbuses just for the occasion. I was kneading dough in the kitchen, pounding it harder than necessary as I held my mental conversation. I could never forget Arvil's mission or how ruthless he could be in obtaining his goals.

We have your location pinpointed on the Zephili map, Lendill informed me. *We wanted to wait until the shipping station got the first crates so we can get the shipping addresses. Anyone expecting seed will get a visit from the ASD instead. This is too perfect, Reah. I think we can arrange for a surprise for Arvil's visitors while they're looking over his fields. Keep up the good work special agent Nilvas, I think I can get you a promotion and a pay increase.* Lendill was gloating. Well, that was easy for him—he wasn't neck deep in the middle of this.

On a personal level, I merely wanted to come out of this alive and intact. I also wanted Farzi, Nenzi and their brothers to get out of this alive as well. I wondered if I could skip them away somewhere, just so they could be free for a change. I grabbed my comp-vid after putting the dough to rise again and started looking for likely places that would be safe for them.

"Reah, you look tired." Teeg held my face in his hands when Astralan folded me to Campiaa to pick up the wine and arrange for the kitchen staff and servers. Kiasz was going to help me out with my mission. He even offered to come and help out on Zephili, but I told him he was needed where he was. I didn't want any more friends' deaths on my conscience. Kiasz looked disappointed, but I gave him a hug and hoped he'd get over it. He was far safer where he was, although Campiaa wasn't very safe to start with.

"Teeg," I bumped my head against his chest.

"What's wrong with my baby?" His fingers stroked my jaw and neck before he bent down to kiss me. Tory, Ry, Astralan and Stellan were all with us inside Teeg's new study; he'd set it up inside Arvil's palace, not far from Arvil's office.

"Boss, do you want us to take care of that problem over at SG-2?" Stellan asked. I lifted my head—Stellan had called Teeg boss. Apparently, there was a problem at *The San Gerxon II*, Arvil's casino on the opposite end of the curving strip of sand that housed all of Campiaa's casinos. Of the thirty-eight casinos on that quiet bay, Arvil owned thirty-two of them. Word had it that he took payments from the other six owners for the privilege of having a casino on Campiaan soil.

"I'll come. Astralan, take Reah back to Zephili for me."

That was it? Take Reah back to Zephili? What was going on? Tory couldn't even offer me a shrug as Astralan came to haul me away. I hadn't gotten any mindspeech from Tory either—was he afraid to tell me something? I went cold for a moment, worried that there was indeed something more happening than I realized.

"Come along, short one. You can drool on the boss later." Astralan took my arm and folded me away.

"Reah, will you fix lunch?" That was Arvil's greeting to me the moment Astralan landed us inside the main kitchen. Therefore, it was justice, perhaps, that I was set to preparing lunch for Arvil, the Hardlows, three of the four warlocks, all three of Arvil's newly hired wizards and my reptanoids. I hugged Farzi, Nenzi and the others who jumped in and helped with sandwiches while I put soup and a fruit dessert together. Fruit and rum drinks were also served—I didn't like how grumpy the wizards seemed to be.

"Lack of female companionship," Astralan jerked his head toward the three wizards when I set his plate in front of him. Giving the barest of nods, I went to serve Celestan and Galaxsan next. Arvil and the Hardlows had been served already. I didn't want any of them upset over who got served first.

"Don't worry," Celestan whispered as I handed his plate over, "we're instructed to fry them if they lay a finger on you." He gave me a crooked grin as I lifted an eyebrow at his comment.

"Reah, this is excellent," Galaxsan was already sipping his drink.

"Then you should only have one; I put a double shot of rum in there," I replied, wrinkling my nose at him.

Nearly everyone was finished eating when Farzi, Nenzi and their brothers sat down with me to eat our lunch. Only Astralan and one of the wizards were still at the island, lingering over their food. I sat between Farzi and Nenzi while we ate. I was almost too exhausted to eat and knew I'd have to start dinner soon if we were going to have rolls and something for dessert.

"Reah, you teach us more so we be more help for you," Farzi dipped into his soup. Our meal was a quick one, with pasta and vegetables added to seasoned broth.

"You've been a big help already," I rubbed Farzi's back affectionately.

"I'll pay if you'll put your hands on me," the wizard pushed his plate toward the center of the island.

"I'll kill you if you say anything like that to her again," Astralan examined the fingernails on his right hand. "Master San Gerxon has already issued that warning. I will make sure it is enforced."

My food had suddenly gone tasteless. Arvil's wizards were criminals, it was easy enough to see, but for someone to die over a comment? I wasn't sure how I felt about that. Paltis the wizard gave Astralan a dark look and stalked out of the kitchen.

"Farzi, make sure someone is with Reah at all times," Astralan went on. "If any one of those fuckers makes a move toward her, kill them.

Bite first, ask questions later." Arvil was in too much of a hurry to hire replacements." Astralan rose from his seat at the island. "Lunch was good, Reah. I'll look forward to dinner."

Farzi and I just stared at each other after Astralan left the kitchen. I couldn't even put words together to say how I felt. Puzzled and afraid were the two emotions closest to the surface. Slipping off my barstool, I headed toward the door that led to the back of the house and the pool area. Farzi and his brothers were right behind me. I kept walking until we were halfway between the plantation and the barn area. Stopping there amid a profusion of tropical plants, I turned to Farzi, Nenzi and the others.

"Farzi, if I ask you to do something sometime, will you do it and not ask questions?"

Farzi blinked at me, completely puzzled. Eventually, he nodded his head. "Reah, I know this is trust. We do this, because you ask."

"Good." I hugged Farzi, then Nenzi and each of the others. "I love you. All of you, and I worry about how things are going to turn out."

"We worry too." Nenzi gave me a second hug. I held onto him for a while.

"We'll have the reception around the pool—the weather is too nice to have this indoors," Arvil informed me after dinner. He'd called me into his temporary study; he looked at home there already.

"Of course, Lord Arvil," I agreed. "I think I saw extra tables in the shed near the barns. I believe Grish did this sort of thing before. All we need are some nice tablecloths and napkins to go with what we already have. Grish only bought the best dishes and crystal." Arvil was expecting a hundred guests or so to show up. I'd already brought in menu comp-vids for each table. The main unit would be stationed inside the kitchen and each table would be registered with the proper items. The staff that Astralan and the others would fold in already knew what they were doing—I was bringing them from Arvil's casinos.

"Teeg will stay on Campiaa and make sure everything there is running smoothly during the event. You can give him updates as soon as the whole thing is over." Arvil was smiling. "I hope you have something nice to wear, Reah. I'll be introducing you as one of my heirs."

"I have something." Teeg had made sure I had something. He'd bought the midnight-blue gown himself, along with a necklace and bracelet. Arvil must be paying him generously. I hadn't even had time to look at my credit chip, I'd been so busy. But that gave me an idea. As soon as Arvil was done discussing plans for the reception and tour of the fields, I picked up Chazi and Hirzi, who were waiting outside Arvil's study. We went toward my suite where the other reptanoids were already gathered to go to bed.

"Farzi, take this," I said, handing over my credit chip bracelet.

"What is this?" He looked at me in alarm.

"Just in case you need it for anything," I told him. Farzi's face was troubled as I walked into my bathroom to clean up and dress for bed.

The next three days saw the biggest burst of activity. Tables were hauled in from the shed and the reptanoids and I worried over placement in the pool area. The flagstone base was large but still required some tactical decisions on where everything should go so that none of Arvil's guests would feel crowded. A bar was set up and stocked so the staff wouldn't have to run to the kitchen whenever a guest asked for something. I showed the bartenders how to make the rum and fruit drink at Arvil's insistence. The wizards Arvil employed all came to test the results. They were quite drunk afterward. I hoped Arvil didn't need them for anything.

Arvil was busy arranging for his personal stable of courtesans to be brought from Campiaa—I heard that Teeg was instrumental in making those arrangements. I got mindspeech from Tory twice, but both times I'd been so busy I'd barely had time to talk to him. He was only making sure I was all right anyway. Hoping that Lendill and Director Keef knew what they were doing, I kept up with my work, making sure that Arvil and the Hardlow's guests enjoyed what I hoped was their last meal outside captivity.

~

Barely a breeze was blowing as we covered tables with beautiful champagne colored cloths and set out napkins to match. Crystal champagne flutes and water glasses were added, in addition to polished silver place settings. Plates and chargers came next—Grish's place settings would impress just about anyone. I wondered briefly what the warlocks had done with his body. Rushing to get ready after the last table had been dressed and the menu items and appetizers checked in the kitchen, I barely arrived at Arvil's elbow as he greeted his guests.

The Hardlows stood opposite Arvil, greeting guests just as we were. My head was swimming with names as Arvil took hands, slapped backs and did whatever he could to make them feel welcome. Some names were familiar—names that had been spread across the Alliance as the worst criminals that the ASD hunted. If the Vice-Director could pull this operation off, it would be the biggest arrest he'd ever made, more than likely.

"Reah planned everything and these are her recipes," Arvil boomed to the guests who sat at our table. The yaris fish was such a hit that some were sending back to the kitchen to get a plate after they'd ordered one of the other dishes. Couples were sharing what they had —half of the ox roast for half the fish or fowl dishes. The staff didn't even blink, bringing out extra plates and serving utensils to make the exchanges. Drinks were flowing and Arvil was extremely pleased. I was shaky, if I were honest with myself. The warlocks were scattered through the crowd—Astralan ate at the Hardlows' table; Arvil's three wizards were on the perimeter. I hoped they knew what they were doing in case someone caused trouble. The courtesans were paired with the single males Arvil designated.

The moment everything slowed down, Arvil invited his guests to the waiting luxury hoverbuses and they climbed aboard, evening gowns and all, for the trip to view the drakus fields. The first fifteen fields had been harvested already and the crates shipped to the station. Lendill hadn't given me any update on that but I figured the addresses had been copied and the seed confiscated. No doubt, the ASD agents would be arriving at those addresses quite soon to make arrests.

We were driven out to a preselected field—a deck and walkway had been built so expensive shoes wouldn't sink into watered soil. A separate bar had also been set up so more drinks could be served. Nenzi was driving the bus I rode in—Farzi and his brothers loaded into the back with me. Arvil, Wilffox, Wilffin and most of the guests were in eight other buses headed toward the fields.

"Farzi," I whispered to him and his brothers as the last of the six guests riding with us got off, "I want you and your brothers to go back to the plantation now. Take one of those other vehicles the farmhands use."

"What you want us to do then?" Farzi was nodding at me.

"You know what I look like when I change." Farzi and the others nodded. "Wait for me to come back like that. I'll take you somewhere safe."

"Reah not get hurt?" Nenzi was worried.

"I'll try to make sure of that," I leaned in to kiss his cheek. "Don't worry. Any of you. Be discreet when you leave."

"We will." Farzi was already laying out mental plans, I could see it.

I got off the bus and walked toward the knot of guests who surrounded Arvil and the Hardlows. Arvil was already describing the shipments and the harvesting of drakus seed. Figures—staggering figures—were mentioned, while eight reptanoids turned and slithered away from us, heading toward a vehicle that was almost obscured in the distance.

"I have work to do, why don't you two take the night off?" Teeg nodded toward Ry and Tory. "I can make do with the security around the walls."

"Are you sure? We can stay within shouting distance," Tory offered, though he was itching to get away. Lendill had already told him and

Ry that this was the night Zephili would be taken. The Vice-Director had instructed both his special agents to fold or skip away at a designated time. They'd been recalled to Le-Ath Veronis; Lendill and Norian already had plenty of agents in place to take the drakus seed fields and many of Arvil's guests. Not all of them came with powerful warlocks, as the Hardlows employed. Lendill and Norian's hopes rested on a fast strike and the element of surprise.

Ry and Tory nodded to the gate guards as they left Arvil's palace behind, heading toward The San Gerxon I. "Time to get the hell out of here," Tory muttered as they walked through the casino's doors. Both of them headed toward the men's bathroom located near the front. As soon as they were inside, both disappeared.

The field that Arvil had chosen to display was two away from where the brown and dry-leaved drakus plants were. Not that far, really, but none of his guests would be seeing any of that. Farzi, Nenzi and the others had gotten away—I saw the top of the vehicle as Nenzi drove them at a reasonable pace toward the plantation. The plants were as high as my shoulder in the field—they were scheduled to be harvested in two days. More than tall enough to hide eight lion snakes as they made their way toward an old bus. I was thankful for that. I'd found a planet not far away—one that held mostly jungle around the equator. Farzi and his brothers could live there until something else could be done. I had no intention of handing any of them to Lendill Schaff or Norian Keef.

"Of course you may take a pod, my dear," Arvil was smiling at one of his guest's pretty companion. "What you hold in your hand is worth one hundred thousand Alliance credits," Arvil went on when the woman broke off a branch of a plant.

"This one branch?" She sounded surprised.

"Just that branch," Arvil chuckled. His chuckle was cut short as bullets started flying.

I was frightened out of my wits when I saw the hovercopters flying toward us, heading straight for the plantation. I had to do something and fast to keep them occupied and pointed in a direction away from Farzi and the others. The fields containing the brown-leaved plants were near and in the right direction. Everyone around me was screaming and shouting as bullets continued to spray around us. I expected the warlocks to send blasts toward the Alliance attackers or the hovercopters. I was shocked when nothing of the sort came as I skipped away.

"ASD!" Arvil shouted at those around him, "Get down. Head toward the buses!" His words were proven useless only ticks later as all nine buses were firebombed by the attacking hovercopters. Bullets were raining from the hovercopters too, as Wilffox and his brother looked around for their warlocks. This should be a simple matter for those four, except they couldn't be found.

Wilffox was shouting for Astralan, even as he died in the midst of a drakus seed field. Others were screaming and running now, while bullets brought anyone down who ran at the rear of the fleeing crowd. Expensive heels stuck in damp soil and were left behind as women ran shrieking from the attack. Wilffin was firing the pistol he'd carried inside his jacket when he was hit in the chest. He fell, bleeding from a wound dangerously close to his heart. More hovercopters came, herding the crowd before them. Lendill, in the command copter, was shouting to keep as many as possible alive for questioning.

I was turned to Thifilatha as soon as I landed in the field. What I reached out for after turning was the heat beneath the ground. It leapt to do as I bid—a volcano in its infancy. Lava would have taken perhaps ten or twenty turns to make its way to the surface, but some power I held while Thifilatha reached out toward it, calling it to the surface in a matter of ticks. Still, it felt too long as the cone rose around me and the air grew hot and stifling. I urged it on, forcing it to answer my call. The cone roared to life, lifting me with it. I could feel the molten rock and ash beneath my feet. The hovercopters were whirring overhead as I commanded my volcano to erupt.

I didn't know until then that heat, even the heat of a volcano, cannot hurt any High Demon in their other form. Ash and fiery, molten lava spewed from the newly formed crater and fountained upward, forcing the hovercopters to veer away. I could hear the screams of people coming toward me—they would be compelled to find an alternate route to get away.

Night was falling around me and the light from the eruption was spectacular, calling out to me to come and play within its heated frenzy. I forced myself to ignore the call. Instead, I focused on the reason I'd done this in the beginning—my reptanoids. I had to get back to them. Take them to safety before the ASD came and took them away. It made my heart sore to think of Farzi and his brothers, locked inside a cage.

The kitchen was quiet as I landed inside it. My clothing had been burned away the moment I turned, so I stood naked upon the tiled floor. The staff must have run the moment the ASD attacked—piles of dishes and glasses were everywhere, tossed aside by servants in favor of saving their lives. I couldn't blame them—I would have done the same. Grabbing one of the white coats the pastry cooks had left behind, I tied it around myself and went to look for my reptanoids.

"Farzi! Nenzi!" I shouted, ghosting quickly from room to room. Wiping frightened tears away, I frantically searched for my friends. I needed to hurry and get them away; the Alliance and Lendill could come at any moment. When I raced into my suite, hoping they'd gone there to wait for me, what greeted me instead shocked me to my core.

CHAPTER 15

Astralan, Celestan, Galaxsan and Stellan all stood beside Teeg, who held a pistol in his hand. What truly shocked me, however, was that Galaxsan and Celestan had Farzi and his brothers gathered and held in a tight knot. The two warlocks disappeared with the reptanoids as I skidded to a stop inside my suite. "No!" I screamed. "Bring them back! Teeg, bring them back!"

"Too late, Reah Nilvas of the ASD," Teeg checked the charge of his ranos pistol. The moment he'd said my last name and ASD, I'd gone cold. Was he going to kill me? Ask one of the warlocks to try? I had a defense against the warlocks. I had nothing against a ranos pistol. I wondered if turning Thifilatha would do any good, but Teeg's next words stopped me.

"Arvil and the Hardlows are already dead, Reah. Your doing, no doubt." His dark eyes were hard as he stared at me. He hadn't pointed the pistol at me yet. *Yet.* "I have to thank you for that," Teeg went on. "That leaves me everything. The warlocks know where everything the Hardlows have is located; all I have to do is take it. They're willing to work with me on this." Teeg offered me a beautiful smile. If I wasn't so stunned, it might have brought an answering smile from me. Teeg had planned this and I should have seen it. The warlocks calling him boss and asking him what he wanted, instead of consulting Arvil or the Hardlows. I should have seen it coming from clicks away. I'd been foolish enough to think he loved me, when all he truly wanted was everything the biggest criminals on this side of the galaxy owned. Now, as Arvil's heir, he would get it, especially if he were backed by the four most powerful warlocks anyone might find to hire for that sort of thing.

"Where did you take Farzi and his brothers," I demanded, stalling for time. Perhaps Lendill would show up soon, although I had my doubts that he could capture Teeg if he were supported by the warlocks.

"They're on Campiaa," Teeg's voice sounded different—harder.

"Set them free, Teeg," I begged. "They don't belong to you or anyone else, and they certainly don't belong on that cesspit of a planetoid."

"That's for me to decide," Teeg snapped. "Don't be so shocked, Reah, there's more," Teeg's lip curled in a nasty grin. "What you just did—getting Arvil killed—well, that voids your claim to any of his empire. It all comes to me now. I'm his sole heir and I have the records to prove it."

I gaped at Teeg, I know I did—mouth open and everything. I could hear gunfire in the distance; the ASD was coming closer. I didn't have much time.

"You did this purposely, just so you'd get it all," my voice quavered. I didn't give a damn about anything Arvil had. What I'd cared for was Teeg. Now, he was pulling that rug from beneath my feet and allowing me to hit the floor hard, knocking the breath right out of me. My heart squeezed in my chest and it hurt. "And I thought Delvin was the real betraying *difik*. Too bad he's dead now or I'd go and apologize to him for calling him the blackest of betrayers." I wanted to throw Teeg into a wall. I wanted to curl up in a corner and weep. I did neither. "I hope you enjoy it," I said and skipped away.

～

Shouting and crying from the moment I landed at the palace on Le-Ath Veronis, it took Karzac and a Larentii to place me in a healing sleep. I didn't learn until later that Tory had sent mindspeech to Vice-Director Schaff, telling him I was safe and there with him. Lendill and his operatives had cleaned up bodies and arrested the others, making a complete sweep of all of Arvil's guests. The ones he didn't get, of course, were Teeg San Gerxon, his four warlocks and the eight reptanoids.

I didn't want to do anything except be by myself for the next moon-turn. The only person welcome anywhere near me was Gavril. He truly was my best friend. He never told me I shouldn't behave as I was, or eat more or sleep better. He just huddled with me most of the time when he was free, or asked about his research as he worked on an assignment for Master Morwin. Finally, after the moon-turn was up, he spoke.

"Reah, you can't let this ruin your life. Tory and Aurelius are just about to go crazy without you."

"I know," I muttered. We sat on the tallest, widest dome that covered the central hall of his mother's palace. I'd skipped us there—he'd asked me to take him somewhere so we wouldn't be bothered. Chash I would humor. Even Vice-Director Schaff was wary of approaching me. He did try to ask me to dinner one night, though. I'd slammed my bedroom door in his face. That was probably a black mark on my record, but right then I really didn't care.

"I'll be thirteen tomorrow," Gavril went on, bringing me back to the present.

"Chash, I didn't know," I sighed, pulling his head over and planting a kiss there. He grinned and looked flushed when I let him go. "Can I take you to Casino City tomorrow and buy something for you?" I focused on his dark eyes.

"If you want to. What I'd like most is for you to feel better, Reah."

"I know. I don't know when that's going to happen, Chash."

"Reah, must I fold myself to the tops of tall buildings, just so I can court you?" Wylend Arden appeared from nothing and sat down on my other side.

"King Wylend," I nodded respectfully. He wanted to court me? I swallowed nervously. That was unexpected. He had come and given me spelled jewels on Zephili, though. Now I knew why.

"Reah, that fool of a Director is refusing to allow you to leave the ASD, even if you might come to marry a King. He tells me Karathia is not an Alliance world and therefore that particular rule does not apply."

"What rule, Em-pah Wylend?" Gavril leaned around me to look at his great-grandfather.

"The one that allows any Alliance conscript to leave the Alliance's employ if they marry into royalty. As you see, he has already found a way around that piece of legislation." Wylend was frowning as he leaned against the curve of the dome at our backs. We all stared at the stars overhead for a while, until Wylend's warm hand slowly moved to grasp mine. *I already love you*, he sent the mindspeech. *And I am more than content to wait.*

"We don't have a single thing to charge him with," Lendill tossed the comp-vid onto Norian's desk. "Even the crime rate is going down on that side of things if my sources are correct."

"Then there's nothing we can do," Norian grumbled. "I can't find his name anywhere—it's as if he appeared from nothing. He must be operating with an alias, but even his description doesn't fit any known criminal. Teeg San Gerxon has a clean record, as far as the ASD is concerned."

"And that makes me angry," Lendill snapped. "After what he did to Reah."

"Well, you still have making up to do, as do I on that front," Norian pointed out.

"She slammed the door in my face," Lendill whined.

"What did you expect? Besides, you're not allowed to get involved with an underling. You know the rules."

"Oh, throw *that* in my face," Lendill snapped.

The End